T0285355

THE CONDOR'S RIDDLE

MARCELO ANTINORI

SECANT PUBLISHING
Salisbury, Maryland

THE CONDOR'S RIDDLE

ISBN: 979-8-9851489-9-2 (hardcover)
ISBN: 979-8-9886410-0-1 (paperback)
ISBN: 979-8-9886410-2-5 (ebook)

Library of Congress Control Number: 2023922941

Secant Publishing, LLC
P.O. Box 4059
Salisbury MD 21803

This book is a work of fiction. Names, characters, places, events, and incidents are either the product of the author's imagination or are used fictitiously.

Cover design by ebooklaunch

Before we start, let me tell you something. Everything you will read here is true. Trust me. I lived in Santa Clara for three years, and I can confirm it. I spoke with each person quoted here, and that is what happened to the Condor. Not the official version, and neither one of the fake ones repeated in the streets, but the truth. I just had to change a few names to preserve privacy. Other than that, I'm telling you exactly what happened, and now, let's move ahead, and enjoy it.

1

Bebéi marches with the band. On a sunny Saturday, Bebéi joyfully strolled through the cobblestone streets of the old quarter, his eyes wide open, feeling the sun's embrace. He was the archivist at the French Embassy, an older man who saw the world with a child's candid eyes. That morning he was ambling by, enjoying the friendly streets and the calmness of the old colonial neighborhood. He greeted everyone and he was happy to notice each one waving back and smiling.

He was born far away, in another country, in another time. His father was Algerian and had fought alongside De Gaulle and the Free French Forces during the Second World War. After liberation, and while still in France, his father was awarded with French citizenship and married a young French woman who was an idealist and revolutionary like him. From their love, Bebéi was born in the town of Malakoff, south of Paris, and he was barely two years old when his parents left him behind to fight to free Algeria. That's a long story, which I may share later, but the important thing here is to understand his mood as he walked through the streets of the old city, since it was the pounding he felt inside his chest that explained everything that happened next.

Bebéi was a serious and dedicated worker. He spent his days in the Embassy quietly searching for, and filing, papers with such efficiency that there was no cause for complaint from anyone. When he was not at work, he relished every minute of his free time walking the cobblestone streets and cruising along with his daydreams, always peripherally related to reality.

He fancied Santa Clara from the time he got there. He noticed that every house had a story to tell, and each story, true or not, could feed his imagination. He seldom spoke – *better be unnoticed* – that was the first lesson he got from his uncle. He learned to think and dream in silence, without bothering to explain himself.

Bebéi enjoyed looking around and appreciating details of what he saw to later relish every image, color, and movement in his mind. Where others would simply regard the sea, the sun, and a few fishing boats, he would note every color change brought by the moving clouds. He would patiently watch the flight of the birds and follow each fisher in their boats: some clearing up the deck and others just staring at the dock. He learned to commit to memory every detail as if his life depended on it.

That morning he was distracted by reminiscing about his childhood. He was a French citizen but had been raised by his uncle, who taught him that immigrants had to be careful to survive – *the less they see you the better it is.* His childhood had been lonely but smooth until his uncle found out that he was sick and didn't have much time left to live. He had been afraid to leave Bebéi alone in the world.

That morning, as Bebéi meandered through the streets of the old quarter, he recalled, with a smile, his uncle's desperate efforts to find him a suitable job, one about which he could be inspired and passionate.

They both knew that what he loved to do most was daydream. Bebéi was always good at that – but one can't make a living of daydreams, his uncle would say. Amidst those worries, Bebéi had started to help the nuns at the school to file papers and notebooks. That was something he was good at – filing what should not be lost and finding papers which were needed.

Thanks to his ability, and the help of his uncle's friend who knew someone who played cards with the minister's son-in-law, Bebéi got a job in Paris as an assistant archivist for the Ministry of Foreign Affairs, and there he worked quietly for many years with more than enough salary to live on. Every day he would wake up, take the metro, and, following his uncle's advice – *work as a submarine* – so quietly that no one would notice him, and with such diligence that no one could complain. At the end of each day, he would return home, a place he would rarely leave. This is how he survived for nearly three decades without making a single mistake but with no mornings of happiness like the one he was having that Saturday greeting his neighbors in Santa Clara by the Sea.

Bebéi walked, remembering the day he heard his boss, Madame Roisson, mentioning there was a vacancy for an archivist at the Embassy at Santa Clara. The idea had immediately caught his attention and triggered his daydreaming: Santa Clara, a Caribbean village in the Caribbean – *certainly a meeting place of adventurers*. His days in Paris were lifeless, and nothing could make him dream anymore; he felt dismayed in his apartment, on the metro, and at work.

Walking and greeting his new neighbors in Santa Clara, he remembered that the idea of travelling had excited him so much that he had decided to risk everything. He knew that one day he would have to retire from the Ministry. What would he do afterward if he didn't know how to do anything else? At the Ministry, very few people noticed him, but those who worked by his side knew he was an excellent archivist, and that was what they were looking for at Santa Clara. He had landed the job; and that is how on a sad and cold Parisian evening, he'd boarded a plane and flown for the first time in his life to a place that was neither near Rue Jean Moulin, where he lived, nor close to Quai d'Orsay, where he had always worked.

It had taken him twelve hours to cross the ocean, and before landing, he had seen through the window the small peninsula crammed with colonial constructions which soon would be familiar to him and the old city of Santa Clara by the Sea, where the French Embassy was located and where he would soon be living.

Those were his thoughts that Saturday. He had taken a risk, and thanks to his choice, he was living with pride in a place where he could happily stroll through the streets and where everyone greeted him with a smile.

That morning as he walked before the local school admiring the sun's brightness reflecting off the roofs and on the colors of the old houses, Bebéi heard a *doum doum dacadacadá, doum doum dacadacadá*. The school band was rehearsing their drills.

He had heard them before, but that morning the kids wore their white gloves and proudly carried new instruments; the lyres were polished, the baton twirlers sported new uniforms, and all marched spiritedly with their heads held high.

3

Hector, the band instructor, yelled last-minute instructions while everyone listened carefully. It was their general rehearsal before Independence Day and a chance to march through the familiar cobblestone streets of the neighborhood before facing the parade in the capital's main avenue.

At Hector's signal, the drums started rolling. Then the lyres chimed in, and the enthusiasm increased. The baton twirlers led the march, and alongside them went Bebéi, attracted by the joy of the music and the band's festive mood. *Doum doum dacadacadá, doum doum dacadacadá.*

They went down Central Avenue towards the Cathedral. The lyres gave the melody, the batons jumped in the air, and the drummers beat with all their might.

Just as they were about to enter the main square, Bebéi surprised himself and those around him. He went to the front of the line, and to everyone's astonishment, he marched at the head of the band, sporting his worn suit, his out-of-style hat, his chubby belly, and his faded brown tie. With great enthusiasm beaming from his soul, he marched with exaggerated military posture, saluting the city and all who watched and applauded him from the sidelines. The energy he emanated was overwhelming. He was venting his deep emotions about having ventured out and started a whole new life. His euphoria became contagious. Perched on the steps of La Merced Church, the drunkards of the Brethren, who were used to watching his timid figure pass by, were dumbfounded to see him leading the parade. La Pajerita was the first one to get up and follow the band. After her, La Trotska, who was so drunk that she thought it was a protest against the government. Farther down, even the municipal policemen interrupted their card game to walk out and applaud, and Bebéi saluted them with all seriousness and respect.

The band marched with passion through the streets, and leading it, the archivist was balancing his body with long steps in rhythm with the drums and the lyres' melody. Grená, the shaved ice vendor, immediately realized that it was more than just a mere rehearsal. She abandoned her stand and the syrup bottles, to run and march alongside Bebéi, imitating his exaggerated steps and marching with pride, inviting everyone to join them on that unexpected patriotic march.

4

When the band passed his bookstore, Joseph the Princess put on his colorful hat, approached Bebéi and Grena wearing flamboyant dress, and marched alongside them. They formed the trio that would lead the parade throughout the neighborhood. Even the puritan widows who were leaving the church kicked off their heels to accompany the band, and one by one, those who had something to do and those who did not, joined the march.

The workers who were restoring the hotel abandoned their posts and followed the band with red union flags, which led drunken La Trotsky to wave in solidarity with the red grocery bag she carried.

Everybody, those who were readying their tents for the Sunday market, the grumpy men who gather in the square to complain, and the kids who bother them with their noise, gladly joined Bebéi and the band.

Bebéi, with his extravagant steps and martial air, surrounded by the joy of Grená and the colorfulness of Princess, was leading the band. Full of confidence, he guided them triumphantly into the French Square where his colleagues from the Embassy greeted him, impressed. Bebéi saluted them as if he was France's Field Marshal rendering honors to the emperor.

Doum doum dacadacadá, doum doum dacadacadá, the band continued uninterrupted, drums, lyres, baton twirlers, all ready for the big parade. *Doum doum dacadacadá, doum doum dacadacadá,* they marched back through Central Avenue, ready for the parade and the festivity. *Doum doum dacadacadá, doum doum...* The rehearsal was about to conclude, just a block from the school, when the news came, and Hector, the instructor, gave the signal for the band to stop. All the neighborhood quieted down. A dead body had been found in front of the ruins of the Old Archway.

2

A dead body and an annoying dog. I apologize for the ending of the first chapter. Those are things one has to get used to when writing about Santa Clara. The original plan was to write a little more about Bebéi's background and continue introducing other characters of the old city: the five members of the Brethren, Diocles, the walking philosopher, and even Ilona, the restaurant owner. I was also planning to acquaint you with the chats in front of Grená's shaved-ice stand, the nightlife in Pigalle Street, and the wild clashes between the church ladies and bums on the steps of La Merced church, but all of a sudden, an unidentified corpse showed up in the middle of the street, completely changing the narrative.

The people in the city weren't even sure if the man was dead or not. In any case, I am compelled to abandon my initial plan so I can help you to understand what happened. This complicates the writer's job, and it may confuse the reader, but in Santa Clara that's how it goes. People there are utterly undisciplined, and their charm comes precisely from their surprises. And don't worry if there are too many characters. What can I do? It's a whole city. More than fifty people were involved in the Condor's story. You deserve to know everything each one did, and if you follow along with me, you won't get confused.

"A tourist dropped dead near the ruins of the Old Arch!" The news spread like wildfire.

"He looks dead!" some were saying. "No... he's not from here, it's a tourist," yet others said. "He was alone. No one knows who he is."

"The police are here; they are waiting for the ambulance to arrive. Hurry!" And everyone hurried along to the Old Arch; those who had marched in the parade, those who had just watched from the storefronts and applauded from the balconies, and even those who had held back on Bebéi's call but couldn't control their curiosity as death visited the neighborhood.

It bears mentioning that death was not usual at those premises; however, on that particular morning, someone chose to die in front of the old Dominican convent. And that's where everyone was headed...

No, that's not right, sorry, almost everyone. La Trotska couldn't go because she was too drunk and wholly drained by the parade. Grená was also exhausted and went back to her shaved ice stand, but not before making sure that one of her sons, Lieutenant Pirilo, was going to head towards the Old Arch and report back the news. Joseph the Princess did not go either; he remembered that he had left the bookstore unattended. Aside from them, everyone else ran there.

Explanations, theories, and doubts circulated among the crowd: "It's a man ... An older tourist ... He looks sick." "I remember him, but I thought he had died a long time ago." "He fell, and he isn't waking up... Who knows if he is dead or not."

Bebéi also ran towards the ruins, but he couldn't get close. Many were already there, and he stood at a distance fanning himself with his hat and trying to understand what was going on.

The corpse was sprawled out in the middle of the street, and Arcadio, a well-known petty crook tried to resuscitate him. Those who knew Arcadio found his actions intriguing since no one imagined he had nursing qualifications and much less to be a good Samaritan. La Pajerita had her strong doubts on the matter. The Spaniard, with her madly unruly hair, wasn't easily fooled; she knew Arcadio had not a streak of good in him and must have had an ulterior motive up his sleeve.

The street was packed, and everyone was speaking at once. Next to the body, two cops were standing guard waiting for the ambulance to arrive. What caught everyone's attention was a black dog trying to approach the body. It would try to approach from one end, and people would buzz it off, then it would try to approach from the other end, and once again it was shunned. It would bark, be shushed, and try again. At times it would get close, but there was always someone pushing it away.

Arcadio shooed it off, he didn't want anyone close, but the dog would not leave. The German tourist, who had a fear of dogs, shooed it off and it returned. The cops shooed it away without knowing why they were shooing, and even the photographer kicked it because he didn't want a dog in his shot. Everyone pushed it away: the church ladies, the priest, the girls from the Music School, the Mayor's chauffeur, and the gypsies. For thirty minutes, everyone tried to get rid of the dog, but the dog always returned.

Bebéi watched and wondered if the man was really dead. He began to follow the progress of the black dog. Everyone else saw the dog as a nuisance; nobody wanted it around, but it kept insisting. It would poke its head between the legs of those standing around the body, bark, growl and try to get closer. It didn't matter how many times the dog was shooed away, it would always try again. Bebéi was impressed by its perseverance.

Its canine efforts finally bore fruit, and the dog was able to escape from those trying to catch it and get close to the body. It was then that Bebéi realized that what was attracting the dog was not curiosity. When the dog finally broke through the circle and got close to the body, it caressed the man's face with its snout as if to calm down the deceased.

Arcadio insisted on scaring the dog off, but the animal made it clear that it would not back down. Not now. The dog barked viciously at Arcadio, ears perked up, fangs bared. Bebéi understood that the dog belonged to the man lying dead, and with the same resolve and energy he had led the band with, he made his way through the crowd and helped the dog remain by its master.

The animal lay next to the body and placed its head over the dead man's chest. It was only then that all present realized what Bebéi had already perceived. Suddenly, the rush of questions and speculations ceased and was followed by a deep and respectful silence. Everyone looked at the dog, and the dog looked back at the crowd with mutual compassion.

The sad eyes of the dog had transformed the festive mood of the city into one of respectful mourning. On San Domingo Street, a man was lying dead. His yellowish skin and bald head seemed to indicate that he had been ill, and the whole old colonial neighborhood was saddened: residents, tourists, poets, and beggars. All present, reunited in silence, looked at the dead man that no one knew except for the dog and the dog could not explain who he was.

Today, knowing everything that happened, I wonder if it wouldn't have been best to ignore the man's identity. However, that was a sorrowful day, and Bebéi felt for the dog so that when the ambulance arrived Bebéi approached the dog, trying to calm him.

From a distance, La Pajerita followed Arcadio's every move, and by her side was Diocles, the philosopher, with his brown raincoat, white beard, and wise expression. Contrary to everybody else in Santa Clara, Diocles didn't spend his days concerned with himself. His pleasure was to observe others – what they did, how they did it and why.

Bebéi's behavior had surprised him. On his daily walks Diocles had crossed paths with the French archivist, but he never caught his attention. That day, however, Diocles was impressed. Bebéi, the shy foreigner, had become the protagonist. First, by leading the band during the parade and later, at the Old Arch, by protecting and caressing the dog that everyone found annoying.

It was then that something equally unusual happened. Ibrahim, the Egyptian whom Diocles had frequently seen at Ilona's restaurant, arrived. He looked at the body with a stupefied expression. He started to walk away with a worried look as if he hadn't liked what he saw. Diocles and Bebéi both noticed it. The Egyptian's face was not just surprised; he seemed fearful.

Ibrahim left but came back as if he didn't believe what he had seen. He approached the body and looked one more time. Diocles tried to speak to him, but Ibrahim didn't respond. He looked disturbed and left in a hurry as if he had to go and tell someone else what he had witnessed.

Diocles remarked on his odd behavior. He had seen Ibrahim before chatting with Ilona at the restaurant. and Ibrahim was usually a calm and discreet person.

Bebéi was also puzzled by the Egyptian's behavior, but since he didn't know him, he kept petting the trembling dog. Bebéi's hand seemed to calm him, and so they remained until the cops began to disperse the crowd, making way for the stretcher. Then, in a matter of seconds, what was a peaceful silence turned to an atmosphere of angst. The dog grew nervous and began to bark. Bebéi tried to calm him down, but when the dog sensed that the cops were putting the man inside the ambulance, he barked with more determination. He jumped and slipped from Bebéi's hands, and in one leap got into the vehicle, but the cops threw him out.

Bebéi tried to intercede, but no one understood his confusing words in French. The dog barked more energetically, and his desperation began to overwhelm Bebéi. The dog ran back and forth, and when they shut the door and the ambulance started to move, the dog grew desperate and ran to Bebéi, barking vigorously. Bebéi understood that the dog wanted his help, but he didn't know what to do. The vehicle drove off and the dog took off after it.

Bebéi felt helpless and lost. He mumbled some words that no one understood, and awkwardly ran after the ambulance and the dog. He kept going and going, beginning to resign himself that he might not reach them, until he heard the howling.

The animal wasn't running anymore and was limping and heaving heavily. Someone was yelling that a car had hit the dog while he was racing down the street, and the dog's loud and hysterical howl pierced Bebéi's heart.

He hugged the dog, and a crowd gathered around them, helplessly watching their desperation, until a taxi stopped. Out jumped La Pajerita, who gestured to Bebéi, inviting him to climb in along with the dog.

Once inside the vehicle, the dog stopped howling. He was still in pain, but when the cab speeded up, he didn't feel alone. By his side, Bebéi was crying, sharing his agony.

3

A cast and a new beginning. I will begin this new chapter by informing you that the black dog is doing fine. That same evening, after an extended visit to the vet, countless x-rays, and a cast, the dog finally got to rest at Bebéi's apartment. He had calmed down by then. A Saturday that had begun festively with the band's parade turned tragic with the death of the unidentified man and the howls of the nervous dog. But thanks to La Pajerita and Micky, the taxi driver, Bebéi and the dog had arrived safely at the vet and later back home.

It is important to highlight La Pajerita's behavior; it surprised everyone. It's true that Micky was the taxi driver and everyone in the neighborhood knew him; but no one could have imagined that La Pajerita, in her permanent state of dementia, would have ever taken such an initiative at a time of so much stress.

In the old neighborhood, everyone knew of her walking up and down in a hurry, carrying prayer cards for the Virgin followed by her skinny female dog, both competing for who sported the crazier tangled hairstyle.

By her accent, one could figure out that she was a Spaniard, and some even said that her arrival to Santa Clara many years ago was due to the Franco regime's persecutions, but no one knew for sure. La Pajerita didn't speak much, and almost nothing of what she said made much sense, but she didn't bother anyone, and nothing really bothered her either. She was one of the five members of the Brethren. Contrary to the other four, who spent their days and nights on the steps of La Merced Church, La Pajerita slept on a particular bench in the boardwalk, always alongside her bitch and away from everything and everyone. She would walk around every day with no real destination but always in a hurry, and to rest, she would hang out at La Merced with the Brethren, not because of the alcohol since La Pajerita rarely drank, but because she was crazy or perhaps lonely. Her attitude never had any connection to reality, but the good side was that she was always smiling.

That noon, everything ended differently. She was not smiling, but she knew very well what she had to do. Once she saw Bebéi running after the dog, she convinced Micky to go and find them in his taxi. And when they found them, she helped Bebéi and the dog get settled in the cab. But she didn't go along with them. La Pajerita never left Santa Clara. Her world began and ended in the old neighborhood. There, she lived alone, and she couldn't be happier. She knew the place and its people like the palm of her hand; those who lived in houses that opened their windows and the others who remained cloistered to keep secrets under lock and key. However, she didn't know anything or anybody outside of the old quarter.

Her choice of Micky as the taxi driver was not a coincidence. He was the one who always picked up the bums at the jail every time the police would book them. Micky was the best friend of Rasta Bong, Grená's older son, and since they were kids, people were used to seeing them together on the streets of the city. Micky had never been able to keep a steady job, and he survived thanks to the taxi that Rasta Bong had bought for him.

Nobody knew for sure, but it seemed that his permanent nervousness was due to the blows he received during his disastrous and short-lived boxing career as Micky, the Lefty Beast. Whatever caused the nerves, Micky could never control himself, not even for a minute. When he wasn't moving or walking back and forth, he would talk and torture any poor soul in front of him with endless questions. Not even when he was driving would he shut up. If he didn't have a passenger to talk to, Micky would rattle off to himself, and when he stopped at a light, he would get down from his car and start talking to the driver next to him or at least interrogate them through the window.

Knowing Micky's restlessness, it is interesting to imagine the scene at the vet's office: the black dog howling in pain, Micky going around with his non-stop chatter, and, behind them, Bebéi moving around trying to understand what everyone was saying.

At first, Micky took La Pajerita's request as routine. He planned to take the chubby man and the dog to the vet's office, charge his fee and be back on his routes, but he ended up staying. He realized that Bebéi could not understand what people were telling him, and Micky stayed, asking questions and talking to anybody who would approach them. Next to him, Bebéi watched and smiled, distracted by his own uneasiness.

Later that evening, once the dog's leg had been put in a cast, they went back to the old city; and after so much excitement: the parade, the death, the running about, the howls, and the vet visit, Bebéi was finally able to relax.

It had been an intense day, and there was much to think over, but for once Bebéi wasn't alone in his apartment. Ever since he walked in with the plastered leg, the dog had stayed near the door, following Bebéi's movements from the corner of his eye.

He only has a broken leg. Three weeks in a cast, and he will be as good as new, the vet had told him.

Bebéi knew that the dead man would never reunite with the dog, so he tried to pet him, but the animal ignored him and remained quiet. Not even the food he brought interested him; the dog barely lifted his head to sniff the food before he went back to looking out of the window. Maybe he thought that his friend would return, and Bebéi didn't know how to explain otherwise. He continued to pet the dog's neck, and the dog kept ignoring him. They remained like that for a long time until they both fell asleep on the floor.

The following morning, Bebéi woke up staring at the dog. He noticed that a subtle change had come over his life since the arrival of the dog the day before. Until then, everything had been a series of knee-jerk reactions, starting with the desire to march alongside the band. One thing leading to another without even a second to decide. Still, this morning there was no impulsive behavior nor desperate events. The only thing that was real was the black dog lying next to him with his leg in a cast and his sad eyes piercing into Bebéi's soul.

Bebéi had never before shared his home with anyone, and even though his new roommate remained quiet and still, he now had someone to spend time with. He didn't know what to do with his new friend, but it was Sunday, and the sun rose in its splendor, inviting them out onto the street, so they headed out.

Bebéi changed his suit for another brown one that looked exactly like the one he was wearing before but was clean and didn't have dog blood on it. He put on another tie, same color, adjusted his hat in front of the mirror, and opened his apartment door. He wanted to start the day by walking the dog through the neighborhood. He, the embassy's archivist, was no longer Bebéi the loner, walking quietly through the streets. Now he felt different; he felt like the Master of Ceremonies of the band, walking proudly behind the black dog, who was limping and sniffing right and left, looking for the right spot to pee.

The dog didn't belong to him. He knew well that he would have to find out more about the dead man; he must have relatives or friends waiting for him. The problem was, how would he go about finding them? Bebéi only spoke French, and the few Spanish words he knew were barely enough to say hello to neighbors, but one way or another, he would have to find out who the dead man was. While he did this, he was also committed to help the dog get over his sadness. That's what he promised himself, and that is what he was going to do.

Walking the dog was a brand-new experience. Before, his walks were limited to greeting and being greeted by passersby. That was it. Greet, smile, and keep walking. With the dog the walk was more pleasant. After the greeting and the smile, there was always something else. That morning he heard many comments, which he couldn't completely understand, first from the cops, then, from the Mayor's driver, and later, from the principal who was rushing by to open up the school on a Sunday, and from some girls whom he almost bumped into as he rounded the corner pulled by the dog. He picked up on the jokes by the well-dressed woman going to the church, which he pretended to understand, and returned the smiles of the sensual ladies from Pigalle Street, who had just ended their night shift, with their make-up smeared across their faces, and who stopped briefly to pet the dog.

One of them asked the dog's name. Bebéi was caught by surprise and didn't want to admit he didn't know. How would they believe it was his dog if he didn't know his name? He answered with the first name that came to his mind, Zoubir, his uncle's name. That was how the black dog got its Algerian name.

When Bebéi got into the main square, he was approached by a group of backpacking tourists moved by the dog's leg in a cast. One of them, Diana, came close to him. She had blue eyes, looked like an angel, and spoke French. Never, since his arrival, had Bebéi stopped to chat with someone. Still, that Sunday, he told Diana that the dog's owner had been taken away in an ambulance and that the dog's leg was broken. The story moved her, and to Bebéi's surprise, she kissed him on the cheek. It was such a sweet kiss that he continued on his walk even more joyous than before.

Leaving the main square and climbing the Central Avenue, he came across Hector, the band instructor, who greeted him and caressed the dog, saying something that Bebéi didn't quite catch but which he assumed was related to the parade the day before. Later, while passing by the corner where Grená was readying her shaved ice stand, she jokingly indicated to him that she wanted the dog for herself. He smiled and rapidly excused himself, pretending he didn't understand her proposal. How could she dare want his dog?

Walking with Zoubir was entertaining. Before, Bebéi walked about the neighborhood streets, but he hadn't felt as though he belonged; he was just a spectator passing by and greeting the people. With the dog, it was different. Bebéi was becoming part of the neighborhood. And the irony was that he was so distracted by his thoughts that he didn't even think to pick up Zoubir's mess, leaving it behind on Central Avenue.

Bebéi was smiling. Now he was not just another foreigner. He continued along, greeting people as if he was no longer Bebéi the Archivist, nor Bebéi the Adventurer, but just Bebéi; no more, no less. Perhaps, Bebéi, the good Mayor waving at his voters on his way to Mass, or who knows, Bebéi the Detective, on his way to search for clues regarding the dog's owner.

His imagination kept running wild when he passed in front of the steps of La Merced Church, where he heard something that caught his attention.

"Sale chien!"[1]

It was one of the members of the Brethren standing on the church steps who had shouted out. Bebéi had always been scared by that group of men and women who he didn't know for sure weren't beggars or drunkards. The one who spat out Sale chien! that morning had an aggressive look on his face, but Bebéi only cared that the bum had spoken to him in French.

If he was alone, he would have walked on by without batting an eye, but Bebéi felt brave with Zoubir on his side and approached the bum to confirm what he had heard.

Robespierre – that was his name – reacted in a threatening manner walking towards him cursing at dogs that pooped on the street and at their owners who ignored the pile of shit left behind. He kept shouting and insulting Bebéi, who stood there listening calmly, protected by his dog. In reality, Bebéi was happy, although they were insults, that drunkard was the second person who had spoken to him in French that day. It was something new and pleasant, but his smile and simplicity weren't enough to disarm the irate Robespierre.

"Un sale chien et un sale con!"[2]

According to Grená, Robespierre came from one of the traditional families of Santa Clara, rejected for the embarrassment of his mental state. He was always very aggressive when he wasn't drunk, a rage that immediately disappeared after the first drinks turned him into a gentle lamb. This was Robespierre's ritual every single day: aggressive before he started drinking and later, when he was drunk, as affable as a nun. But that morning, he had just woken up.

Robespierre kept on with his shouts. The black dog growled, protective of Bebéi, and Robespierre raised his voice even louder. Zoubir growled fiercely, looking Robespierre directly in the eye, which in turn enraged him even more. Both kept defying each other in front of Bebéi, who had turned into a spectator, until Zoubir began to bark in a fit of rage, the unmistakable signal that he was ready to attack. Robespierre had enough common sense to shut up and

---

[1] Dirty dog!

[2] A dirty dog and a dirty idiot!

retreat, sitting between Null-and-void, the older bum who snored away in his drunkenness, and Henry Moriarty, the Canadian who observed the spectacle under the guise of being in a deep trance.

Bebéi smiled at the exchange before him. He still didn't know for sure who the bums were, but even without knowing it, he sensed that along with Zoubir, he was part of the city. The drunks wouldn't intimidate him anymore, and he sat next to them on the church steps.

He felt brave next to his dog, and for the first time, he heard a mysterious violin playing a Gypsy melody. He was beginning to unveil secrets only a few knew about, sadly, secrets that would bring him and the old city of Santa Clara by the Sea a full measure of grief and regrets.

4

The Brethren's Sunday gathering. It's nine in the morning, and the church bells ring and clang and chime away. The old city of Santa Clara by the Sea calls its faithful to Sunday Mass, while on the steps of La Merced, the bums argue about the dead man's identity.

Robespierre calmed down after the dog growled at him. It's not that he had changed his mind, but he realized that it would be better to keep his mouth shut, hiding behind Henry Moriarty, the old hippie, who still hadn't said a word with his gaze lost in outer space.

I know I could elaborate on the chubby Canadian with a long beard and hair, a mix between blonde and grey, who is always sitting on the steps of La Merced with a blank look on his face. But to call him an old hippie is a good start.

Moriarty is a poet, despite not having published anything, claiming that Walt Whitman had written everything that there was to be expressed. As he said: "To be a poet, it's not necessary to write, but one must live the vital expressions of emotions that flow through every moment." With phrases such as these, he would justify his permanent catatonic state, which to him meant nothing more than "the expression of a deep and nostalgic rebellion."

He is the one who invented the name, the Brethren. According to him, it was inspired by the Persian Brethren of Purity, a secret society created by Ikhwan Al-Safa in the eleventh century. But none of the other members care about Moriarty's words, and all of them blatantly ignore that name, which was nevertheless adopted by the rest of the city to identify the La Merced bums.

Nobody in Santa Clara seemed to pay much attention to Moriarty, and the reason was that one hundred percent of the time, he was completely stoned. He rarely drank but was always high, smoking joints and drinking teas and portions that he prepared following mysterious recipes combining ayahuasca, other exotic plants, and strange mushrooms he harvested. Everything he consumed was absolutely organic, and according to doctors, he is a healthy man, as his exuberant belly can prove. However, to talk with him is a waste of time; his eyes are permanently bewildered, and words only come out of his mouth on rare, but significant, occasions.

The old hippie was leaning against the church's wall when Robespierre sat down, looking for protection between Moriarty and Null-and-void, the Brethren's dean, who kept snoring and farting from all the beans he ate.

Bebéi stared for a while at the three of them until he saw the slight figure of La Pajerita. She was climbing up the street, followed by her skinny bitch that began wagging her tail at the sight of Zoubir. La Pajerita approached and, without a single word, sat down besides Bebéi to watch the dogs at the church entrance. La Pajerita's bitch was hyper-excited, but the dogs could not horse around too much since Zoubir could barely walk with his leg in a cast.

Bebéi thanked for her help. He spoke in French with words La Pajerita did not comprehend, but she understood what he was trying to say and was pleased. And while the two struggled to communicate, the young priest, who had arrived in Santa Clara a few months before, came to the door to welcome the honorable ladies who daily attended the morning Mass.

As soon as Robespierre saw the priest, he stood up and began with his revolutionary atheistic blasphemies. "Hypocrite! Crow! Merchant of false redemptions!" Robespierre then turned to target the women who were arriving and scudding along. "Shit-infested Eucharist eaters! Ask for forgiveness for your obscene lust for this castrated priest!"

Please forgive Robespierre, but it's impossible to ask him to be polite when he isn't yet drunk, especially when dealing with the new priest or the honorable ladies. In any case, this gives you a good idea of how a Sunday morning starts in Santa Clara by the Sea. Inside the church, the priest and the ladies fall to their knees before the altar reciting their prayers, while back on the steps, the irreverent drunkards blaspheme their abominations; a spectacle that entertains the residents and scares the tourists. In the midst of all this, Bebéi smiled while petting Zoubir, and La Pajerita looked on with a deranged expression.

Micky, the taxi driver, arrived after the Mass had begun. First, he passed by Grená's stand. Before we continue, let me explain that this corner with its four cardinal points—Grená's shaved-ice stand, the La Merced church steps, Rasta's barbershop, and the Chinaman's grocery—is, undoubtedly, the busiest place in the city. And mainly because of Grená, since everybody in sunny Santa Clara passes, at least once a day, to drink a shaved ice refreshment prepared by her, despite the dangerous exposure to the unpredictable mood of the Brethren's bums.

While having his refreshment, Micky told Grená the previous day's adventures. He knew that nothing mattered more to her than to hear a story, even if it was just gossip. Grená was the most beloved, and respected person in town. She was Black, tall, and always dressed in colorful African colors, except for the twelfth day of every month, when, to honor her dead husband, Grená only wore white.

She was the widow of the African Barber, a man who owned the barbershop and was also known for his ties to the Revolutionary Party. He and Grená had three sons, and each chose his own distinct path. One was Rastafarian, the other a police lieutenant, and the third a petty thief, but all three were very close to Grená.

Under the big yellow umbrella covering her stand decked with all those colorful fruit syrup bottles, Grená prepared the shaved ice refreshments. Her stand was a main gathering point in the neighborhood. She spent all day there, and I can assure you that nothing, absolutely nothing that happened in the old city of Santa Clara by the Sea, went unnoticed by her.

She listened to Micky's stories, while her oldest son, Rasta Bong, briefly joined them in a hurry to open the barbershop. And I must pause again to explain since I know it's unusual to think of a Rastafarian barber, and much less a pothead, anxiously tending to his business.

The African, Rasta's father, died of a heart condition, but before passing away, he made Rasta promise that he would keep the barbershop going. A task which in the beginning seemed complicated, not because of his long Rastafarian dreads, which he always kept neatly tucked away inside an enormous Jamaican Rasta tam, but because of the bits of holy herbs he liked to smoke. This problem had been overcome after he and Grená had a serious chat. He committed to work every day with the same energetic zeal as his father, on the condition that as soon as night fell, he would light up his joints, and do whatever he pleased. Rasta Bong has always been a firm believer in One Love, a Rastafarian commitment of passion and pride in honor of the great Haile Selassie, Lion of Judah.

That morning, the identity of the dead man was discussed on that corner, and Bebéi was among the people there. After a long debate, Grená and the bums concluded that Bebéi couldn't go alone to the hospital looking for more information on the deceased, and Micky would have to join him. And as speaking French was a must for Bebéi's understanding, they even briefly considered Robespierre as a possible companion, but almost immediately, the idea was thrown out; Robespierre would have to get drunk to calm down and that could cause more problems than necessary.

That's where they were when Bebéi, who more-or-less understood what they were talking about, saw Diana, the foreign backpacker who had petted Zoubir. She was coming out of the Chinaman's store, and Bebéi approached her. He explained that they needed help from someone who could speak French to figure out who and how the dog's owner had fared, and since she was on vacation, she agreed to accompany him.

Once the decision was made, Bebéi left Zoubir's leash in La Pajerita's hands and jumped with Diana into Micky's cab, leaving Grená and the others surprised by his initiative.

The twenty-minute trip was exhilarating with Micky behind the wheel, narrating stories and asking all sorts of questions, and Diana juggling between the Spanish that she understood, the English in which she thought, and the French in which she translated Micky's stories to Bebéi, who watched and smiled, enjoying every minute of his new adventure.

First, they went to the police station and later to the hospital, where they heard the grave news: "He was dead upon arrival." Few words, but quite clear.

The trio kept digging for information and met the doctor who had received the body the day before. Luckily, the doctor knew Micky from the ring, and he explained to them that the cause of death was cerebral hemorrhaging.

"Something he most likely was aware of. He had cancer that had spread all over his body, and a large tumor in his head, which he probably understood would sooner or later cause a blood vessel to burst." All three listened attentively to the doctor's explanation. "He had gone through an aggressive radiology and chemotherapy treatment."

Bebéi was impressed by the doctor's revelation, which he understood via Diana's interpreting. It reminded him of his uncle, who also knew he was going to die when he bade farewell and traveled to Argelia, leaving Bebéi alone in the world.

The doctor believed that they were the man's relatives, and they were shown the few belongings the dead man had on him, among them a hotel key.

"This is all we have," said the doctor. "We couldn't find any documents to identify him. The police came to take fingerprints in order to ID him, but they forgot to take the key."

Diana translated what she heard to Bebéi, who then asked if anyone else had come to find out about the dead man.

"Yes, two men, who didn't identify themselves," replied the doctor. "An interesting pair. One was an elegant foreigner, not too tall, dressed in a suit and tie, and the other, an older one with a long white beard wearing a ragged raincoat. They came, asked questions, and left."

The three departed the hospital with more questions than when they arrived. Now they knew for sure that Zoubir's owner was dead, and that two people had stopped by to ask questions. Bebéi had a hunch that the one with the raincoat was Diocles, and the other, with a suit and tie, was probably the same man who approached the corpse in the street and had appeared to be puzzled and fearful.

Bebéi and Diana were deflated, but not Micky. He was all smiles while crossing the hospital entrance. He had something hidden in his pocket, and when they left, he showed them the hotel key.

At first, Bebéi was frightened, but Diana was pleased.

"Don't you want to know who the dead man was?" she asked.

"If you want," added Micky, "now, we can go to his hotel and find out. What do you think?"

Bebéi knew it was the fastest way to go, but he had never come close to doing such a thing. Micky was the one who explained how easy it would be to find out the dead man's identity. The key came from a hotel in the capital not too far from the old city. A hotel that had been very prestigious but was now a little run-down, receiving businesspeople from the rural area and tourists traveling with their pets.

Micky insisted, "We can tell them that we are his friends and want to foot the bill and take his things. They will, certainly, let us into the room."

The idea was risky, but Bebéi was yielding to his new reality. To foot the bill would not be a problem – he had never spent all he earned. What was missing in his life was action and since he marched with the band, he had been caught in a continuing adventure. Besides, he needed to know about the man; he had promised it to Zoubir.

Micky and Diana were smiling during the journey. Diana was impressed with the shyness hidden in Micky's blue eyes, and Micky glanced over at Diana, thinking what a pretty foreigner she was.

The three returned to Santa Clara to discuss their new plans with Rasta and Grená, and Bebéi sat in the car in silence. He was not thinking, just feeling, and enjoying an unknown euphoria. Poor Bebéi, little did he know what he was getting into.

5

Was he a saint or a criminal? On Sunday afternoon, tourists walked along the boardwalk dividing their attention between sailboats and the arrival of the Chinese acrobats. In front of the Cathedral, the plaza was packed with little girls competing for the attention of the Mayor's wife, who was handing out colorful sweets. The boys ran around after a ball, exasperating the older men playing dominoes. At the Grand Colonial Theatre, everyone waited anxiously for the afternoon exhibit of the Spanish Theatre, which was widely promoted thanks to La Pajerita's effort in distributing the flyers. But none of that mattered to our three friends; they headed directly to La Merced.

Null-and-void had just woken up, and as usual, he was in a foul mood. From a distance, one could hear the yelling and insults between him and Frida La Trotska, the fifth member of the Brethren. Nothing out of the ordinary to those who lived there and were used to such flowery dialogues each time the two had hangovers that coincided.

Null-and-void was the senior member of La Merced Brethren; every time he awoke from a drunken state, he felt he had the right to insult everyone, but this didn't apply to Frida. Before arriving in Santa Clara, the German woman had faced much greater odds than the insults from an old drunk who could barely keep his pants from falling down.

What they said to each other is better not to repeat. The important thing is that as soon as the taxi halted in front of Grená's umbrella, the insults ceased, and they both approached with curiosity. La Pajerita also came running, and behind her, the two barking dogs.

The other two bums, Robespierre and Moriarty, remained on the church steps with their eyes and ears wide open.

Micky narrated what had happened at the hospital and their plan to go to the hotel to discover the dead man's identity. Null-and-void heard and commented with his peculiar wisdom.

"And why the hell do you want to know who the dead guy was? He's dead, nothing more to it. Is he related to this Frenchman, who doesn't even understand a damn word I'm saying? Just take care of the dog! Forget about the dead guy! End of discussion!"

Like always, Null would make a decision that everyone ignored. Rumor has it that he used to be a powerful and wealthy banker, a respected citizen, and an exemplary family man until he threw it all away and chose to be free and live as a drunk on the steps of La Merced. Too bad no one bothered to listen to what he had to say.

Micky and Diana were enthusiastic, and the taxi driver kept talking fast, insisting on taking the dog with them to the hotel.

"Even though he was there for a short time, the hotel is small, and with luck, someone at the reception will recognize him."

Grená agreed. Bebéi was still suspicious, but Diana's smile and eagerness helped him overcome his fears. For her, everything there was daring: the colonial city with its ancient houses, the narrow cobblestone streets, the black dog with his leg in a cast the chubby dude who spoke French, and the handsome taxi driver with blue eyes. All was good.

When Bebéi saw the dog get into the taxi following Diana, he couldn't resist joining in, and against Null's advice, they headed out, and the bums kept on with their discussions. The truth is neither Null nor any of the others cared much about the whole thing: the dead man's identity, the dog's future, and Bebéi's doubts were utterly irrelevant in their world. For them, the only urgent thing was to share the booze that Frida pulled out of her enormous red bag. That was life for them. One day after the other, pushing their passions to the limit and celebrating, no matter what, with any booze they could get their hands on.

The taxi pulled up at the barbershop so that Micky could explain to Rasta Bong what was happening. Rasta was upset. He had a lot of business to take care of. In addition to the barbershop, the taxi with Micky, the reggae bar with his Rastafarian friend, and the ice cream business with La Pajerita's son, Rasta was helping Rita, who worked at Ilona's restaurant, to open a stand to sell Mexican tacos at Pigalle Street. Micky was his right-hand-man, but despite Rasta's complaints, his mother's wishes always came first, and Rasta's errands could wait. Grená had her priorities clearly defined. Her main interest was to have something to talk about, and Rasta Bong knew it.

Rasta asked for them to go fast and come back soon. That suggestion, combined with Micky's natural anxiety, forced the group to move quickly. On the road, Micky kept talking, but was distracted by Diana's legs. She noticed but didn't mind. Zoubir, with his head out the window, barked at every car that passed by and next to him, and Bebéi was lost in his thoughts, fantasizing about being a detective on a new assignment with his two assistants: the speedy Caribbean taxi driver who knew all the ins and outs of the city, and the beautiful American who could solve any problem with her smile. He wanted to find out the dead man's identity. And the best part: if no one claimed the dog, he could keep him.

As soon as Micky parked at the hotel, Zoubir began to bark, wagging his tail, and making it evident that he knew the place.

Bebéi and Diana got down and walked toward the reception, where everything happened as Micky had predicted. They explained to the doorman that they had come to pay the bill, offering the excuse that their friend had to fly out on an emergency trip. The receptionist recognized the dog and even petted him.

"What happened to the poor dog? Did he break his leg?" he asked.

Diana explained he'd had an accident, and they quickly entered the elevator.

"No time to waste," said Micky.

Zoubir was hyper, jumping around and barking at the apartment door, which they opened with the key Micky had pocketed.

Inside the room, they noticed a small array of belongings: a few changes of clothes, an old suitcase, a bag of dog food, and an old worn rug where the dog must have slept.

For the dog, it was as if everything was back to normal. The same room where he had been with his friend, and all his things and food were to be found. Zoubir wagged his tail, showing his hope that the dead man could return at any moment.

Next to the bed was a book of poems by Fernando Pessoa, a Portuguese poet. The book looked worn and had a few notes and comments written in its margins. In the closet, the few clothes indicated that the deceased wasn't much of a dresser, and inside, only a suitcase with a few medications, a key chain with a bunch of keys, and a Florida driver's license with an American name and address. The dead man had been traveling with only the bare essentials. They looked inside the bathroom and didn't find anything else.

Micky was in such a hurry that he barely let them talk, and they quickly left carrying all they had found.

While throwing the man's belongings in the taxi trunk, Micky spoke with a smart face, probably trying to impress Diana. "The room was very spartan. Was he a saint or a criminal?"

Neither Diana nor Bebéi dared to reply.

Inside the car Diana mentioned that at least they had the name and address on the driver's license.

"And the telephone number," added Micky, after a pause. "It's in the receipt we got when we paid the bill."

"We could call it," Diana proposed. "Who knows, perhaps the dead man had a relative we could notify about what happened."

Bebéi didn't like this, but he agreed. He was committed to do the best by Zoubir.

Diana called the number and reached an answering machine. She Googled for more information and discovered that the address corresponded to a residency condominium in Florida. Now hooked on Bebéi's detective mission, she called the condo's office number, saying that she had some medicine to drop off for her uncle who lived there.

"No one is at home. He lives alone, with his dog," was the answer. It was Sunday, and the Lady who picked up didn't seem to have anything better to do and kept talking out of boredom. "There are a lot of people here who live alone. Although your uncle does have his dog, who everyone adores!"

Diana translated for Bebéi, who smiled. As there was nothing else to do, and Rasta was waiting for them, they returned to Santa Clara craving shaved ice. The sun was incandescent, and when they got to La Merced, Null, Robespierre, and La Trotska were already drunk. Moriarty remained stoned, and Grená kept asking questions that Diana patiently answered while subtly touching Micky's arm. But just for a few minutes. As soon as Rasta saw Micky, he called him to work.

Bebéi listened, petting Zoubir, cozily settled on his lap. In his mind was a single thought: maybe the dead man had no survivor, and he would be able to keep Zoubir for himself. But it was crucial to be sure. Maybe Diocles knew something more? Why did had he gone to the hospital? And who was the other man – the one with a suit and a tie? Could it be the same man who went to the hospital? According to Grená, his name was Ibrahim, a friend of Ilona, the restaurant owner. What did he know about the dead man?

Bebéi felt anxious as he thought about all that was happening. He didn't want to lose Zoubir, so he had to find out everything he could about the dead man.

With this thought in mind, he left La Merced to walk through the streets of the neighborhood. He started by the Cathedral Plaza, where the children were still playing. There, he met up with Doña Cecy, the cook at Ilona's restaurant, who was heading towards her sister Lais's house. She greeted him, but Bebéi sensed fear and apprehension in her face.

Further on, he saw Arcadio, *the bad guy*, as La Pajerita had told him, the one who had tried to resuscitate the deceased. Arcadio was walking alone and had no friends, but Bebéi noticed he was wearing new shoes.

Bebéi kept walking, thinking that Ibrahim knew something about the dead man. *Was he a saint or a criminal?* Micky's question kept bouncing inside his head. *He lived alone with his dog.* Isn't that what the lady said over the phone? And just like his own uncle, Zoubir's owner knew he was going to die.

Bebéi greeted Princess, who was closing the bookstore wearing his colorful wardrobe, and he stopped a moment to pet the dog. Up ahead, Bebéi saw Diocles. Why had he gone to the hospital? Bebéi wanted to talk to him, but he didn't know what to say.

He kept walking and crossed paths with Colonel Viera, who was leaving his niece's house with a little Swiss hat covering his giant head. Colonel Vieira didn't greet him back; he seemed distracted by his thoughts, and Bebéi kept going. Maybe Ilona could tell him why Ibrahim and Diocles were interested in the dead man, and he could ask her. Bebéi had been at the restaurant before; he knew Ilona and she spoke French.

Bebéi walked toward the restaurant, which was closed. What a surprise! *My restaurant never closes!* At least that's what Ilona always said. But that Sunday evening, the lights were off.

He kept following Zoubir and had the impression that Diocles was nearby. Perhaps he also wanted to approach Bebéi but was intimidated too and preferred to watch from a distance.

The restaurant was closed, he had seen Doña Cecy with fear on her face, Arcadio sporting new shoes, and Diocles following him – those weren't regular events in Santa Clara. Bebéi decided to stop thinking and headed home.

When he passed the ruins of the Old Arch, he suddenly remembered that Ibrahim was not the only one who had recognized the dead man.

Bebéi had a good memory, and he recalled that when he arrived, coming from the parade, he crossed a tall, Afro-Caribbean walking away from the body and speaking to his friend. Bebéi had heard him explaining who the dead man was. On Saturday, whatever the tall man was saying didn't seem to matter, but as Bebéi walked on Sunday evening, that flashback changed everything.

Bebéi realized that someone else could help him find out who the dead man was, and he knew that to keep Zoubir he first had to fearlessly dig out the whole story. Whatever it took!

6

Sniffing along the street. On Monday, there was the start of a new week and a fresh new life for Bebéi. As he left his apartment very early in the morning to walk his dog, he wasn't thinking about the documents he had to file for the Ambassador, nor about the new efficient and modern mail logging system being introduced at the Embassy. His life was different now. He no longer had to spend his mornings cooped up in his apartment reading news in the Parisian newspapers – all old news by the time it reached him. In the afternoons, he no longer had to sit on the balcony and watch the rain, the boats docking, or just stare at the city to calm his anxiety. And at night he would not have to follow through his window the women who combed the streets, the bars, and the hotels on Pigalle Street. Now, everything was new. With the dog, he had a much more enjoyable priority: to slowly wander along the cobblestone streets of the old neighborhood, tagging along with the languid rhythm of the dog with the cast on his leg.

The sun was not yet out, and the dog was already sniffing along the curbside wagging his tail. Bebéi, attentive behind him, was observing and keeping a certain distance. When the dog stopped, he would wait respectfully; when it was his turn to guide, Zoubir would walk beside him. They had left the apartment when the city was still in its slumber to stroll by the seafront, watching the sun as it started to rise above the sea.

The limping dog would sniff, rest his leg, and then carry on. Bebéi, right behind it, was enjoying the hike and thinking about his own priorities. He wanted to find the tall Afro-Caribbean man he had seen Saturday after the parade and planned to go to Ilona's restaurant to ask Ibrahim why he had freaked out when he recognized the corpse. Most importantly, he was determined to challenge Diocles, who was undoubtedly the raincoat-wearing man who had been with Ibrahim at the hospital.

It was with those thoughts in his mind that he sighted Diocles sitting on one of the benches of the Cathedral Plaza, corralled by his cats. Bebéi noticed that Diocles spotted him too, and stared over as if he had something important to tell.

Diocles did not belong to the Brethren, but many in Santa Clara believed he did. He slept amongst the cats under the bandstand and spent his days meandering aimlessly through the streets like a vagabond. But he would reflect about life and its contradictions, like only lunatics dared to do. It wasn't unusual to see him sitting on the steps of La Merced, plotting with Null-and-void. However, in contrast to the others Diocles did not share the same ethylic habits. He sported his white beard, but he was not as dirty or unkempt as Null or Moriarty since he would shower every other day – a condition imposed by Ilona if he wished to dine with Doña Cecy, the cook, in the restaurant kitchen.

Like Bebéi, Diocles greeted everyone with respect, but more discreetly – no waving, only nodding his head. He was refined in his manners and language, which didn't surprise anyone since, according to a story that Grená could not vouch for – but others swore true – before he arrived in Santa Clara and began sleeping among the cats, he was president of a tiny Caribbean Island, and did such an outstanding job that people begged him to keep running the country. Diocles, however, hadn't accepted. He had done his job, and it was time for others to replace him. That is what he said. The pressure, however, had been so intense that he had to compromise by staying four more years, not as a President but as Vice President, and that was all. After being President and Vice President, he wanted to become a nobody, which is why he ended up leaving his island.

Bebéi, who didn't know about his past, had always felt intimidated by Diocles' silent and sober expression. Still, Diocles knew something about the man who died, and Bebéi walked toward him with a severe expression on his face and sat down on the bench at his side. Zoubir sat peacefully at Diocles' feet, as if waiting for him to talk, and all three fell silent. Diocles said nothing, Bebéi didn't ask, and the dog just stared at both men. They stayed side by side until the birds grew tired of chirping and the cats vanished, hunting for secret adventures. They remained silent until all dogs grew tired of their laziness and began barking, and the pigeons started to shit out the breadcrumbs they had eaten. That is how they remained for almost an hour. Diocles and Bebéi didn't uttered a word until the sun warmed the square and everyone went looking for shade. They felt each other's presence, and Bebéi realized that Diocles preferred silence to a lie, and he understood.

That same morning, after his silent encounter with Diocles, Bebéi went to work and received a call from the police.

"We only have your name as friend or relative and no one else showed up to claim the body." That is what the policewoman told him.

Bebéi answered with the help of Carmela, one of the Ambassador's assistants, who had a desk next to Bebéi's, and understood when the policewoman added, "The fingerprints were identified since they were registered at the Interpol and belong to a South American. We have the name and his date of birth, but it's intriguing since the fingerprints matched a man who died thirty years ago in a motorcycle accident in Italy."

Both Carmela and Bebéi shrugged their shoulders. How was it possible for the dead man to be alive on Saturday morning if he had already been dead for thirty years?

On that same evening, Bebéi had the idea to call the archivist at the American Embassy. He wanted to know more about the name on the driver's license they had found at the hotel. The American had called him weeks before, inviting Bebéi to an archivist conference in Miami, and although he had no intention of going, Bebéi had kept his number. During the conversation, Bebéi mentioned the dead man, his driver's license, and even what the police had discovered about his previous death.

It's unfortunate that Bebéi made that call. In his world, he never heard that IDs could be falsified, and that even deaths could be faked.

For him, the death of his parents and especially his uncle were very real and painful events.

He was reflecting on what he had discovered when he left his office and took his dog for a walk. Zoubir was excitedly sniffing around, while Bebéi observed attentively everyone who worked at the construction sites nearby. He was well aware that the tall Afro-Caribbean man wore a hardhat like the construction workers. He remembered his face and height and he knew he would be able to recognize him. He kept his eyes open, following his dog along the streets and also up to some open doors that Zoubir walked through without asking for permission.

That Monday, they invaded Rasta Bong's barbershop, and Rasta welcomed the dog kindly with a big smile. On Tuesday, his dog jumped into Ling's shop, and Ling's daughter Kay gave him two cookies. On Wednesday, Zoubir intruded into the bookstore and was rewarded with sunflower seeds that Princess kept next to the medicinal herbal teas and organics.

At the end of each afternoon, Bebéi and his dog would slip by the Cathedral Plaza for Zoubir to play with other dogs gathered near the ice cream vendor. While the other dogs barked, Zoubir attempted, unsuccessfully, to chase the pigeons with the cast still on his leg. Either walking or sitting on the square bench, Bebéi attentively observed every person that passed by, searching for the tall, skinny Afro-Caribbean man who knew something about the man who had died.

On Friday, Bebéi was called up to visit the morgue. Following Grená's advice, he went with Diana, who was still in Santa Clara. She hadn't stayed there for Bebéi or the dog, but mostly for the blue-eyed Micky, and his gentle hands.

They went, signed the release papers, and waited until the body was cremated. The dead man's ashes were handed over to Bebéi inside a cheap metal can that Bebéi immediately replaced by a blue Algerian pot he had in his apartment.

"He deserves more," Bebéi said to Zoubir.

He placed the pot next to a candlestick holder his uncle gave him before leaving for Algeria. He remembered his uncle saying, *All you need is to trust in the candlestick holder you have inside your chest. It will always enlighten your path and help you find what you are looking for.*

Bebéi never completely understood those words, bt as he wanted to find out more about the deceased, he put the ashes beside the candlestick holder.

That night he left his apartment, and he carefully carried the pot. With the ashes in his hands he continued his mission – walking his dog, searching for the tall Afro-Caribbean man, and thinking about Ibrahim, who never again showed up.

According to Grená, Ibrahim was Ilona's friend and, when in town, he used her restaurant as office. Bebéi wanted to ask him why he had gotten so uneasy when recognizing the corpse, and every night he passed in front of the restaurant he got the same answer:

Ibrahim isn't here, and we don't know where he is, nor when he will return.

Bebéi was intrigued and couldn't understand why any of the waiters would not explain to him why the place was closed Sunday after the stranger's death. Without understanding, he kept walking around the neighborhood, carrying the dead man's blue pot and following Zoubir's limping gait.

Grená observed him anxiously walking but could not help him. She was also intrigued. Ibrahim's disappearance, Diocles' silence, and Ilona's angriness clearly signaled that, somewhere, a secret was hidden. She knew how to be patient; the truth would come, and she watched Bebéi walking and walking around.

Bebéi walked every night until no one was out. And, on Friday, in the deep of the night, he passed by the old house in ruins where Doña Cecy hid her four children. From afar, he listened to the Gypsy violin.

He would not give up and he kept walking until the dog grew exhausted, and they went back home to sleep.

7

Is it reality or delusion? In Santa Clara by the Sea, reality goes hand in hand with delusion, was a statement once made by Henry Moriarty. The line was now being repeated over and over by Frida La Trotska on that Saturday morning while she tippled a bottle of vodka at the Cathedral Plaza in front of Lais's window. Next to her, Hector, the band instructor, wanted to confront reality but recognized the delusion of his dreams were a comfort compared to the reality that left him older, frustrated, and distant from everything he fought for.

Colonel Vieira, the retired military with rigid principles, passionately discarded the idea. He said, "Delusion is a subterfuge for the weak." But he then grew silent as he recalled his delirious desires for Riquita, his first cousin's stepdaughter, who had left the university and returned to Santa Clara. The old Colonel couldn't get her image out of his mind – sweet Riquita with her oversized glasses and huge tits peeping from her low-cut top, suffocating the crucifix buried between the boobs. *What a pleasant delirium*, thought the Colonel.

Frida was just drinking; her mind was left blank. In the past, she had thought a lot. Like that afternoon, or perhaps it had been a nightmare, where a young woman detonated a bomb inside a train station in Germany. That had been the maximum expression of delirium trying to transform reality. After that, she had stopped thinking – it only increased her pain – and without thinking she gave her body to survive, succumbing to her torturers' desires. That was how she ended up as a prostitute in Santa Clara before becoming an alcoholic and turning into a deadbeat drunk, and one of the Brethren on the steps of La Merced. And now she was getting drunk in front of Lais' window – to bear that she was still alive.

Next to her were her two friends, also foreigners working at Pigalle Street. Ludmilla, the Russian acrobat, and the little Chinese Doll, the master of ceremonies at *La Vie en Rose* with her minute body and doll-like face, and who, according to Grená's strong opinion, was neither a prostitute nor stupid.

"She works for the Chinese as an informant getting tips from captains and sailors docking at the port," stated Grená adamantly.

You might be getting confused with all those new characters in our story, but let me explain. The corner of La Merced where Grená has her stand is not the sole gathering point of Santa Clara. Every morning, in Cathedral Plaza, you could see a line in front of Lais' window. People start to gather there around ten-thirty, since every day at eleven, Lais opens the window of her apartment on the first floor, to sell empanadas.

That Saturday, the first group in the line contained Princess, Hector, and the Colonel. The three friends got together every day at the square to talk about politics in the world. And right behind them, Frida was happy to enjoy the company of her best friends from Pigalle Street.

Bebéi was never there; he didn't like empanadas. Too greasy and heavy, he once confessed to Carmela and, following her advice, never repeated the words elsewhere.

Bebéi was not delirious that morning; he knew he must speak with Ilona. Perhaps she could tell him where Ibrahim was and why the restaurant was closed after the stranger's death. He was very suspicious. He thought again of what Ilona had once told him, proudly - that her restaurant never closes. Not even on Carnival or Christmas, but on the day after the man died, all of the lights had been off.

Bebéi had a secret admiration for Ilona. She was an attractive woman, inspiring desire in both men and women. What made her even more special was how she treated her customers. She had a natural kindness with which she handled everyone, a unique gift of making anyone feel like royalty at the restaurant, and that is how Bebéi felt when he went there.

The last time he had dinner there, she had approached him as if he was an old friend and took him to one of the tables out on the terrace. They chatted in French, and she suggested, "J'imagine que tu veux Doña Cecy's pulp risotto, n'est pas vraie?" And Bebéi had nodded with a bemused smile.

He had already been there a few times, but on that Saturday, he didn't want Doña Cecy's risotto or Ilona's smile. He wanted answers, but so far, he had had no luck.

When he got inside, he immediately sensed that Ilona was acting differently. He noticed she was in a foul mood and was snapping at the waiters. For some reason, she seemed to be filled with angst. Bebéi tried to approach her, but Ilona ignored him.

Bad luck for Bebéi, but good luck for the dog. As soon as Bebéi sat down on the terrace, one of the waiters approached him and asked if he could take the dog to Ilona. "The boss wants to meet him." And Bebéi didn't protest.

The dog followed the waiter limping, and Bebéi was left alone. On a table nearby, he saw Gigi. She was Ilona's close friend, and she seemed upset. Bebéi was used to seeing Ilona and Gigi laughing and drinking together, but that Saturday, Gigi was alone, and Ilona was inside her office with the black dog.

Bebéi ate in silence, confused about what was going on.

The terrace became crowded, and everything was almost normal, but Ilona was not greeting her customers, making rounds at every table, chatting, and smiling. No one played the guitar, no one danced, and no one sang. The food was good, but the restaurant lacked her joy and magic touch.

After eating, Bebéi decided to find out for himself, and without asking anyone's permission, he went up to the small office at the back of the restaurant. He had been there before when Ilona showed him pictures of her friends but that Saturday she was not smiling. She was sitting on the sofa with puffy eyes as if she had been crying, petting the dog.

Dazed and without knowing exactly what to say, Bebéi asked about Ibrahim. She said he was out on a trip and wasn't sure when he would return. He then mentioned that the dog belonged to the dead man.

"I know," was all she said.

He hesitated, but then he told her it seemed as if Ibrahim had known the dead man. Ilona ignored his comment.

Bebéi noticed that some of the photographs he had seen before had been removed from the wall.

"If you don't want this dog, let me know," Ilona said. "I can keep him. I've been thinking about getting a dog."

Bebéi's reaction was harsh. He put the collar back on the dog, said goodbye to Ilona, and left the restaurant. Zoubir was his new friend, and he wasn't planning to give it to anyone, not even her, whom he considered a respectful woman.

Following Zoubir, Bebéi went back to meandering through the old neighborhood streets. He thought about how Ilona had shown affection towards the dog, but how she had ignored Bebéi and Gigi. He couldn't wrap his head around this. He wasn't yet aware of the hidden secrets, and he couldn't even begin to imagine how much passion, tragedy, and hate the dog and the dead stranger would bring to Santa Clara.

The city was quiet in slumber under a light rain that kept falling. In the Chinese grocery store four guys played dominoes and Bebéi stopped to watch. He liked dominoes and became engrossed in the game until suddenly his heart started to beat faster; one of the players was the skinny tall man he had seen when the dead man was found.

Bebéi felt euphoric. He needed to speak with the man, but he didn't know how. No one around the table understood him, and after a few seconds of floundering about, he ran with his limping dog towards Frida who was still in the square, chatting with her two friends under the roof of the bandstand.

Bebéi approached them and began to mutter in confusion, trying to explain, but his anxiety didn't let him. It was the Chinese Doll who took his hand and calmed him down with a sweet kiss on his cheek.

Calmer now, Bebéi was able to ask for their help to speak with the tall Afro-Caribbean man who was playing dominoes.

The three women agreed to help him and they headed back together to the Chinese grocery store. There after questions, answers, interpreting and explanations, they finally understood that the tall man was a carpenter who worked on house restorations in the neighborhood.

"Yes, I met the dead man," he said while still playing.

"And who was he?" Bebéi asked anxiously in French.

After the corresponding translation, the man replied, "I met him while on a job assignment restoring his house. He lived not too far from here." The tall man paused, studied the dominoes in his hands, and slapped one down on the table with a splash. He then smiled and continued. "That was more than five years ago when he wasn't bald or sick. He was Doña Ilona's husband."

"That's impossible!" exclaimed Bebéi, who didn't need Ludmilla's help to understand the last statement.

"Yes sirrrreeee. I never forgot his face, even though earlier he was much stronger and happier, but it was him, Doña Ilona's husband," the tall man insisted.

Bebéi shook his head from side to side in disbelief while he listened to Ludmilla's translation.

The tall man, without missing a beat in the game, kept on. "How could one not notice if the job at their home lasted many months? They lived at the end of the boardwalk. He would spend all day at the house and always made coffee for all of us workers there." After he spoke, he raised his gaze to watch Ludmilla translating. When he deduced that Bebéi was up to date with what he had said, he added, "I was surprised to see him that day because a while back I heard he had died, but it wasn't true; it was he who was face down on the streets the day the band paraded."

Bebéi was still in disbelief, but he wasn't the only one. Ludmilla and the Chinese Doll were also in shock. Not only with the story but with Frida's reaction. As soon as the man stated that the dead man was Ilona's husband, Frida had got up and left. She didn't say where she was going. She simply got up, forgetting that she was drunk, and ran away as if she had something urgent to do.

Bebéi and the other two women went back to the bandstand. He was confused by the unexpected news, and the women were uneasy about Frida's reaction.

Ilona couldn't be the dead man's wife. Her husband had died four years before. Nothing made any sense, and what made Bebéi more uncomfortable was the fact that since he arrived in Santa Clara, the two people whom he appreciated most were Ilona and Diocles, and neither one was telling him the truth.

Why were they lying?

The two friends were also wondering about Frida's sudden disappearance. She never acted that way before. Frida always seemed aloof to everything and everyone; nothing seemed important to her. But that evening she left in a hurry with a worried look.

Bebéi, absorbed in thoughts, gazed at his dog sniffing around. He didn't have anyone he could trust in Santa Clara by the Sea. Sad, but he would not give up, and with the candlestick holder and Zoubir on his side, he would keep looking for the truth.

8

A blind girl who could see. Bebéi was upset about Diocles' silence and Ilona's lies. But he couldn't complain. He knew more people in Santa Clara than in all those years living in Paris. For the first time in his life, he had a friend who wagged his tail when he came home, and he slept peacefully with the dog's snout on his legs. And on Sunday, while following his sniffing dog through the streets, Bebéi reflected on his new friendships.

Organizing files at the embassy was a lonely job, but he had Carmela sitting next to him. She was a teacher, and, after retiring, she was hired by the French Embassy to adorn with her elegant writing the invitations they would send out. She was a lonely woman who was kept entertained thanks to Bebéi's company and stories.

Bebéi also felt that after the parade, people in the neighborhood were greeting him warmly, including the Brethren members, who let him sit next to them on the steps of La Merced and listen to their ranting. Of course, Frida still scared him, now more than ever after her strange behavior when the tall man mentioned Ilona's husband.

Frida was a strong German woman who, when sober, would amble with her shoulders hunched and a sorrowful expression on her face. Looking at her, one would think that all world's griefs were in the bags she carried in her hands. Nevertheless, after a few drinks, depressed Frida would become Trotska Frida. Rebellious heiress of the European revolution, who, along with Robespierre, would storm the Bastille, break down the Brandenburg Gate, and sing the International Socialist Anthem at the top of her lungs.

Robespierre was a different case. He was also aggressive, but only when he was sober. He took it upon himself to insult everyone, mainly

Joseph the Princess. However, he was sweet and harmless when drinking and would enjoy waltzing across the streets with children and pigeons. In this sense, he was the opposite of Frida, since while drinks calmed down Robespierre, the more the German drank, the more revolutionary she became. More often than not she would end up at the police station, not for her words, since no one could really understand Frida's speeches, but for fear of what her enthusiasm and powerful arms could do.

Frida's and Robespierre's friendships were crucial to Bebéi since they both knew French and helped him keep up to date with the happenings in the neighborhood. Henry Moriarty, the Canadian, had also mastered the French language, and Bebéi liked to sit in front of him returning his stare and trying to make him smile. The Canadian was either stoned or reading his torn pieces of papers filled with Walt Whitman's poems. For some inexplicable reason, Bebéi felt a great appreciation for him and also for Null-and-void, with his useless instructions and haphazard pants, which were constantly falling down.

Null was the Brethren's dean. According to what Grená explained, before, he had been an important businessman. A man of great power in foreign lands, but, apparently, no one in Santa Clara seemed to know his real name. For everybody there, he was just Null-and-void, a name he christened himself upon his arrival. Bebéi loved watching him when leading the Brethren's meetings. Null would listen patiently to all comments until he got bored and then end the meeting presenting his decision: "The two of you will go ask the nuns for a plate of food. You there will go to the Chinese grocer's asking for a bottle of hard liquor on credit and this Algerian here who just sits there smiling and doesn't understand a fuck we are talking about can provide the money we need for the next bottle. And now I don't want anyone else to bug me, I'm going to take a nap."

Rarely were Null's decisions carried out. After giving his verdict he would retreat, and the others would continue arguing, calling out the politicians and criticizing everyone else. They would rant and rave to the tourists who would drop alms into their hands, insult the priests who lent them a hand, and curse the Mayor's wife who brought them food. They'd insult the police, blaspheme the days gone by, and curse even more the days ahead. All this with the utmost passion.

There was never a dull day on the La Merced Church steps. Things there weren't as bureaucratic, logical, or insipid as in the Ministry in Paris or at the Embassy where Bebéi worked, and this is what he loved the most. On that corner everything was confusing, intense, anarchic, and yet full of life. The bums would fight passionately over the bottles they'd drink and would come close to fist fights arguing over who was the best in handing out the food around the old quarter, whether it was the church ladies of Saint Francis Church with their Tuesday soup, the Mayor's witch wife with her Wednesday chicken broth, or perhaps the Asturian Association with their Thursday stew.

Among others who lived in Santa Clara by the Sea, Bebéi also admired the bookstore owner, Princess, who marched with him and was always nice to Zoubir. Bebéi was mostly impressed with Princess's knowledge. There was not a single question that he did not know how to answer. Having arrived in Santa Clara after being shunned from other lands because of his forbidden sexual preferences, Princess had come to live and be happy there, where he proudly professed being gay, and was a bookstore owner.

During the day, Princess could be found at his bookstore reading on a stool or tending to customers. But at night, he sang in a cabaret at the port and went by the name of Lola Marlene, the Blue Angel, decked out with a blonde wig, a silk dress, and high heels. However, that wasn't something to be talked about in public.

Princess's best friends were Colonel Viera and Hector, who were forced to bend their rigid moral code to keep his company, recognizing that no one knew the history of Santa Clara better than him. Both preferred to ignore that their chatting companion was the blue-eyed drag queen with false tits, the main attraction at La Gata Caliente. Neither of them had stepped foot in the place: a cabaret of ill-repute and damnation.

"I'm telling you all this, but keep it to yourself," Grená whispered to Bebéi as he struggled to understand what the word 'secret' meant to the old lady.

Like everyone there, Bebéi had learned much of what he knew from Grená. She was always sitting with her colorful dresses behind her shaved-ice stand, listening to what the others wanted to tell and telling what she wanted everyone to know. Grená always knew who owed money and who was spending beyond their means. She knew who had just gotten a job or had a fight with their boss. Which man was after which woman. And which women lusted after Chombo, the Zen yoga teacher, who was always strolling shirtless through the streets sporting his sensual physique. Grená knew who was on good terms with the Mayor and those who would backstab him. Grená knew all and would tell all, and that's why any day and any time there was a buzz around her yellow umbrella. Always dressed in colorful African colors, but on every twelfth of the month, Grená would wear those dazzling loosened white clothes, making her look like the mother of all African gods.

Bebéi also liked Rasta Bong, Grená's son, and his friend Micky, the jittery taxi driver. Many nights, while walking, Bebéi saw them both coming out with eyes brightened by marijuana, marching towards Pigalle Street to meet up their girlfriends. Bebéi sometimes followed them, smiling at their slow swinging pace while high.

Bebéi thought about all these things, trying to relax after an intense week filled with discoveries, new friends, and some disappointments. He looked with sympathy at his dog, his main friend, who kept sniffing left and right, probably looking for the dead man or someone who might know where he was.

It was still early, and Bebéi was strolling while the city was lazily awakening for another Sunday, when the dog got inside the old and ragged house where Lais and other less wealthy families lived.

Lais already had her apartment door open and when she saw them, she invited Bebéi to have a coffee she had just brewed. Lais was not a talker and never gossiped, but she was famous for her cooking skills. The coffee smell and the little cookies she offered him were enticing, and Bebéi realized his dog had stepped out of Lais' apartment and climbed the stairs while he was distracted and enjoying his coffee. Other families lived in the building, so he needed to get the dog back. Bebéi went after Zoubir up to the third floor where, at the end of the dimly lit hall, he saw his dog standing in front of an open door. Bebéi approached and looked inside a small room that could barely fit a bed, a chair, and a table. There were no lights, and once his eyes adjusted to the darkness, Bebéi could see an older man sleeping on the bed and, on a chair, in front of an empty table, a little girl.

Zoubir went inside and snuggled up to the girl's feet. The window was closed, but a meager light had trespassed through a small hole, and Bebéi could see that everything inside the room was clean and tidy. The floor, the table, the bed, everything was well taken care, in stark contrast to the room's simplicity.

The girl couldn't have been more than ten years old and was dressed like the indigenous Kuna women. She wore a bandana on her head, and Bebéi noticed some jewelry on her arms and legs.

She spoke first.

"My name is Irigandi."

Listening to her words, Bebéi contemplated her face. The little girl looked like paintings he admired at the museums of his old city.

Irigandi remained seated, petting Zoubir, and Bebéi stayed at the door. The image of the girl in that little room made such an impression on him that he was speechless, staring at her. The only sound inside the room was the breathing of the older man sleeping, and the only movement was offered by Zoubir, happily wagging his tail.

Bebéi had seen many Kuna women on the streets wearing colorful dresses and selling arts and crafts, but none were as angelic and beautiful as her.

Irigandi was in Santa Clara, far away from her family, keeping her grandfather company as he went almost daily to the hospital for hemodialysis.

She kept petting the dog, thinking that if she had a dog, she would go out and feel the warmth of the sun that reminded her of the island where she was born. By her feet, Zoubir was quiet, enjoying Irigandi's tiny fingers and trying to lick his leg beneath the cast. Bebéi was just staring at her, and without words, all three became friends and decided to go out together.

When Irigandi stood up, she extended her arm to let Bebéi know she needed help.

"I can't see," she said, smiling sweetly.

He understood what she was telling him, and as if he had spent his entire life caring for the blind, he passed the dog's leash to her and helped her walk by following the animal, wagging its tail.

All three went down the stairs towards the street, Zoubir ahead, followed by Irigandi holding the leash, and behind them, Bebéi, alert to every move, protective of Irigandi's steps.

When they reached the door, the sun illuminated Irigandi, revealing the colors of her clothes, the designs on her blouse, and the gold jewelry on her arms and legs. She was even more angelic than Bebéi initially thought.

That was the first time they walked together, sharing their emotions and the sweet sound of their silence. They marched one behind the other, and Irigandi seemed to levitate with her long dress and tiny steps. Their quiet march attracted everyone's attention, interrupting conversations, stopping cars, and even quieting down the birds.

Since that first Sunday, Irigandi learned to understand what Bebéi was feeling. She couldn't comprehend his words, but since the day she was born, her entire village knew that Irigandi was a Nele, and true to all Neles, she could see the light emanating from people's hearts.

Irigandi was born blind, and although she had the gift to see the emotions of others, she couldn't admire the colors of the ocean, but she learned from her grandmother how to walk amidst the darkness and to interpret what words could not express.

That is how she knew that Bebéi was a good soul, and she didn't need to understand his words to know that they should find out who was the dead man, and what Diocles was hiding.

Irigandi also knew that she and the black dog had always been linked by something stronger. She didn't understand the reason yet, but ever since the dog walked into the tiny room, she immediately knew that they both had the same roots, and together they would continue on their journey. That is why, from that day on, Bebéi never walked alone again. After he met Irigandi, they were no longer two walking but three – the dog always leading the way, followed by Irigandi seemingly floating in the air, and behind them, Bebéi, who couldn't understand where they were headed, but still kept pursuing his path passionately.

When they passed near the restaurant, Ilona watched them from a distance and silently thought to herself that perhaps that dog, the Kuna girl, and the chubby sweet foreigner, were the only hope she had to understand why that son-of-a-bitch had lied, and left her, only to return to Santa Clara by the Sea on the day he would die.

9

Ilona, betrayed by love. On the steps of La Merced Church everyone was confused. No one understood why Frida had vanished when she heard that the dead man was Ilona's husband, the same man who had been dead for four years, or perhaps thirty if one believed what the police had said.

The residents of Santa Clara had no idea that the dead stranger was none other than Don Francisco Lacayo or Julio, as his closest friends called him. Everyone there knew that Don Francisco had died when his plane split in two before landing in the Dominican Republic. They even remembered the sadness that had engulfed Ilona after hearing about his death.

The sudden disappearance of Frida La Trotska perplexed her friends. They sensed that finding out about Ilona's husband had frightened her somehow.

Grená noticed something serious was going on and made an important decision. There were way too many unanswered questions that could complicate things even more. She asked Micky to bring some chairs from the Chinese grocer, the same they used for domino tournaments, and place them in front of her stand. It was going to be a long talk.

As it was the twelfth day of the month, Grená wore white – a full white skirt, white blouse, and a white scarf covering her hair— honoring her husband, the African Barber, who died on the twelfth day of the month.

Sitting next to her were Bebéi and Irigandi, with the dog curled up at her feet. Right in front was Ludmilla, who, according to Grená, was charmed by her son Rasta. And standing next to her, Null-and-

48

void, who always found an excuse to get close to the Russian dancer. Robespierre was also around but didn't seem interested in what Grená started to explain.

"Ilona was born in Maracaibo and comes from a very wealthy family there. She studied at an all-girls school and was among the best students."

Grená was doing what she loved best, talking, and being listened to, and she continued. "You should see the picture Doña Cecy has of Ilona when she was fifteen. She was a beautiful girl, but her brother was a problem."

At this point, Grená put on a worried expression, indicating that she was about to say something dire.

"Her brother fell in love with her, and not only that, but he was unstable and vigorously possessive," she said. "A madman."

Null-and-void, distracted by looking at Ludmilla, pulled his pants up, and Robespierre left the group to follow a pigeon.

"The brother caused her problems. He didn't let anyone look at her, much less talk to her, and then he got into drugs, and his insanity got worse. He went berserk and kidnapped Ilona; he wanted her to be his lover." And Grená clarified, turning to Irigandi. "It's best not to get into details because Ilona has suffered greatly by it. He kept her as a hostage for many weeks until the police rescued her and took him to jail. He was sick and swore he would never let any other man approach her, and Ilona remained in a clinic until she was able to go home. Even though she was deeply disturbed by it all, she was willing to live her life, and accepted an invitation from a young man who was a friend of the family to go to a party. Big mistake. Soon after, the boy was found dead."

Grená paused to emphasize the seriousness of what she had just shared.

"From jail, her brother led a handful of thugs who would carry out his orders and follow her. Ilona was furious and ran away. She was barely eighteen when she left her family house to live in Cartagena, and the first year went by without incident."

At that moment, Grená noticed Null engrossed in staring at Ludmilla's cleavage and yelled at him. The bum lowered his head, embarrassed, and Grená continued.

"When she heard that her brother's orders were to threaten all her boyfriends, she went for full revenge. She became a prostitute and let him know that he would have to kill all sailors along the Caribbean since she was going to sleep with all of them."

Grená told them that with a proud expression.

"Ilona wanted to take control of her life. If that is what she had to do; she would do it. She traveled as a prostitute through Cartagena, Barranquilla, Aruba, Trinidad, and Barbados until she reached Santa Clara and headed straight to Pigalle Street, where there had never been a more respected woman than her."

Robespierre came back, and the pigeon he was following also got closer.

"As soon as she arrived," Grená continued, "she met Doña Cecy, who cleaned one of the women's houses, and since then they have been close friends."

While Grená was talking, all others kept listening in silence. Even La Pajerita, who had also joined in, could not take her eyes off Grená, despite her own delirious mind.

"At that time, life for the women on Pigalle Street was different. All brothels belonged to pimps who would exploit them and control every woman's move. But Ilona didn't lower her head and defied them by opening her own house together with three friends. It was the first house owned and controlled by women without depending on any man. Two of them no longer live here, but the old-timers know who the third one was."

She cleared her throat to add to the suspense and let the bomb drop by.

"Frida... Frida La Trotska." And Grená paused, enjoying the surprised looks that her words had caused.

"Frida had arrived in Santa Clara before Ilona, and they quickly became friends. They made history in the city. Their house, Cloud Castle, was the best, and Doña Cecy was with them, helping with the management. Even though Ilona and Frida always got along quite well, there was a big difference between them. Ilona knew how to control her drinking. Not Frida. The ghosts Frida harbors inside were too strong to be overcome by any therapy. They cared for each other, but their lives took different paths, and they rarely see each other today."

50

While speaking, Grená caressed Irigandi's arm, and the little girl, in turn, spoiled Bebéi's dog by combing its fur with her tiny fingers.

"It didn't come easy for them," Grená continued. "All the other cabaret owners – all pimps – were determined to destroy them. They didn't know that Ilona, stubborn as she was, was determined to hold onto her independence. Null-and-void here, who now can barely keep his pants up, knows the story very well since he was once an important man who had lent Ilona and Frida a big hand for their house."

Null remained silent, lowering his gaze.

"The example they gave inspired many women. Today, it should be no surprise that women control all houses on Pigalle Street," she said, smiling at Ludmila.

"Ilona kept the Castle open for many years," continued Grená with a proud expression. "It wasn't rare to bump into renowned politicians, famous artists, and also the adventurer type – Ilona's favorites. The ones that stood out. The others, as she preferred to call them. Those that had stories to tell after risking their lives globetrotting around the world. As Ilona used to say, 'Better broken than boring.'"

Listening from his chair, Bebéi was fascinated by Ilona's story.

"She also helped us a lot," said Grená. "When my husband passed away, Rasta Bong was a total pothead. She helped to convince him to take care of the barbershop, and to this day Ilona is a partner in all my son's investments."

Rasta, who had also approached the scene after spotting Ludmilla, added for confirmation, "Yes... Ilona is one love."

"Ilona had many lovers," continued Grená, "never an exclusive one. She knew that her brother was still keeping a close watch from prison, and she was afraid that he could kill her boyfriends." Grená turned her head to Irigandi. "Her brother became more powerful and violent as a head mobster, and made constant threats, but then Ilona met Don Francisco."

Honestly, Grená was getting tired of talking so much. Her specialty was quick-to-the-point gossip, not long stories, but she had to finish to help them understand.

"Don Francisco, who was called Julio, was a friend of Theo Cavafys, the Greek sea Captain, a great friend of all of us in Santa Clara, and it was through Cavafys that she met Julio."

She paused to rest her voice.

"We know very little about Ilona's husband. It was always a big mystery. Rumor has it that he had something to do with drug trafficking, but we never knew for sure. Whatever he did, he never did it around here. We rarely saw him here in the streets. He was always traveling, and when he wasn't, he was taking care of his own life, next to Ilona and far away from everyone. He helped her open the restaurant, and for that, he had to be someone very powerful because one way or another, he was able to settle things with Ilona's brother, who never bothered her again. At least not while Don Francisco was alive."

Null-and-void kept holding up his pants and glancing at Ludmilla's tits. Ludmilla noticed and smiled back, teasing, for having caught him in the act. Robespierre thought the smile was for him and got closer to Ludmilla.

"Alongside Don Francisco, Ilona changed and became a calm and composed woman. They were very happy until he died in that plane crash in the Dominican Republic. Ilona was depressed. It took a while, but with time she regained her self-esteem and went on with her life."

Then Grená paused. She was also confused about many facts that didn't seem to make sense.

"You say," she said, looking at Bebéi, "that a carpenter swears that the man found dead on Saturday was Don Francisco Lacayo, Ilona's husband. That is hard to prove, and to make things worse if it is true, it would be difficult to understand."

After pausing again, and caressing Irigandi's arm, Grená concluded by saying what was also on everyone else's mind. Something that even Irigandi was beginning to realize.

"La Trotska knows more about Ilona's life than we do, and if she took off running after hearing it, it's because she knows something that we don't. And this may mean that Ilona is in danger, big danger."

She didn't say anything else; Grená had already told all there was to tell.

10

And now they were four. The three of them were strolling along the streets of the old city of Santa Clara by the Sea. Nothing significant happened throughout the whole week. The calm that precedes the storm, predicted Frida.

Bebéi continued his work at the Embassy, and each morning, before going to the office, he would walk Zoubir to Irigandi's apartment, and as soon as he left his work, he would run back to pick up Zoubir and Irigandi and walk with them.

It was always the same, the dog walked ahead and behind was Irigandi with a firm grip on the leash. Closing the line was Bebéi, with his body leaning forward and hands clasped behind his back.

They walked in silence every evening, captivating those who watched them. Irigandi, with her colorful clothes and her head held high, had an air of fearless dignity, and seemed to be floating on air, guided by the dog. From a distance, Diocles watched them.

He wished he could approach them. He knew what they wanted to know but he had to keep it secret: the dead man was indeed Ilona's husband. That's what Ibrahim, said when Diocles went with him to the hospital. He was also there when Ilona broke down in tears and wails as Ibrahim confirmed the dead man was Julio.

Diocles had never met Julio, nor did he know who he was. Julio was known as Don Francisco Lacayo and according to Ilona, Ibrahim, and everyone else in Santa Clara, he had died in an accident four years before. Impossible to understand. Julio was Ibrahim's business partner and Ilona's husband and was already dead when he died again that Saturday a few blocks from the restaurant.

Diocles could feel Ilona's tension as he held her in his arms in front of Ibrahim.

"If they find out he was alive, they will think he was hiding something. And if he died here, they will think we knew about it," said Ibrahim.

Confused, Diocles remembered Ilona's desperation as she realized that her once-dead husband, the one she loved so much, had still been alive. But Diocles didn't understand why Ibrahim was so scared and kept repeating that the dead man's death would bring great danger for all of them.

Diocles was one of the few who knew why the restaurant closed that Sunday. He and Doña Cecy spent the entire day trying to calm Ilona. Diocles saw Ibrahim leave hastily that Sunday, saying it was best to hide since they are going to kill us. He also heard Ilona's friend Gigi suggest desperately that it would be best for her to flee. Diocles knew about all this, but he couldn't tell.

The more people who know the greater is the danger, Doña Cecy had said.

Diocles felt bad because he could see how much Bebéi wanted to know what he couldn't reveal. That's why he was reluctant to approach them and was watching from afar as the trio walked through the cobblestone streets of the old city.

The three kept marching with their worries, and as they passed at the Cathedral Plaza, Princess, Hector, and Colonel Viera watched them go by. They, too, couldn't understand what was going on. They knew Don Francisco Lacayo was involved in drug trafficking but was well respected and kind to everyone. They knew as well that, four years before, upon his death, some shady characters appeared in Santa Clara asking questions.

"Who were his friends?" they asked, and, without a doubt, the friends belonged to the drug cartels.

The police and some well-dressed Americans had also roamed the neighborhood, asking *Who was he? What did he do?*

Julio's death had fooled them all: the police, the Americans, his friends, and the cartels. And his death had also fooled Ilona, who was his wife and loved him.

From her window, where she sold chicken soup and empanadas, Lais also watched them in silence. She knew what was going on. Don

Francisco Lacayo was, in reality, Julio; and Julio was actually the Condor; and the Condor was more powerful than any of Ilona's brother's thugs. Because of that fear, her brother didn't dare threaten Ilona. All the cartels respected the Condor. Lais had heard this from her sister, Doña Cecy, who had shared this, sobbing, mentioning that Ilona was in great danger.

Lais knew that Ilona's desperation wasn't because she found out that Julio died that Saturday – whenever he died, it didn't matter to her. She was suffering because, perhaps, Julio hadn't loved her the same way she loved him, and Don Francisco, who was Julio, had betrayed her by faking his death in the plane crash. Lais also understood that Ilona could care less if the cartels were wondering if she had fooled them. What infuriated her was to believe that that son-of-a-bitch, whom she had loved so much, might have faked his death to leave her.

Arcadio, who knew something but kept it to himself, was also watching them from afar. Arcadio hated everyone. He was neither a drunk nor a beggar; he was just Arcadio, with no friends, family, dreams, or joy.

While everyone was lost in thoughts and doubts, Irigandi, who was a Nele and could feel everything, sensed Diocles' presence and knew that he had a good heart and wanted to approach them. She also sensed Arcadio and knew that he was mean and had something that had belonged to the dead man. And she even felt the presence of La Pajerita, who secretly followed Arcadio from a distance.

They kept walking, with many eyes following them closely, until Irigandi, the only one who couldn't see, felt another presence. Ilona was hidden behind the church columns.

Irigandi wanted to meet her, and that's why she let go of the leash.

Zoubir limped towards where Ilona was standing, and she crouched to pet the dog while Irigandi approached them and gently touched Ilona's back. Bebéi came quickly behind her. "C'est vraie qu'il était ton homme?"[3] Bebéi asked without hesitation.

Ilona nodded slightly with her head. Yes, Julio, that son-of-a-bitch was her man. However, that's all she could say. Julio's real story could put them in danger.

---

[3] Is it true that he was your man?

Diocles came out from the shadows approaching Bebéi and revealing his secret:

"I couldn't tell you," he said, pointing at Ilona, "It was her secret, not mine."

Bebéi understood Diocles' words and Ilona justified them. "I hid it to protect you."

She kept petting the dog in silence until she took off toward the restaurant.

The dog had stopped sniffing and Bebéi was still puzzled, but Diocles felt at peace now that he no longer had to harbor any secret.

Irigandi was smiling happily; she had sensed that Ilona was a respectable woman and Diocles was a trustworthy man.

Irigandi could feel all the love Ilona had when petting the dog that had belonged to the man she had loved so much. That damned lying son-of-a-bitch whom she had loved like no other, and she would love again as many times as she could.

They stood there until Ilona disappeared inside the restaurant. Only then did they start walking again, but they were no longer three. From then on, they were four. Zoubir, sniffing and leading the way, followed by Irigandi, holding the leash, Bebéi, with his hands clasped on his back and, Diocles, lagging behind, watching the three of them and thinking, since thinking was what he could do best.

Diocles knew that very soon many would find out that the Condor had not died in the plane crash, and dangerous and powerful people would be coming to Santa Clara to check if Ilona indeed had known that his death was faked. And most of them wouldn't believe that he did it without telling Ibrahim, his business partner, or Ilona, his wife. Diocles also understood that Ilona would not run away.

Hard times were on the horizon, and to help, Diocles needed to find out more about the dog's owner, Don Francisco, also known as Julio or the Condor. A mysterious man who had died after the band's parade, a man whose absolute power was now no more than a pinch of ashes resting in an Algerian pot in Bebéi's apartment.

11

Saturday, it's time to act. It was Saturday again, and the sun was about to rise over the bay. Two weeks had passed since the corpse had shown up in front of the Old Arch. The sky was cloudless, and the ocean extended, absolutely calm, without a single wave. The only movement across the entire bay came from a fishermen's boat approaching the harbor, followed by a flock of noisy birds.

Bebéi was already out walking with Zoubir, but that morning he didn't watch the ocean nor the wharf waking from its slumber. Instead, he walked directly to pick up Irigandi and meet Diocles. It was going to be a busy morning.

Irigandi was already at the door wearing an immaculate and colorful dress. That morning the patterns on her blouse were yellow and purple, the same colors as her bandana. When her family decided that she would travel with her grandfather, her grandma asked her to always show with pride that she was a Kuna.

Diocles was also waiting for them. The old ex-president was anxious and had spent the entire night awakened among his cats, worried about what he was sensing.

"Ilona is in danger, and we cannot simply wait if we know that something bad is about to happen."

It was still too early; people were barely coming out of their homes when the four of them gathered on the street; the only sound was the hymns from early mass. At Saint Joseph Church, the mass began at six, the favorite service of the Pigalle Street women who fancied to be forgiven for their sins before returning home.

The four of them crossed the Cathedral Plaza, and at Central Avenue, they helped Rasta Bong open up his barbershop. Saturdays were always busy. The little bus transporting the Gypsy band was returning from playing all night long. The musicians were either drunk or asleep, except for the accordion player, the band leader, who kept playing non-stop as they left the bus and assembled in front of the barbershop.

Next to them, La Pajerita's son was readying his ice cream cart, dressed as a clown with multicolored balloons tied to his back, and a group of church ladies approached La Merced Church in a hurry for the mass with the young priest whose angelic face was secretly desired by many devotees.

According to the church ladies, the young priest was much better than the previous one, who spent all his energy helping the poor and had no time to attend the parties they organized. Instead, the young priest spoke eloquently, spewing phrases in Latin, unlike the foul street talk of the other one. But of course, Robespierre thought differently, and from the top of the steps, he insulted the priest and the church ladies, for all to hear.

Maybe, it's good to pause here and add that Robespierre was more than just a crazy drunk. In truth, he was indeed crazy and a drunkard, but in his youth, he was a renowned professor at the National University until he was expelled due to insanity in extremis. Afterward, he suffered pitfall after pitfall and ended up living atop the steps of La Merced, where, while sober, he would express severe aggression and, when drunk, would waltz around with pigeons. That morning, however, he was annoyed and ready with insults.

A pandemonium was building at the church door, and Bebéi struggled to understand what Robespierre was saying. Zoubir, unleashed, went playing with La Pajerita's bitch while Irigandi and Diocles crossed the street to watch Grená lecturing Micky, the driver.

"When you're on marijuana, you go nuts. You go out with the whores who take you god-knows-where, and now you come complaining, they robbed you. That's not fair!"

Micky kept insisting that he had been robbed, and according to him, the problem wasn't the money, since he didn't have much, it was his documents.

"It's useless to speak with Lieutenant Pirilo," said Grená. "He won't be able to find your documents. The one you have to ask is Silvino. He might know who robbed you. Speak to him!"

Seeing Irigandi's stupor upon hearing those words, Diocles tried to explain to her.

"Lieutenant Pirilo and Silvino are both Grená's sons; Pirilo is the chief of security at the Mayor's office, and his younger brother, Silvino, heads a gang of thugs." As Irigandi looked at him still puzzled, Diocles added chuckling. "One protects, and the other robs."

While they were talking, Ludmilla, the Russian dancer, and the Chinese Doll arrived bringing Frida with them. The German was drunk and joined Robespierre in insulting the priest, increasing the ruckus on the church steps.

"Confess that you dream of Magdalene's tits and St. Theresa's legs, you hypocrite!"

Bebéi watched Zoubir jumping, despite his cast, with La Pajerita's bitch. They were both trying to tear up a purple piece of fabric La Pajerita had thrown them, which Henry Moriarty claimed was one of the t-shirts he kept amongst his things.

It's important to note that the t-shirt was very dear to the stoned Canadian, as one of the few that had survived from the Mayor's last election campaign. On it, a slogan saying Esperanza is back was stamped over the smiling, fat face of the municipal chief. It was a hugely successful slogan until his wife discovered that Esperanza not only meant hope in Spanish, but was also the name of a Spanish dancer who had returned to Pigalle Street to be her husband's mistress.

The couple's crisis was epic, and the poor Mayor was forced to sleep out of the house until he promised to collect all t-shirts and burn them in public. Luckily for him, he won the election with a sweep. Thanks to the popular vote he kept his cunning smile and his battalion of mistresses. And despite all promises, he never stopped the corruption that prevailed in Santa Clara. On the contrary, he increased it with brand new creative scandals that he constantly denied to the media.

The Saturday morning ruckus at La Merced intensified as the sun rose over the city and a group of Rastafarians showed up at one of the corners to greet Rasta Bong, their leader and friend. It was then that Diocles decided to intervene. Enough was enough. Insanity was an old friend of the neighborhood, but Ilona was in danger, and she needed help. Diocles climbed to the top of the steps and yelled, "All of you! Stop right now with your yelling and insults. We have something more important at hand today."

It wasn't every day that the morning fuss would get interrupted that way, so all stopped and paid attention. Diocles was a man of few words, and if he asked to be heard, it was for a good reason.

The bums stopped their morning insults, the church ladies ran inside the church, the Rastafarians approached quietly, and even the Gypsy with the accordion paused his music. All on the street approached the steps in front of Grená's yellow umbrella, where Diocles explained the situation.

He told them Ilona was in danger. Don Francisco had outsmarted everyone with his death in the airplane crash, and the cartel kingpins would likely come looking for her very soon. He explained Ibrahim's getaway, reiterating that Ilona did not want to leave Santa Clara.

Frida, who was listening with her eyes closed and her temples pulsing from a severe hangover, spoke up to say in a sad, hoarse voice, "Ilona is as stubborn as a mule. She needs to get out, but she won't. I tried, but she told me she won't abandon her restaurant."

Her words seemed to offer a signal to all to speak at once in an explosion of opinions and comments. Grená insisted that they had to convince Ilona to disappear, and Frida confirmed that it would be impossible. Ludmilla argued that the women of Pigalle Street were ready to help hide her, but Diocles reminded them that the drug kingpins had friends everywhere and would not have a problem finding her hideout. Robespierre proposed to defend Ilona in arms, but the proposal was so absurd that no one paid him any mind. The Gypsy accordionists start to play again, and there were so many people asking for shaved ice that Micky and a few Rastafarians approached to help Grená.

Henry Moriarty, the old Canadian hippie, a pacifist by conviction, surprisingly got out of his trance to propose a dialogue with the drug traffickers but was ignored. Null-and-void opted to remain silent; he didn't know what to say.

La Pajerita began to dance with the dogs and Ludmilla insisted that Ilona should hide, saying they would help Doña Cecy keep the restaurant running, and the dogs started to bark loudly. Still, Frida kept reiterating her friend's stubbornness and declaring that she would never leave.

Diocles tried to reestablish order, saying that he didn't have a solution either and that the only thing to be done was to find out what happened to Don Francisco Lacayo.

Just then, Frida murmured in his ear, "Fine, but while you find out, let's get Ilona out of here because they won't be merciful with her."

Everyone kept arguing and arguing over what could be done. The Chinese Doll, who had been having a secret affair with Grená's thug son Silvino, remembered that they could ask him to help them to contact the drug traffickers. Grená shook her head; she loved her son but was always suspicious of the Chinese Doll's intentions.

It was then that Henry Moriarty spoke again. He kept sitting on the church's steps but shouted, "We know what no one else does." It was odd to hear Moriarty speak twice in one day, so everybody paused to listen to him. "We know where he lived, and we have the keys to his house. We can go there and find out more about his life."

Initially, it seemed an absurd idea; everyone knew the house of the deceased was in the United States, miles and miles away, but it was Diocles, known for his realistic positions, who replied.

"Maybe Henry is right. It would be useful to find out more about Don Francisco, and his secrets are likely hidden in his home."

They discussed other ideas, some fantastic, others ridiculous, until all had been laid out. Robespierre, who hadn't been able to find anything to drink and continued to be in a foul mood, proposed a Florida invasion to knock down the dead man's house door, and with a sarcastic smile, Frida egged him on.

Rasta Bong, who was more pragmatic since it was too early and he hadn't smoked any joints, proposed to hire some "break-in specialists" in the United States. He remembered that Silvino knew of a pair, but his suggestion was ruled out by Diocles, who knew too well that to have Silvino's friends involved in matters overseas would just make things worse.

Micky, the cab driver, who was overwhelmed helping Grená with the shaved ice, made a rational proposal.

"What if we ask Diana to help us."

He had kept in touch with the American backpacker and knew she would help. They had the dead man's key, and that would give them access to the house.

Everyone kept arguing over different alternatives, and that's when Bebéi, who had said nothing till then, decided to speak up.

"I can go with her."

Frida let out a yelp of amazement, but mostly everyone was astonished at hearing Bebéi speak in a meeting. They were happy that he finally understood, and, for the first time, expressed himself publicly – they knew how much effort it took for him to say something more than *good morning*, greeting everyone on the street.

Starting with Grená, everyone applauded, and the Chinese Doll kissed Bebéi's bald head. Still, in all honesty, they didn't take his proposal too seriously. It seemed impossible for Bebéi to travel to Florida, but he insisted.

"Mon ami at the American Embassy invited me pour aller to Florida for an Archivist Conference in Miami…"

At this point, they were all ears. Bebéi wasn't talking nonsense. He had an official invitation, and he could travel with a diplomatic passport as a French Embassy member.

Diocles knew it was risky, but they really had no other option, and if Diana could go with him, who knows?

Frida commented that if Bebéi could understand what was being discussed in La Merced, he could do anything anywhere in the world. That was all it took for Null-and-void, true to his old habits of a businessman, to take the last word and sum up what had been decided.

"The Algerian goes to Miami for the conference. Micky talks with the American woman to go along with him. They both go together to the deceased's home and solve the mystery. It's decided!"

Having done his job and having nothing else to add, he turned to his bottle to resume drinking.

Frida, who was slowly getting enthusiastic about the idea, whispered to Diocles, "It's important that we stay one step ahead of the cartels. Right now, only a few of them know that Julio died again, and this may buy us time to save Ilona."

There was nothing left to discuss, and that is how Bebéi, the archivist, became a secret agent on an international mission.

Diocles, however, remained silent, thinking on Frida's words.

"We need to get Ilona out of Santa Clara," Frida insisted when they left.

He knew that Frida was right, but how would they convince Ilona?

12

Bebéi's international mission. Bebéi spent most of his time getting ready for the trip. The Ambassador was delighted since one of the subjects to be covered at the Miami convention was precisely the archiving of historical documents — a field in which Bebéi was currently working. The diplomat knew that the Bebéi was not used to traveling, but he was the best archivist he knew, and he did not foresee any risks on the trip since someone would pick him up at the airport and he would stay most of the time at the hotel. At least that is how the Ambassador saw it, unaware of the alternate plans of his subordinate.

Diana had agreed to meet him in Florida, excited about the idea. It was an opportunity to reunite again with her friends from Santa Clara. The only one worried about it was Diocles, who knew that Bebéi didn't understand what it took to travel to another country and break into a stranger's home. Diocles felt it was risky, but it was the only possible alternative to help Ilona.

The uneasiness heightened when two men visited Bebéi at his apartment, identifying themselves as government employees from the embassy of the South American country where the dead man was born. Supposedly they were there because of the fingerprint ID. They asked him some questions, but in all honesty, they seemed clueless about what they were looking for. They had orders to question Bebéi and to confirm the dead man's ID. According to them, the deceased's fingerprints coincided with a Julio Silva who had died thirty years before and was considered a terrorist for his involvement in the assassination of a military general during a time when street clashes between young guerrilla fighters and South American generals were common in the region.

Bebéi listened quietly and luckily, he didn't blurt out that it was not the first time he heard that the deceased had already been dead, but he did explain that he had kept both the dog and the ashes, showing them the Algerian pot in the living room beside the candlestick holder and his parents' and uncle's photographs.

Actually, the two men were not interested and simply followed bureaucratic orders without meddling any further. That's how Bebéi narrated it back to Grená and Diocles without hiding his pride for having received unexpected guests. He was happy: he had a dog with whom he strolled daily, he received guests at his apartment, he had friends like Diocles, Grená, and the bums of La Merced, and was going to travel to the United States. He even felt that it was possible to become Ilona's friend again.

Diocles, however, was worried. The visit confirmed that Julio was Don Francisco Lacayo's real name. It could be that Julio's past was more complicated than he was imagining, and there were now too many people who already knew that Julio had returned to Santa Clara before dying.

Bebéi didn't ponder those things; he was anxious to begin the trip, and nothing worried him. All of it was new, and he liked it. The fact that he had left his dull life in Paris to become an adventurer in Santa Clara was an enormous step, and it was mind-boggling to travel as some sort of a secret agent on an international mission.

Bebéi's thoughts sometimes ran in an imaginary parallel universe. It was a universe only he knew about and one he didn't mention to anyone. That's how it had been since childhood, a lonely kid, floating in his thoughts while reality was a mere supporting actor, a prop to help him dream. It didn't even faze him that in the U.S., they spoke a different language since in Santa Clara, they spoke Spanish, and in no time, he had made friends. Also, Diana, the American tourist with her clean smile and her muddled French, would always be with him.

The dog would stay with Irigandi, and Diocles promised to help with everything. Diocles was also feeling responsible for the little Kuna girl; little by little he had begun to understand what it meant to be a Nele, but he was still intrigued. Irigandi had some physical traces slightly distinct from other indigenous women, which led him to believe that perhaps she wasn't full-blooded Kuna, but that wasn't a subject he should be worrying about, especially now that Ilona was in danger, and he had to try to convince her to leave Santa Clara.

Bebéi flew to Miami where he was picked up at the airport by the conference organizers and dropped off at the hotel. Even though the speeches were about something he liked, he found them quite dull, and for three days, he counted down the hours to when Diana would pick him up.

Finally, she arrived. They both went by car to the deceased's house and as soon as they got there, they noticed the house was inside a gated property, and they would have to go through a security checkpoint – something unforeseen in their planning. Unperturbed, Diana kept driving towards the entrance as if she would have done so every morning and calmly told the security guard that they were headed towards the address she had noted and showed him the key.

It was an excellent strategy, but it failed miserably.

The rules were strict, and no one could enter without prior instruction from the proprietor. Diana explained that her "uncle" asked her to come; he was overseas and wanted her to pick up some things he needed. The security guard checked over the key again and peered at Diana's fresh and smiling face. But it was the pleasant smile of the foreign gentlemen inside the car that convinced him that they were indeed telling the truth. However, the rules were the rules, and he asked them to pull aside while he spoke to the supervisor. Clueless, of what was happening, Bebéi showed no sign of worries.

"Keep smiling," Diana recommended, "Somehow, he trusts you."

They waited a few minutes, and the guard returned with good news.

"The supervisor authorized your entry, but as a precaution, he wanted me to escort you."

While driving inside the condo, Bebéi was awed by what he saw: huge properties facing the ocean, and all houses with well-manicured lawns, swimming pools, and access to an enormous golf course. The one belonging to the deceased was relatively small compared to the others but located at the top of a hill, isolated from the rest and surrounded by a breathtaking view, which included the entire bay with waves breaking against breakwaters along the shore.

In the house – comfy though not at all lofty – there was a great living area, a single but large bedroom, and a studio with a desk, a comfortable armchair, and a few books on the shelves. The living room walls were covered by a few paintings and photographs. The first one, which caught Bebéi's attention, was a picture of Ilona's restaurant, the same one he had seen at her office which Ilona had removed after the appearance of the corpse. In it were a younger Ilona, the deceased with long hair, Ibrahim, Gigi, and someone else wearing a captain's cap. In another picture, he noticed the dead man and the black dog standing in front of a snow-covered mountain.

In the living room, above the fireplace, there was a large and imposing picture: the dead man with Ilona at the beach, and inside the bedroom, next to the bed, Diana found a photo where the dog and the deceased appeared to be standing in front of a temple in the Far East. The security guard was distracted, and she put the photograph inside her purse.

They didn't find anything else that could be interesting. There were few objects left, which prompted Diana to remember what Micky had asked at the hotel: *Was he a saint or a thief?* From what they had now seen, the only thing they knew for sure was that the house belonged to a lonely man and his dog.

In the studio, there were numerous books, well-organized and lined up. Bebéi stood in front of them, motionless, reading the spines. Diana didn't want to disturb him and preferred to keep roaming the house with the security guard at her side. She pretended to look for things for her "uncle" while really looking for any clue as to how the dead man lived. Maybe the computer could be a good source of information, but she couldn't check it, with the guard so close.

After taking his time admiring the bookshelves, Bebéi moved to the desk where some loose sheets of paper – some printed and others handwritten – were left. On the top there was a page where the word "Takarkuna," with three exclamation points, was handwritten. He browsed through them, one by one. Diana caught what was going on, and to buy Bebéi some time, she went to the bathroom, where she took some medications, supposedly requested by her "uncle." She kept talking to the guard and went with him into the kitchen, where she saw two bowls, one that was still filled with water and the other empty. She took the empty bowl with her as a gift to the black dog.

On her way back to the studio, she noticed Bebéi holding a bound book about the Kuna which he took to give to Irigandi; the little girl would be happy to know that the dead man was interested in her people. Then they left and returned to Miami.

Diana was thinking that except for the few belongings salvaged, the investigation was unfruitful, especially considering the risk involved. But on the drive back, she understood why Bebéi was known as a great archivist and why he had stood in front of the bookshelf. At first, she thought it was some kind of routine he had, but to her amazement Bebéi began to spew out the names of each book the dead man had on the shelves, as well as the phrases he read on the notes over the desk.

Bebéi had a photographic memory and never forget what he saw. When he was a kid, he would entertain his uncle by telling everything he had seen at the school. Even the minutest of details would get lodged in his memory.

Diana dropped him off at the airport, and the international secret agent returned to Santa Clara with all data stored in his head, ready to share it with his friends. He now knew, after having visited his home, that the dead man had lived alone, and Ilona was his one and only true love. And from the books they saw in his studio, they could also say that he was an avid reader. Bebéi was happy to realize that he knew some of the books on the dead man's shelves.

Still, something was puzzling him, but he didn't tell Diana; it was part of a secret he carried. At the embassy, he was working on some special files. They were highly confidential, and according to the Ambassador, Bebéi should be the only one to know about them. But what intrigued him was that some of books and documents he found on the dead man's shelves were also part of the files bought by the Ambassador from Monsieur Le Breton's niece.

What a coincidence! Both men, who had never met, and didn't know Irigandi or her grandfather, were interested in knowing more about the Kuna's sacred lands.

13

A hero's welcome. Bebéi returned to Santa Clara and received a hero's welcome at the airport. Word had gotten out about the adventure, and Bebéi's memory capabilities had impressed everyone. Almost all his friends were present, including Null-and-void and Frida—sobered up. Well, not quite. Colonel Viera went in a coat and tie. Ludmilla had bought herself a miniskirt, causing a stir wherever she passed by. Princess sported a shirt more colorful than a rainbow. Even La Pajerita, who never left the neighborhood, decided to join in and was beside herself waiting for Bebéi. She left behind her little bitch tied side by side with Bebéi's dog at the leg of Henry Moriarty, who did not go since he was stoned.

Given such a large posse, Rasta Bong drove them all in the Gypsy band's van, and Bebéi was welcomed with hugs, applauses, and a musical performance of Mesecina, the Gypsy song to praise the moon, played by the Gypsies and danced by the Chinese Doll. This was a welcoming second to none at the airport.

Everyone was curious to find out the news. Micky asked about Diana, Ludmilla inquired about the condo, and Diocles wanted to know in detail how the deceased had lived and what they had found inside the home. The Chinese Doll asked about the photos, Princess about the books. La Pajerita didn't utter a word; instead, she looked proudly at her hero.

Bebéi was a tad euphoric as he shared the recent events and so anxious that he couldn't even organize his thoughts. This might have been to do with the fact that the band kept playing inside the van while Frida poured her heart out singing some Turkish songs she had learned while locked up in German prisons.

When they arrived in Santa Clara, they went directly to Rasta's barbershop, where the party continued, with the Gypsy band getting out of the van without missing a beat. There, Bebéi reunited with his dog, who jumped happily, excited by the music.

Those strolling by got closer to look, and the well-dressed church ladies interrupted their prayers and walked out of the church to figure out why the heathen carnival. Henry Moriarty was the only one static in his meditation trance.

Diocles and Grená moved away from the turmoil to observe the celebration from a distance. "At least we know that he didn't lead a double life and that Ilona was the single love of his life," Grená said.

"He lived alone. It didn't seem as if he had any friends, nor lovers," Diocles added, repeating what Diana had said over the phone.

"But it looks like he was expecting to find an answer among the history books," added Princess, who joined them. And this, in particular, contrasted with the image of Don Francisco Lacayo they knew; a man of action, always on the move, with no time to waste reading. It was hard to figure out why he kept so many books.

Irigandi arrived a little later with her grandfather. After the brief hug, Bebéi gave her the book he brought on the Kuna, and Zoubir became even more excited when Bebéi showed him the bowl, which he remembered well. Everyone crowded around to see the photo of Julio and the dog in front of a temple. In the image, Julio had long hair and was healthy, with the same expression as the Don Francisco Lacayo they all knew. The Chinese Doll suggested that the temple was Japanese.

Ludmilla asked for the book titles, but when he began reiterating them one by one, Diocles interrupted. "It's best that Bebéi sit down with Princess, alone and in a quieter place. It may take longer than we anticipate and should be done very carefully."

The next day, Bebéi repeated for more than an hour, and Princess wrote down, the hundred or so titles the deceased had on his bookshelf. However, before that meeting, Bebéi fulfilled a critical duty. Diocles had agreed with Ilona she would be the first to meet him, but not at her restaurant. Diocles had insisted on a more discrete location, which ended up being an abandoned house not too far from the Cathedral Plaza.

Diocles didn't go in; he took Bebéi there and waited at the door. "She's waiting for you on the second floor," he whispered.

Bebéi knew Ilona wanted to hear about the dead man, and he carried the pot with the deceased's ashes. After visiting the man's home, Bebéi was sure Ilona was his great love, and she should be the one to keep his ashes.

The house wasn't completely abandoned as Bebéi had initially thought, and some people lived there. After climbing the stairs, he saw a few chairs, a table, and four small beds. Intriguing, but Bebéi didn't had time for distractions. Ilona was there waiting for him, and as soon as Bebéi stepped inside, she got up and hugged him.

"I'm sure you're upset with me for hiding you the truth."

Bebéi was so happy with the hug that all previous sorrow immediately vanished.

"You need to be careful. Getting close to Julio can cause a lot of harm. It was like that while he was alive and worse now after his fake death."

"In his maison he has a picture, just like the one you had in the restaurant, ou vous are with Ibrahim, Gigi and un autre at a table on the terrace," Bebéi mumbled shyly.

The words were confused, but Ilona understood and began to cry while listening. Bebéi put his hand on her shoulder and waited patiently until she calmed down.

"Few people knew he was alive," she said, trying to control her tears. "It's better that way. Please, I beg of you, don't speak to anyone about Julio, but before I go, tell me how he lived," and her expression changed to a smile. "Can you describe his house for me? Tell me everything and after this, don't mention it again to anybody. Never!"

Bebéi told Ilona what he had already told the others, but her curiosity was more profound. She wanted to know it all.

"The pictures, where they were placed? And tell me about the picture where we were on the beach, where it is? And which photo is in front of the bed?"

Ilona wanted to know about the clothes in the drawers and what he had in the fridge.

"Wait, let me guess, he had strawberry yogurt and French mustard, right?"

Bebéi confirmed this, making Ilona's smile shine.

"And I bet he kept a bottle of Haitian rum somewhere in the house?"

Bebéi nodded and confirmed the exact location of the bottle.

"And the cigars? Where did he keep the cigars?"

"Inside a carved wooden box, in the living room," answered Bebéi.

"And where was the big ashtray with a cigar rest? I'm sure he had one of those."

"I saw an ashtray, but it was outside on the terrace."

Ilona began weeping again, bringing her hands to her face. After a moment, she clarified.

"He did it for me; it was the only thing I asked of him: not to smoke inside the house."

Ilona was smiling and crying all at once. She wanted to know every detail of the bedroom, the bed sheets, the comforter, and the pillows. Bebéi smiled. She wanted to know about the car parked in the garage, the flowers around the house, the view from the terrace, the birds, and the sounds in the garden, and Bebéi told her everything.

She kept asking, and he answered, until she paused and regrouped. "It's best we stop here. What use is it to keep talking about what isn't ours?" She then looked straight into Bebéi's eyes and thanked him, insisting that he must not speak about Julio to strangers since it could cause him a lot of pain.

They got up, and she walked down the steps with him. That's when Bebéi tried to hand over the ashes.

"I think these belong to you."

Ilona took the pot, thought for a moment, and kissed it, but returned it to Bebéi.

"It's probably better these ashes stay with you. I won't be able to keep them where I'm going, and now you must leave. I need to protect myself."

Bebéi looked at her, curious.

"Are you leaving?"

"Yes, but don't mention this to anyone. I have to go."

When Bebéi left the house, he no longer felt like a secret agent returning from a successful mission. Ilona hugged him; she was his friend, but her life was in danger, and he didn't know how to help her.

He went back home with the ashes, convinced that there were still many mysteries he wanted to unveil in Santa Clara by the Sea.

14

Now Ilona is gone. Once Bebéi returned, life seemed normal again, at least that's what La Pajerita thought as she woke up on her bench on the boardwalk. But Diocles, surrounded by his cats on the bandstand of Cathedral Square, knew things wouldn't be so simple. The worst was yet to come.

According to him, the peace and harmony in the old neighborhood depended upon Ilona. There, bums, crazies, and drunkards all survived thanks to her and her restaurant: the food distributed at night at the restaurant's back door, her clients' used clothes she collected, the medicines and the doctor's appointments she finagled, and even the food Diocles delivered to his cats would vanish without her.

She was also partner in all Rasta Bong's crazy ventures, alongside Micky and his cab, and the Gypsy band. She was the only help that came forth when Princess needed a loan for his bookstore. Not to mention all money she gave for many years to Cloud Castle and other brothels and cabarets along Pigalle Street. They all existed and survived, thanks to Ilona.

Diocles knew that most people he loved and respected depended on her, and she was in grave danger. The unexpected return of Julio had raised unanswerable questions. Many people would think she was an accomplice of his betrayal, and that is something that the drug kingpins would certainly make her pay for.

Diocles had done his best and had finally convinced Ilona to leave. With everything that Diana and Bebéi shared, she knew that Julio didn't have another love. Why he abandoned her was still an open question, but at least she knew he never stopped loving her, and this was important. With all the men she had in her life, she chose Julio, and it was a relief to know that she was also the only one for him.

"Could it be that he just returned to Santa Clara to see you before he died?" Diocles suggested. But deep down, he felt it was not true. If Julio wanted to see her, he could have walked into the restaurant, and he didn't.

"I feel they are coming soon," he had confessed worriedly to Grená. "We must get Ilona out of Santa Clara right now."

It wasn't easy to hide her. The cartels knew how to rip the truth out of anyone in their way. She would have to leave without anyone knowing her hideout. Diocles was conscious that the cartels would make him yodel even if he were the only one to know.

Null-and-void was the one who had come up with a clever proposal. He was so wasted one night that he ended up passing out at the foot of a Jamaican dancer's doorstep, irritating the security guards responsible for managing the Mayor's escapades. Diocles was wandering by and had helped Null to return to La Merced. There, after he threw up over Henry Moriarty's feet, Null sketched his idea.

"You choose five people you trust and ask each one to draw out a plan to hide Ilona. But you do not discuss or even ask what they will propose. Ilona should be the only one to talk with each of them and choose which plan she wants. That way, nobody than her would know where she is."

The proposal had seemed wise, Diocles would be the only one to know who the five were, and even if they made him talk, he could not tell where she chose to hide. He liked it but he had to carefully select the five names. Who in Santa Clara would be reliable and capable of hiding her?

In the end, he only chose four. He told Null that he was the fifth to make him happy, but Diocles knew that the old bum couldn't hide his own shoes.

When each of the chosen drew out a plan, he shared the names with Ilona. She chose by herself. That's why he was relatively at ease. He didn't know where she was, but he knew she was, temporarily, safe.

For a while, everything could return to normal – at least before the big storm arrived – and he could feed the cats, walk around the neighborhood, and gaze up at the sky, trying to foresee early signs of thunders.

At the steps of La Merced, Henry Moriarty was stoned, Frida was eating, and Robespierre was walking back and for in front of the Church Door. Diocles greeted them. A little further, the Chinese man was opening up his store, and Grená was setting her stand, and Diocles greeted them too. That's when he heard.

"Ilona disappeared!"

The first one to notice was Pirilo. Afterward it was Micky the cabbie who ran to tell Rasta at the barbershop, and from there Rasta shouted to Grená —and Diocles heard—and the news took flight and spread far and wide all over the city.

The official version and buzz were that Ilona had decided to take some time off.

Frida went frantically to the restaurant asking questions, and little by little, everyone showed up looking for an update. Some thought Ilona had been kidnapped, but Doña Cecy cleared things up.

"Last night, Ilona followed Ibrahim's suggestion and decided to go on a trip. No one, not even me, knows her whereabouts."

Those who heard pretended to believe, but they all knew Ilona was not vacationing, and no one could tell how long she would stay away.

Doña Cecy clarified that the restaurant would be open as usual but that she couldn't manage it all by herself. She said that Ilona had indicated how each one of her friends could specifically help, and she explained, "In the kitchen, I don't need any help. I've always done this job, but Ilona told me that Colonel Viera could help with the groceries."

Many there knew that Colonel Viera loved to fill his time shopping at the Santa Clara market, where some stands belonged to the retired military like himself. Sometimes he would even accompany Ilona, which gave him some knowledge about the restaurant, and it wasn't a bad idea. The truth was that lately the Colonel was a little uneasy and no one knew why. He was usually a very calm man, spending his days in front of the City Hall, listening to the latest from Lieutenant Pirilo, his former assistant, and sharing it at Lais' window with Princess and Hector. Still, something was affecting his behavior, and helping Doña Cecy would undoubtedly be good therapy.

Doña Cecy kept talking on the terrace, but she sat with her swollen feet propped up on the small resting stool that Rasta had made for her.

"At the restaurant, we need Gigi's help to assist with the customers."

Gigi promised that she would show up every night. Still, both Doña Cecy and Ilona knew that with her drug addiction, she was not reliable for the task.

Doña Cecy said, "Ludmilla could be Gigi's assistant." She then turned towards Ludmilla. "Ilona told me to pay you well, it may not be as much as what you get at the cabaret, but at least no one will be groping your tits."

Doña Cecy had been through a lot in her life and was determined to exhibit a sense of tranquility so everyone would assume that Ilona indeed had taken a short vacation.

"Ilona also said that she needed someone with business sense to make sure everything would go along financially smoothly. She trusts Rasta Bong but knowing that he had a lot on his hands, she asked Null to help him."

Null-and-void nodded, agreeing, and everyone was surprised except for Grená and Frida. They both knew that Ilona had known him from way back when he had another name and was a banker who often passed through Santa Clara to visit the Cloud Castle women. Don Francisco himself, along with Ibrahim, had done business with him, but this was before he decided to leave everything behind: his family, his friends, his bank, and even his country, to become a bum on the steps of La Merced.

Lost in his thoughts, Diocles was barely paying attention. He knew that Ilona was fine, and that Doña Cecy could manage the restaurant with everyone's help, but would that be enough to protect Santa Clara from the cartels' wrath?

While all this was happening at the restaurant, Princess was at the bookstore researching catalogs for the titles Bebéi had seen on the dead man's bookshelf. It wasn't until late that afternoon that he called Diocles and Colonel Viera to share with them his initial conclusions.

"The one who died under the Old Arch didn't like to read novels. Among his books, he had more poems than fiction. There were poetry collections in English, French, Spanish, and Portuguese, which most likely meant that he was fluent in all these languages. He also had some books about Buddhism and Zen Buddhism, but what caught my attention was the vast collection of books about colonial times in America, and specifically in Panama. Some of them are ancient books, the kind you can only get from private collectors. He had books which I had never heard of all about the colonial period. Those are precious works describing the religious orders and great expeditions to Venezuela and Colombia, which makes me suspect that he had a keen interest in that region. There were also books about the expeditions by Sir Frances Drake and the pirate Henry Morgan to Portobelo in Panama, and others about the native tribes of the region, particularly the Kuna, and their sacred lands in the Darien."

Both men were confused by all that information, and Princess continued. "I'm going round and round with a theory in my head… Would he have been searching for something hidden there?"

Diocles and Colonel Viera looked at each other, not daring to answer.

15

A dream becomes a nightmare. The next day Bebéi woke up in a happy mood. His life was satisfying to say the least. His job at the Embassy was running smoothly, and the Ambassador was delighted with his progress.

When he started, all the ancient documents he was working on were still in a pile, some stashed in boxes, and most of them damaged by humidity and time. They were collected by a Frenchman named Le Breton who lived in Santa Clara and then abandoned in the attic of one of his daughters' homes. When she passed away, and her son was selling the property, he called the Embassy to check if they were interested in such useless and hefty tomes. And it was because of those papers that Bebéi ended up in Santa Clara.

The Ambassador pointed out that they could have valuable historical significance. Le Breton had spent most of his life trying to figure out some mysteries of a region in South America known as La Gran Colombia. The Ambassador apparently believed those documents would be wasted or squandered within the Paris archives, and that's why he insisted on keeping the documents in Santa Clara, bringing an archivist to organize them.

Bebéi thought it odd that some of the books he saw at Julio's home were also part of Le Breton's archives, and he was thinking about that while bringing over Zoubir to keep Irigandi company while he would go to the Embassy. He felt at ease, with no worries at all. With Ilona safe in some faraway place, nothing bad could happen.

He was ambling along absentmindedly in his happiness when two strangers pulled up alongside him on a motorcycle. One of them got off and approached him with a weapon in hand. Suddenly a car came, and Bebéi was forced to get into it.

Everything happened so fast that he didn't have time to react, and even if he did, there was nothing he could have done. He got into the car and was violently forced to lie on the floor.

Bebéi didn't even think to yell out since he could see two weapons pointed directly at his head. He only cared to shield himself from the stomping he was getting. He didn't understand why they were hitting him with such force. He never had in all his life harmed anyone. Never, not even in his worst childhood moments, had he been mistreated in this way. But for some reason, they were stomping his back with such brutality and rage that he couldn't protect himself.

He couldn't open his eyes and could hardly breathe. One of the kidnappers was stepping on his head, keeping his face crushed against the floor, while the other one held his arms and stomped on his back.

Bebéi felt his nose was bleeding and his face and arm were in pain. The only thing that came to his mind was that Zoubir was left alone on the street.

He tried to let them know that they needed to go back to pick up the dog, but he passed out after getting a hard blow to the head.

He woke up in a dark empty room. His arms and legs were tied up, and his left arm was painfully throbbing. He screamed for help, but no one showed up, and the fear and pain continued until he passed out again.

He was awakened by a kick to his liver, and he tried every way imaginable to ask the kicker to untie his hands to lessen the pain, but they gagged him so he would shut up.

Bebéi had never felt so much pain. His arm hurt, and so did his back and nose. The pain increased while he was held upright in that dark and sinister room. The gag in his mouth made him want to vomit, and he was overcome with panic. Each movement he made only increased the discomfort, making it unbearable. Barely conscious, he understood that he had to avoid any movement. He no longer screamed but whimpered, fearing the gag in his mouth would suffocate him. His weeping seemed to last for hours, but no one came, and he slept.

Later, three men woke him up, shaming him vigorously. The gag had been removed, and the men began interrogating him, but he couldn't understand them. One of them was unmasked; he was tall and strong with a big mustache. He seemed to be the leader and was also the more violent one. Bebéi's arm hurt, and he realized it must be broken. The pain he felt when the unmasked man grabbed his arm was so intense that he fainted.

Later, they woke him up again, asking him about the deceased, and next to the unmasked man, there was a masked woman who could speak a broken French. He told her everything: the parade, the day Julio died, the dog he found, and about Diana and Micky and the visit to the hotel. Everything he said, the woman translated to the unmasked man, and Bebéi was terrified. He also told them about his trip to Florida and the deceased's home. Everything. He told her about Ilona crying and Frida worrying, and he explained that Don Francisco was also Julio and, according to some, the Condor. He told her that Diocles wanted to find out more about the deceased to save Ilona from the cartels, and he told her how Ilona had hugged him before vanishing. The pain became so intense, he could not continue speaking. The unmasked man gave him some pills, which made the pain go away and made him feel giddy.

The questions kept coming, but what Bebéi told them only confirmed what they already knew from word on the streets. He was a simple man and didn't know what was going on. His only immediate concern was to protect Zoubir, the dog who had belonged to the Condor.

They let him sleep for a while, and later woke him up with kicks to his back. Then the tall, unmasked man with the mustache and a tattoo across his chest told the woman to ask about Ilona. Bebéi said he didn't know where she was, but the man insisted and began hitting his arm, seemingly taking pleasure in it. The man gripped and pressed where the bone was broken while making the woman ask Bebéi about things to which he had no clue. The pain was unbearable, and the tall man kept twisting his arm. They continued for what seemed an eternity, grilling him with questions about Ilona and her friends.

Bebéi went missing for two days, which caused a stir in Santa Clara. When Micky found the dog running back and forth loose on the street, he figured out that something was wrong, Zoubir was trembling and barking confusedly. Micky called Lieutenant Pirilo and told Rasta and Diocles. It didn't take long to them to get together, assess the situation, and conclude that Bebéi had been kidnapped.

In a matter of minutes, the steps of La Merced Church drew a big crowd. Everyone was asking questions without answers. No one seemed to know what to do next. Zoubir, overwhelmed, wouldn't stop barking and Diocles took him to Irigandi's house, where he could settle down. He even tried to come up with a fib to appease her, saying that Bebéi was on a trip, but the Kuna girl didn't need anyone to tell her about her friend's suffering since she could sense his pain.

Lieutenant Pirilo told Grená that they couldn't do much at the Mayor's office since they had received instructions from the top that important people would be combing the streets, and as, a precaution, he should retreat his men. She understood what this meant and how things worked in Santa Clara. The ever happy and smiling Mayor had a few close friends who ran questionable businesses at the port, and Pirilo was instructed not to touch them. But the fact was that Bebéi was in danger, and she grew impatient thinking how disoriented Bebéi could feel in the hands of criminals.

She wanted to do something, and she did it. She asked Micky to take her to see Silvino. At first, Micky tried to talk her out of it. He knew that Rasta Bong would not like it, but Grená was determined. Whether Rasta liked it or not, she would speak with her rebel son.

For some reason that Grená could never figure out, Silvino hated his father. He was also cold and distant with his brothers, although he was always close to her. After his father's death, Silvino became even more rebellious and chose to leave the house and live with his friends, all thugs living off of petty crimes.

"If this is what you want, then this is how you will live," Grená told him.

And from that moment on, she had never spoken to him until that morning. She decided that she must intercede for Bebéi; he was an innocent man who shouldn't suffer any harm at all.

Silvino knew all the criminals, and he could help her find out who had kidnapped Bebéi. At least that's what she had thought but it seemed that her effort was pointless. Her son confirmed that powerful drug traffickers were in the city, giving explicit orders that absolutely no one should interfere with their dealings. Silvino explained to Grená that all his friends were off the streets to open space for the cartels and avoid trouble.

Grená understood that there was nothing she could do, and she asked Silvino to pass on the message that Bebéi was a simple person who knew little to nothing about drugs and crimes.

Everyone was on edge. La Pajerita was hysterical, and since she didn't drink, the only way to calm her down was to have her try a special tea prepared by Moriarty that made her stoned.

Colonel Viera tried to calm everyone down at the restaurant, saying that Bebéi would be brought back since the narcs would soon figure out that he knew nothing all along. But each day that went by, the anxiety increased, and it was hard to hide from the people in the Embassy.

Lieutenant Pirilo explained that it would be best if the Ambassador didn't find out about Bebéi's disappearance. It could prompt him to repatriate him back to France. Princess, who knew the Ambassador from being a regular customer at his bookstore, came up with the story that Bebéi had caught a severe cold. Everyone was worried, but they had no choice but to wait.

Two days later, the kidnappers freed him. Bebéi showed up at Rasta Bong's barbershop, beaten up and with a broken arm. Rasta and Micky took him immediately to the hospital, where he was treated and even had a small surgical operation on his broken arm.

In turn, Princess elaborated his story to the Ambassador, telling him that Bebéi had fallen down his apartment stairs. Luckily the Ambassador was leaving on a trip and believed him.

The surgery recovery was quick, and that same night Bebéi was back in the old city, receiving visits by all who knew him. The most excited was Zoubir, wagging his tail and happy that Bebéi now also sported a cast.

Bebéi was no longer frightened. He looked around, and his apartment was full of friends, and Irigandi was there, next to him, holding his hand with her grandfather, who was praying to the ancestors and thanking them for Bebéi's return. The apartment seemed even smaller after the Chinese Doll and her friends from *La Vie en Rose* arrived. They all come to say hello to the chubby foreigner who always greeted them while walking his dog.

Robespierre was enraged and insisted that they should come to heads with the narcs. "If we stand up to governments and armies, why should we fear a couple of bastards?"

Frida, now inebriated by the festive occasion, seconded his motion, and was backed by Colonel Viera.

"When I was in the military, those things were not tolerated. We were the rulers in the country and not those foreign thugs!" he exclaimed nostalgically.

The Colonel missed those days when he was one of the young army officers who had kicked the corrupt politicians out of the country. He was committed to justice and seemed to be a rising star, and many thought he would become the head of the government. But that never happened, and he had to resign himself to an early retirement, powerless to confront the cartels or anyone else who could challenge him in the street.

That same night the drug traffickers also interrogated Ludmilla. The questions were the same: Where was Ilona? Why did Julio go into hiding? No one knew the answers.

At the back of the grocery store, Lieutenant Pirilo played dominoes and eavesdropped. He even pondered – something he didn't enjoy doing. He knew that at times some special cargo passed through the port of Santa Clara, and the Mayor was involved, but until then this had never affected his life. In Santa Clara by the Sea, he and his family, and friends lived peacefully, and the only problems were quarrels among drunkards, and petty crimes carried out by Arcadio, who always ended up in the jail. Bebéi's kidnapping and torture was something new, and it made him uneasy.

Back on the street, the narcs kept asking questions. They questioned everyone except for Diocles. Maybe they thought he was just an older man who lived among cats and talked to himself.

16

And the nightmare had a sequel. After a whole weekend of rest, Bebéi went back to his work at the Embassy. He had to lie, which he didn't like, but no one could suspect what had happened. Actually, he didn't have to explain much, only to Carmela, since no one paid much attention to him at the Embassy. On the streets, he was a hero, but at the office, he was nothing more than an archivist who was taking care of the Ambassador's special files. The only people he really spoke to were the Ambassador, who was always interested in the progress made with the special documents, and Carmela, who loved listening to his stories and sharing his secrets.

Bebéi worked all day, fearing that someone would ask him something. Luckily, they only asked about his broken arm, and he explained that it was due to a fall on his apartment steps.

In the evening, when Bebéi was leaving the Embassy, he noticed an elegant car waiting for him outside. His colleague, the American archivist, was on the curbside, and there were two other people inside the car. One was a very elegant woman who looked like a lady and greeted him warmly, inviting Bebéi to visit the new American Embassy building.

He felt honored with all the attention and gingerly stepped inside the car, chatting with his colleague, whom he hadn't seen since the Miami conference.

"I heard that you were kidnapped and taken away in a car. It must have been awful!" the elegant lady said in flawless French.

Bebéi was surprised that someone from the American Embassy was speaking with him in such a good French, and, as she was polite, he told her about the kidnapping, the men, and the interrogation he was subject to.

The American Embassy was a compound outside of the city and while driving there, the Lady continued to elegantly ask a few more questions. Bebéi answered them without noticing that the sober and quiet man decked out in a dark suit and tie, sitting next to the driver, was recording his every word.

When they arrived, the Lady left him with his friend the archivist and the other man, but before leaving, she kindly warned Bebéi to be patient with the man in the suit and tie.

"I know he can seem a little intimidating and rude at times, so let me know if you have any problems," she said with a reassuring smile. "He would probably like to ask you a few questions about your trip to the United States to the Miami conference."

Bebéi had a bad feeling, but he followed his archivist friend, who escorted him on a quick tour throughout the building that ended in a little room with scarcely any furniture except a table, two chairs, and a large wall mirror. They let him alone for long minutes but offered him tea and some cookies. Bebéi was worried, but he was somewhat relieved by the Lady's kindness.

When the man in the dark suit entered the room, he immediately began asking Bebéi some questions. First, about the day he found the corpse. Who had gone with him to the hospital, and whoever else had gone along? Bebéi answered with few words, and the man asked about everyone with whom Bebéi had had contact. Diocles, Joseph the Princess, Null-and-void, the Chinese Doll. He cross-checked each one of the names on a list he had. It almost seemed as if the man in a suit knew everyone who lived in the old quarter. And it was not just for a few minutes; Bebéi spent more than an hour of ongoing interrogation with them, and he was exhausted when the Lady re-entered the room.

"He must be tired," she said to the man asking questions. "Let's give it a rest."

The man in the dark suit apparently didn't like the interruption. He still had questions, especially about the trip to the United States, but the Lady insisted Bebéi was tired and the invited him to spend the night as an honored guest at the Embassy.

"If you want, we can go get your dog. You will be my guest and there is a nice room here for you and your dog to rest after all this questioning."

Bebéi thought about refusing, but the Lady was so kind to him, and the American Embassy was such a beautiful building, that he decided to accept. He had never been given such an honor before.

The man in the suit insisted on asking more questions, but the Lady held firm.

"Bebéi is my guest of honor, and I won't tolerate anyone making his stay uncomfortable."

She sure was nice, thought Bebéi, and he went with her back to his apartment to pick up Zoubir. Rarely had Bebéi felt so comfortable with someone as he did with her.

They talked about Paris and his uncle, and upon entering his apartment, she immediately took to what she saw and wanted to know everything in detail. It made Bebéi feel proud; it was the first time anyone showed real interest in how he lived. She praised each thing he showed her.

"What a view... Your wardrobe is so classy... What a neat and tidy apartment... Is this your mother and father? What a handsome pair! ... And is this the uncle you mentioned? By far he must have been a very kind man... What a well-trained dog! ... Are these the deceased's ashes? ... You are so respectful! ... Is this the dog's bowl you brought back from Florida? Let's take it with us; that way the dog won't miss it... Are these the deceased's documents and the keys to his house? If you'd like, I can look after them to help you find out more about him..."

Bebéi just smiled, liking her even more.

After the visit, they returned to the American Embassy along with Zoubir, the ashes, and a pile of small things that she wanted to show to her friends.

As soon as they arrived, the man in the dark suit was waiting for them.

"I need to ask a few more questions."

Objecting, the woman showed her annoyance, but the man was persistent.

"We need to know what he did after the conference; we suspect that he invaded a home of an American citizen."

Bebéi answered quickly, clarifying that it had indeed been the deceased's house, and he had only gone there to find out more about him. In his naiveté, he didn't catch on that they were speaking in French to each other purposefully for him to understand.

"Who is Diana? Where did you meet her?" the man asked.

Bebéi gave a detailed answer. He explained how they had reached the house, what they did to have access, what they found, and even offered to name all books on the shelf, which the man began to note down. After listing a few, he asked in amazement how many there were in total, and he was taken aback by the answer.

"One hundred and sixteen," answered Bebéi.

Next, the man wanted to know what he had talked about with Princess, and he kept asking when the Lady showed up again, announcing that it was time for Bebéi to rest. Again, the man in the suit objected, but she paid no heed. She took him to the room – a nice one with cozy furniture and a fireplace which was already lit.

She offered him a glass of warm milk with chocolate cookies, and while sharing the cookies, Bebéi spoke with pride about his friends and told the Lady about Ilona, Irigandi, and Diocles. The Lady listened attentively. Bebéi also mentioned that the man in a suit had asked many questions and he was uneasy about them.

"Why do they make you uneasy?"

"Well, there are things that I cannot tell." "Really? Like what, for example?"

And he kept rattling off what he shouldn't share: That Rasta Bong and Micky were potheads, for example, or that Frida was a terrorist before arriving in Santa Clara. That Silvino, Grená's son, was the leader of a gang of thugs, that Grená suspected the Chinese Doll was a secret agent working for the Chinese Government, and that everything relating to Julio must be kept a complete secret.

Bebéi had never, in his entire life, interacted with an elegant and polite woman who was kind to him, and he was so impressed and thankful that he completely lowered his defenses.

And the nice and kind lady listened keenly with a friendly smile. "Don't worry. You didn't do anything wrong, and nothing will happen to you."

So off he went to bed and slept peacefully, feeling he was in good hands. Zoubir, however, didn't sleep and spent the entire night sniffing the place. He didn't understand where he was and had a hunch that something wasn't right.

The following morning when Bebéi awoke, he was again treated very kindly. The Lady invited him for breakfast and Bebéi was worried that he had to go to his office. She relieved him of this concern by mentioning that she knew the French Ambassador was traveling and certainly, would not complain if Bebéi spent more time with her.

While they ate, she explained to him what had transpired. "We have a bit of a problem."

Bebéi was all ears.

"After the conference, you met up with Diana, and both of you went to Don Francisco Lacayo's home, correct?"

He nodded.

"And got in without permission," she added.

And Bebéi nodded again.

"In the United States, this is a serious offense."

At this, Bebéi's facial expression changed. He tried to control himself, but it wasn't easy, especially knowing he was in trouble.

"Since you were on a diplomatic visit to the United States authorized by the State Department, they wanted to clarify what happened because an unauthorized entrance into someone's home is a crime, and the deceased's family may hold the State Department, which authorized your trip, responsible."

And she said this, looking at Bebéi with a worried expression.

Bebéi tried to explain that the State Department had nothing to do with the visit that he made. "I only went into the house to know more about the dog's owner."

"I understand, but perhaps if you sign a declaration stating that you entered the home by your own will, it would make the State Department agents feel more at ease."

Bebéi immediately agreed to sign whatever was needed since it was indeed the truth.

With that, the situation seemed to have been resolved. Bebéi went back to speak with the man who again was wearing the same dark suit and insisted on asking him about the mustache man's inquiries, showing a few mug shots, among which Bebéi could pinpoint the unmasked man – the violent one who had asked many questions about Ilona and beat him several times.

The interrogation continued until lunchtime when the Lady appeared with a document for Bebéi to sign. It was straightforward, stating that he had entered the deceased's house with Diana without permission and of his own will. Bebéi had no qualms about signing since it was indeed the truth.

Over lunch, the woman brought up yet another "small" problem.

"I was informed that when you were at the apartment, you took a few things that belonged to the deceased, correct?"

Bebéi told her about the dog's food bowl, the book about the Kuna, and the clothes which they took to justify their lie to the security guard, and the Lady interjected worriedly.

"The problem lies in that it doesn't matter what you took, they still deem it as breaking and entering."

When Bebéi realized what he had gotten himself into, he became very nervous, and tears sprang from his eyes. Compelled to help, the woman decided to bring in an attorney from the Embassy to speak with Bebéi, but this just made him panic, even more.

"You will have to travel to the United States and face up for the crime there," the attorney said. Trying to calm him down, he added, "Since this is your first offense, you may not spend too much time in prison."

Even the Lady seemed worried.

"But you see, he works at the French Embassy. What's going to happen with his job?" she asked.

"In these cases," explained the lawyer, "the State Department would have to contact the French Foreign Affairs Ministry, and unfortunately, this may have him expelled from French diplomatic service."

Bebéi began to feel ill, and they had to call in a doctor.

Accompanied by the woman, they whisked him off to the bedroom to rest. The Lady kept trying to help, but what she said next made matters worse.

"There is something else."

Bebéi, now crying, stood up to listen.

"They are saying that since the dog belonged to an American citizen, it will have to be returned to the United States."

With this, panic turned into despair, and the doctor had to give him a few pills to calm him down.

They left him alone in his room, overwhelmed in desperation. He was going to lose the dog, his job and most likely his pension. He would spend time in prison, and what would he do next? All he knew was to file papers, and no one would give an old archivist a job, much less a criminal. He would have to return to France, but he had no one left there. Bebéi kept crying. He wanted to leave, and tell everything that was happening to Irigandi, Grená or Diocles. Staying there only made him feel more desperate.

A long time elapsed before the woman came back with relatively good news.

"I'm trying to convince them to let you go back home and keep the dog. They may accept my proposal and not present the case before the American courts. I told them that you would promise to behave and to keep us informed of everything you hear regarding Ilona, Julio, and the neighborhood residents." Then she added kindly, "My dear Bebéi, you ought to know that they are being extremely generous, and it is of utmost importance to keep this in complete secrecy. That's something I think you can handle, right?"

The archivist nodded repeatedly while she kept on talking.

"You cannot tell anyone what we talked about here, ever. Besides, you'll keep helping us until we resolve in a definitive matter the theft you committed at Don Francisco's house."

Bebéi almost burst into tears again when he heard the word theft. He didn't see himself as a thief. The book was for Irigandi, the bowl was for the dog, but they kept insisting that it was theft.

"They're telling me that if someone finds out about our little arrangement, the case will have to be brought to the courts without any leeway, and there will be no way for you to avoid prison."

Bebéi was scared but grateful for her help. She took him back in the chauffeured limo and brought Zoubir with them, who, without understanding what was going on, jumped into the car and stuck his nose out of the window.

On the ride back, Bebéi no longer saw himself as the international agent. Instead, he realized that he was now some sort of a double agent forced to listen to everything going on in the old city and report it back to the U.S. State Department. That way, at least, he could ease himself out of the big mess he was in, keep the dog, his job, and stay in Santa Clara along with Irigandi, Grená, Diocles, and all of his friends.

Who knows? he thought to himself. *The day might come when everything would go back to normal. The Lady might solve his problem with the man with the dark suit, Ilona might come back, Diocles might figure out why Julio had returned to Santa Clara to die, and Irigandi's grandfather might be cured.*

With this thought, he petted Zoubir and briefly smiled again.

17

Doña Cecy's secrets. Bebéi got back into his daily routine, but it wasn't easy. The least of his worries was his arm in a cast, not to mention the physical suffering he went through at the hands of the narcs. What really bothered him was what went down at the American Embassy.

Thankfully, he thought, the Lady was there to help him, otherwise, things could have taken a turn for the worse. At least he was free, and Zoubir was with him. Now on, he would have to keep secret everything that had transpired and report everything that went on in the old quarter to the Lady. That was the price to pay for what he did.

But how could he not share what happened? The best thing in his new life was just that: friends with whom he could share his experiences. If it had happened before, back in Paris, the Lady wouldn't have to ask him to keep any secrets since he never had anyone to share anything with, maybe his uncle, but apart from him, no one. Back in the neighborhood, it was a different story – he had so many acquaintances.

He thought about it over and over and finally decided he would only share with those he was closest to. He then set out towards the Cathedral Plaza to meet up with Irigandi and Diocles. The indigenous girl and the old philosopher were his best friends in Santa Clara, and they listened to him closely.

Irigandi was proud to be chosen by her family to accompany the grandfather to the city. Still, she often felt alone and that's why a smile always lit up her face when she heard Bebéi's voice approaching with his dog. That morning she was happy and thankful to find out that

Bebéi was doing fine and knowing that Zoubir would remain in Santa Clara, but she was worried. Along with Ilona's disappearance and Bebéi back in town, she sensed that the one who was now in danger was Diocles. Sooner or later, the narcs would come looking for him.

Next to her, Diocles was intrigued. He knew that he should leave, but he couldn't; he needed to understand what was going on. He had a hunch that the dark-suited Americans who interrogated Bebéi were from the DEA, the ones who investigated anything to do with drug trafficking and were always snooping about, asking questions all along the Caribbean. But there was something that he still didn't get.

"Why is Julio so important to them? Don Francisco disappeared four years ago and lived alone in a house back in Florida, having a dog as his only friend. Why is his death causing such a storm?"

Bebéi also told them that the Lady asked him to keep her informed about everything happening in Santa Clara. Listening to that, Diocles kept pondering.

"What exactly had Julio done? The narcs wanted to know why Julio betrayed them. Ok, I understand that, but why did the Americans want him?"

That thought remained in his mind as he spent the rest of the day and long into the night sitting on a square bench with his cats. Later, when he knew that the rush at the restaurant kitchen was receding, he went to visit Doña Cecy. When the hustle and bustle died down, she would always welcome him with a hefty plate of food to catch up with the happenings in the neighborhood.

Diocles' visits to her kitchen had become a habit in the old lady's life. Doña Cecy had her legs propped up on a small bench, finding relief from her swollen legs, and Diocles had loosened his belt buckle.

That night they talked about what had happened to Bebéi and about Gigi and her struggling battle with heroin addiction. They commented on Ludmilla's effort to keep the restaurant afloat even with no prior experience and about Frida. Diocles was surprised by her violent reaction the day before when Colonel Viera commented in front of Lais's window that perhaps Julio was a terrorist.

"I think I can explain why Frida reacted the way she did," said Doña Cecy, smiling and better accommodating her leg up on the bench. She trusted Diocles and knew she could share some of the secrets she was keeping.

"Frida hoards many ghosts inside," she said.

Diocles knew, like everyone in the neighborhood, that when Frida was young and living in Germany, she was part of a revolutionary group that carried out armed activities against the government. Still, there was something else that Doña Cecy shared with him that night.

"Frida had planned an attack on a train station which ended up killing three children. She was the one who planted the bomb, and later on, she found out that one of the children was the daughter of a former classmate. To this day, Frida has the image of the mangled boy tattooed in her heart. No prison, nor the torture she endured, not even the life of a drunkard that she had, has helped her to forget it. The image of that dead boy is stronger than anything and is imprinted with blood in her mind."

After a long sip of wine, Doña Cecy added with a heavy heart, "The day the bomb went off, Frida died along with it."

That night, Doña Cecy needed to talk. Since Ilona's departure, she had felt alone. Many times, the two of them had shared that same table in the kitchen to talk for hours on end, sharing their secrets, dreams, and fears, but now Ilona was not there, and Doña Cecy was scared. Without Ilona, Diocles was a good confidante in whom she could pour out her sorrows, and she shared with him what she knew about Ilona and Julio when they met on Theo Cavafys' ship, the *Ithaca*.

"Ilona was still working at Cloud Castle. She chose to work as a hooker, but she still had dreams, and there was no time to dream at the Pigalle Street. When she was anxious, she would disappear and travel alongside Theo on the *Ithaca*."

Doña Cecy always called Cavafys by his first name, Theo. Only she and Ilona would call him Theo. Everyone else when they'd spot him in the neighborhood, knew him as Cavafys, the Captain.

Doña Cecy continued. "When she met Julio, on one of her many sails, he was a player, even worse than Rasta Bong and Micky combined," she said smiling.

They kept on talking between bites of risotto and sips of wine —leftovers that had returned from the tables. A few clients were still at the restaurant, and Ludmilla was with them, but the kitchen was already closed and almost cleaned.

They talked about when Julio would come to Santa Clara by the Sea and spend nights at Pigalle Street, trying to make all the women swoon.

"Julio was handsome. He played guitar and knew how to tell enticing stories. He had a unique charm that enchanted women, and he attracted Ilona. Little by little, what started as a fun, turned into love. Ilona initially avoided him. she was afraid of her brother and his threats of killing anyone who got close to her. For a long time, she avoided making public her relationship with Julio." Doña Cecy continued. "In those days, Julio was not into drug trafficking. He was a revolutionary who dreamed of waging war against all the tyrants of the world, and he was smuggling weapons to the Sandinistas in Nicaragua, using Theo's boat. Julio believed he was fighting imperialism for people's freedom. And with that aura of romanticism, he utterly seduced Ilona."

Doña Cecy talked about Julio with great affection and added proudly that after Julio left the guerrillas and joined the drug traffickers, he moved up the ranks quite quickly.

"I don't know exactly what happened, but somehow he got frustrated with the revolution, and he joined the cartels and changed his name to Don Francisco Lacayo," she whispered to Diocles. "But I also know that within the cartels, he was respectfully known as the Condor."

She continued to take sips of wine and talk. Doña Cecy was relaxed and told Diocles Julio had helped Ilona leave Cloud Castle and open her restaurant.

"At that time, they each had their own place here in Santa Clara," she clarified. "There was even a time when Julio fell for a Norwegian woman I never met. She lived in Europe, and I only saw her in pictures. She was a very rich woman who befriended kings and princesses. Julio was obsessed with her for a while, and he would tell Ilona everything. At the time, they were nothing more than friends. Ilona loved him dearly, but she was tough and wanted to live her life without men by her side. In truth, she rarely went out with other men, but Julio didn't know that. He thought that she kept receiving friends as before at the Castle and was oblivious to the fact that after Ilona opened her restaurant, he was the only man in her life."

Diocles was attentively listening and eating his second plate of risotto.

"Julio lived the life of a jetsetter, traveling everywhere, like those you see in movies. I know because Ibrahim told me. The Egyptian helped Julio with his drug business. They both owned hotels, land, and big companies, which they bought with the drug money, but I never understood if what they had belonged to them or the cartels. Anyway, Julio lived like a prince, but not here in Santa Clara. Here, he seldom stepped out of the hotel, or if he did, he would be at the restaurant. But when traveling, he would bring us photos showing the expensive hotels and restaurants he frequented. I think Ilona fell in love with Julio early on, but she hid her feelings because of the Norwegian or fear of her brother, I don't know. Until Julio stopped traveling and began spending more time here alongside her."

The glasses of wine had loosened up Doña Cecy's tongue, helping her keep her mind off the pain in her swollen legs.

"One day, when the widow of Lizondo, a politician, decided to sell her house to live in the United States with her daughter, Ilona and Julio bought it to live there together. Julio left his suite at the hotel, and Gigi rented Ilona's apartment. The Norwegian kept the expensive hotels and restaurants for her, and the two of them moved in to play "husband and wife," as Ilona would say. It was the same house at the end of the boardwalk where she lives to this day, Julio came to be known as Don Francisco Lacayo, and the house at the end of the boardwalk was called the home of Don Francisco and Doña Ilona. And her evil brother never bothered her again because the Condor was more powerful than all of his gang."

By now, the wine and the bellyful had taken their toll, and Diocles' eyes began to close. Doña Cecy noticed it was already late, and her mission was accomplished; she had shared with Diocles everything Ilona wanted him to know.

18

Diocles cannot think. The streets were deserted when they stepped out of the restaurant. Doña Cecy's mission was accomplished. As Ilona would often say, Diocles knew how to think things through, and that's why she told him everything. Who knows? Maybe he would figure out why Julio had returned before dying.

Diocles helped her carry the bags of food to the abandoned house, the same place Ilona met Bebéi before she disappeared. Diocles was one of the few in Santa Clara who knew about the four kids that Doña Cecy hid there, a secret guarded so closely that not even Grená would talk about it.

Although there were many rumors, no one knew for sure who the children were. Some say Doña Cecy wanted to adopt them but couldn't, while others would tell they were Gypsies since the Gypsy Band arrived in Santa Clara right after they got there. Diocles knew that their parents had been killed, and the band members were always around them. He even saw the kids inside the *Lion of Judah Artistic Productions* minibus that carried the Gypsies to their concerts. Still, Doña Cecy never wanted to talk about it, and Diocles respected her secret. There were four kids, and the oldest was the same age as Irigandi.

But for the time being, let's respect Doña Cecy's secret, and let's get back to Diocles, who, after hearing so many things and having drunk so much wine, couldn't sleep and wanted to think. He hoped that by thinking he could solve any problem, but this time the problem seemed to go beyond his thoughts.

First, he went with Doña Cecy to the house, and she even invited him to climb the stairs and take a quick peek on the four kids who were peacefully sleeping.

From there, he continued walking and pondering his doubts and concerns on the waterfront until he reached the harbor. A long walk. Then he returned to Cathedral Plaza, taking advantage of the pre-dawn stillness.

As soon as he sat down on his favorite bench, Rasta Bong showed up from a night of partying. His eyes still gleamed from the marijuana, and Diocles smiled. Rasta always amused him. During the day, he was an active entrepreneur always looking for new business, and at night, one love.

"Things are getting feisty," said Rasta with a melodious voice. "Some important men are here... from Colombia, Mexico, and even a few Chinese and Russians. They want to find out everything." He couldn't talk too much; he was high as a kite from his marijuana joints. Before going on his way he added in a whisper, "They were with Silvino. They want all the gangs to help, and they're looking for Ilona."

The storm was brewing, and Diocles knew that if the cartels were in town, it meant they wouldn't stop until they found her. They were going to terrorize everyone until someone would leak Ilona's hideout.

Luckily, the secret was still safe.

Many thoughts were running through his head, and he was planning to spend all day sitting in the plaza, petting his cats, and thinking, until he could figure out why Julio had faked his death.

Just after dawn, he saw some unknown cars driving slowly, perusing the neighborhood, and he wasn't the only one who noticed. Lieutenant Pirilo, who also couldn't sleep, saw them, which made him uneasy and fearful. Diocles saw him from afar, but the lieutenant didn't want to talk. He was embarrassed to be so powerless, and he went straight to City Hall.

Diocles kept petting his cats, enjoying the first rays of light when Micky, who had finished his night shift, dropping off and collecting tourists from Pigalle Street, parked his cab and approached Diocles with a scared look.

"They know who Ilona's friends are! They say they'll pay a nice sum to whoever reveals her hideout." Then he fell silent for a moment as if remembering what he had heard. "They also said that they would kill whoever is keeping the secret." Then he fell silent again, this time for a little longer. "They're telling this to everyone."

They both fell silent, and for Micky to remain quiet and still, something utterly serious must have been going on.

There was no one else in the entire square. Diocles wanted to focus on his thoughts and figure out the reasons Julio could have had to come back, but he couldn't stop thinking about what the cartels would do if they discovered who the five were. At that moment, the Chinese Doll showed up, walking from Pigalle Street. She was worried about Frida after she noticed that cartel people were asking questions. She was walking towards the steps of La Merced, and Diocles joined her. Knowing about Frida was more important than thinking.

They found Robespierre awake, getting ready to greet the church ladies with his insults, and next to him, Frida, completely wasted, slept over Null's belly. She didn't even wake up after the Chinese Doll shook her vigorously.

Diocles was staring at all of them when Grená's voice pierced the scene. She was flustered.

"Rasta Bong told me… we have to protect Doña Cecy." Grená kept on talking without hiding her anxiety. "I'm sure they will soon get to Frida. Everybody knows she's always been Ilona's confidant."

Diocles agreed, but what could they do? How to protect Frida, Doña Cecy, and everyone else who knew Ilona? And that's how Diocles spent the rest of the morning at the steps of La Merced next to Null's farts, paralyzed by fear, taking in everyone's anxiety.

It was almost noon when he noticed Lieutenant Pirilo again, watching them from the barbershop's doorway. Pirilo was also worried and looking for news, and that's when Ludmilla showed up, announcing that Gigi had been kidnapped.

"Two cars stopped in front of her apartment, and I saw her come out escorted by two masked men."

Diocles had not chosen Gigi, Doña Cecy, nor even Frida to be one of the five to hide Ilona. He knew they would be the first the drug traffickers would think of, and he thought that he had the rest of the afternoon to ponder about Julio when, suddenly, a car stopped in front of the steps of La Merced, and four armed men got out, asking for Frida.

They first asked Grená, then Diocles, and then they stopped asking when they saw Frida sleeping atop Null's belly. Without a word, they carried her into one of the cars.

Diocles dared to ask them why they were taking her.

"She's going to tell us where Ilona is hiding," one of them answered.

And Diocles insisted pretending to be naïve. "Why do you want to find her?"

"Because anyone who betrays us doesn't live to celebrate it," answered the same man.

Diocles stopped asking; there was really nothing else he wanted to know.

While they were putting Frida inside the car, Bebéi showed up from around the corner, yelling and running with Zoubir in tow. When he reached them, he was out of breath, yelling in French, not knowing what had just happened with Frida.

"Ils ont emmené Doña Cecy!"[4] Then, while looking around at everyone, including the armed men who were taking Frida away, he said, "I saw them. They put her in a car and left! I yelled, but they kept going."

Diocles didn't move. He tried to remain calm, but inside he was about to lose it. He knew that Ilona wouldn't have told Doña Cecy where she was going, and honestly, they wouldn't believe her. For an instant, he thought about the four children Doña Cecy hid in the big house.

"What will happen to the Gypsy children now?" he whispered to Grená, who stayed speechless. There was no use arguing against armed men. Everything was spinning inside his head, and Diocles could hardly think.

Null-and-void woke up from his drunken stupor, but he kept quiet, and only after the car had left, he whispered in Diocles' ear, "I know nothing. Ilona didn't show up that day, and I don't know where she is."

Diocles was trying to keep his composure and went to Lais's house to tell her that the narcs had her sister. Along the way, he

---

[4] They took Doña Cecy

passed in front of the bookstore where Princess and Hector were chatting away, frightened.

"And you know what else?" Princess was saying, "The French Ambassador showed up this morning asking about Bebéi. He wanted to know what he did back in the United States. Apparently, those from the American Embassy had paid him a visit asking him some questions."

That's what Diocles heard while passing by, but there was no time for chitchat. Up ahead, he saw again Lieutenant Pirilo crossing the plaza with a worried look on his face. He hurried up the pace to Lais's home, and to his surprise, Doña Cecy's sister was not tense.

"We knew this would happen. That's why yesterday, Cecy wanted to tell you everything she knew," she said.

Diocles just listened. He knew he was not able to think anymore and asked, "And who will look after the children?"

"Don't worry. No one will harm them." Afterward, as she got ready to leave, Lais added, "I have to open the restaurant. We promised Ilona that the restaurant would remain open, and if my sister is not there, I have to go."

Diocles knew Lais rarely left her apartment. She would cook her empanadas and chicken soup, and with that small business, she supported her two drunken sons and her two lazy daughters-in-law, who always got wasted with their husbands. But now, she had to go to the restaurant. Ilona and Doña Cecy always helped her, and it was payback time. She had never worked at a restaurant, but she knew how to cook, just like her sister, and she knew she would make it work.

Diocles went with her, unable to even remember what he wanted to think about anymore. It was important to make sure that Ilona's restaurant remained open; that's what they had promised her.

On their way, Diocles met Micky again.

"Diana called me from the States to tell me that the police had shown up at her home. She didn't know why, but she thinks that it has something to do with Bebéi's visit. They even asked if he was still in Florida."

Diocles felt his fear rise with each step he took. The narcs were keeping Ilona's friends hostage while the Americans were looking for Diana.

When they arrived at the restaurant, there was another surprise. At the doorstep was the Greek Captain, Ilona's friend, speaking to Colonel Viera. He seemed to be up to date with what was going on, and he added to the doom and gloom.

"Ibrahim was kidnapped yesterday back in Egypt near Alexandria, where he had been hiding at his mother's farm. The cartels have a wide range of influence, and they have contacts all over the world."

Diocles listened and decided that he wouldn't think anymore. It was too much in one day, and he preferred to seek shelter with his cats under the Cathedral Plaza bandstand.

19

The Greek Captain arrives. Theo Cavafys was the Captain of the *Ithaca*, the merchant boat where Julio and Ilona first met. Physically, he wasn't very impressive. He was short, with unkempt hair and a days-old beard. He resembled a typical seafarer. He didn't look at all like Anthony Quinn's Zorba. However, as soon as he got to talking, his tiny eyes came alive, sparkling with the stories he would tell, making it difficult to resist his charm.

Theo met Ilona when she worked at a cabaret near Port of Spain, and from that day, he had followed her trek across the Caribbean. At every port he stopped, he would ask about her and her adventures, which were many, and he helped Frida and her when they opened Cloud Castle.

Theo had a love interest there, but it was not Ilona. Frida was his occasional lover, which may sound odd, considering his small build and Frida being a robust and tall German. But Cavafys was always attracted to bigger women. Frida was not his only love; he had begotten many offspring around the world during his travels. According to wagging tongues, and there was no reason for anyone in Santa Clara to doubt them, he had solid relationships in Rhodes, Greece, Agrigento, and Sicily, another in Barranquilla, Colombia, and one more in Livingston over on the Gulf of Honduras. And that was not counting his one-night-stand girlfriends throughout the many ports he had traveled.

He proudly shared the same name as the great Greek poet, and *Ithaca*, his ship, was baptized in honor of one of the most famous poems Konstantinos Cavafys wrote, which he knew by heart. Maybe that's why he and Moriarty became friends, and why Theo was one

Harmさ

of the few people able to bring Henry out of his catatonic state. When he was in Santa Clara, the Captain was often seen reading poems with the old Canadian hippie.

For Cavafys, everything was meaningful. He wasn't the kind of poet who wrote verses, but, as Moriarty explained, *He made poetry out of life itself.* He enjoyed each moment, every landscape he encountered, each glass of wine he drank, and he could share that joy with everyone. And when he mixed his joy with wine, rum and ouzo, the terrace of Ilona's restaurant came alive with music and dance.

He hadn't traveled, however, to dance or celebrate. He knew that Ilona was in danger, and this is what had brought him there. Theo Cavafys knew that it wouldn't be easy. He had already lived that same nightmare four years earlier, when everyone thought that Julio had died. That's why when he heard Julio returned to die, he turned *Ithaca's* helm and sailed to Santa Clara. He knew what he would have to confront the cartels, but there were still things unexplained, and maybe Ilona's friends at Santa Clara could help him to understand.

They didn't have time to waste, and as soon as Diocles left, he asked for a bottle of Caribbean rum and sat at the restaurant terrace to share his memories with Colonel Viera, Princess, Hector, and Lieutenant Pirilo, who showed up as soon as they heard that the Captain had arrived.

"Ilona always loved the sea. Each time she felt sadness inside her soul, she would come sail with me on the *Ithaca.* She loved to be on deck just gazing out onto the ocean. The infinite blue seemed to calm her down. That's how she met Julio. He was young like her, a revolutionary full of passion. Julio was able to convince anyone that the world could indeed change. I never understood why it was important for him to change the world, but that's what he wanted, and his passion touched me to the core." He them picked up his glass of rum making a toast and swigged it down in one gulp exclaiming: "Yassu, Julio, my friend. I always respected his dream and his will to live. That's what seduced Ilona."

Each one of his listeners had to drink too. Cavafys didn't respect those who declined his toasts.

"I never traded arms. My business was to carry bananas. That's how I kept the *Ithaca* afloat. Sometimes I would add some small illegal trade here and there." He justified his actions. "I always needed extra cash for my large family, but never the arms trade. I knew that could get me into a lot of trouble." He had a swig of his drink.

"Julio asked me to take a small cargo up to San Juan del Norte in Nicaragua. It was no big deal, but it was risky, and I decided to do it. I could never say no to him. If he was willing to risk his life for that cause, I had no right to hinder his dream. Together we brought arms for the Sandinistas along the coast of Honduras and then along Livingston to help the guerrillas in Guatemala and El Salvador. Back then, Julio had a Peruvian girlfriend, a pretty and wild one indeed. Renata, that was her name." He smiled and invited the others to toast in honor of Renata's beauty.

Theo was known for proposing toasts, but pity the fool who tried to match him! He was able to drink as much as Frida and then get up and dance the hasapiko on one foot, and now that he was rolling down memory lane, he continued to speak.

"Julio and Ilona were made for each other, but it took a long time before they got along. He was afraid of the sea, he only traveled with me out of need, and when he did, he would stay locked up in the cabin. He met her aboard the *Ithaca*, and Ilona was exactly his opposite. On the open deck, she was the queen of the world enjoying the ocean, while Julio got motion sickness with the sway of little waves. At first, there was a huge apathy between them, very intense." He smiled as he remembered.

"In those days," Cavafys continued. "Julio was obsessed with gathering resources to finance the revolution in Central America, and that's all he would talk about. It was in the early Eighties, and Julio thought that by supporting the revolutionary groups there, they would spread the revolution all across the world. The only thing in their way was lack of the damn money as he would say."

"Around that time, he also met another friend aboard, Lara, who would always get his hands on special cargo to transport to the United States. Like Julio, he loved his rum and cigars, a passion all three of us shared. I heard Lara lost his family's fortune back in

Uruguay and went to Colombia to traffic drugs. He would never deal big volumes. He rather made small deals, and this was agreeable for me as well, since I always preferred to work with small amounts – nothing that would cause alarm to some of the friends I had among the North American authorities."

The ease in which Cavafys spoke about his drug trafficking made Colonel Viera uneasy, as he was known for being scrupulously moral, but that didn't seem to bother Cavafys.

"Julio and Lara met in Puerto Cortés, Honduras, and it was aboard the *Ithaca* where they came up with the idea to finance the revolution by the drug trade. The narcs had a lot of resources, but they didn't have control over the region. Instead, Julio's friends, the guerrilleros, were powerful, but lacked the resources to keep the revolution going.

Theo stopped talking for a few seconds to toast once more, although he had nothing left to toast for, so he drank to dampen his throat.

"The Americans, with their people, were supporting the counter-revolution all along the region, making Julio nervous." Every time Cavafys mentioned Julio's name, his face brightened with pride and admiration for his friend.

"They were only a handful of revolutionaries, with a dozen or so boxes of arms, but they believed that they could overthrow the superpower of the United States. They needed resources and men, but they had plenty of balls to spare." This time he raised his drink without stopping for anyone to join in. It was for the memory of his friend.

"Julio dreamed big and would soar fearlessly above the world. He was the Condor."

This time, they all joined in the toast, but just then, Bebéi showed up, and what promised to be a long chat was cut short. Diocles had already warned everybody that no one should discuss secrets in front of Bebéi now that he was spying for the American Embassy.

That evening Bebéi hadn't come alone. Irigandi and the dog were there, as was La Pajerita and her bitch with the disheveled fur. It was evident that La Pajerita, with her mangled clothes and her crazed look, didn't fit in with restaurant's regular customers, but Bebéi could care less. For him, La Pajerita was his friend and owner of the little bitch that played with his dog. This was enough reason for her to be with him at the restaurant, and no one would tell him otherwise.

They sat at a table at the far end of the terrace: Bebéi, La Pajerita, and Irigandi with Zoubir and the little mangy bitch underneath.

Princess explained to Cavafys that the black dog had belonged to Julio, and no sooner had he said this, Irigandi walked directly toward them.

Somehow, she knew who was there, and before anyone could say anything, she placed her hands as if studying the Greek Captain's face and said, "You were Julio's best friend and the only one who can say for sure if he had truly loved Ilona."

Cavafys drank slowly before answering. While he swallowed, he was thinking that the little Kuna with her colorful clothes and her doll-like face wasn't the only one curious to know what Julio felt for Ilona.

"I think Julio loved Ilona like no other woman. He was a passionate man. He would meet someone and fall in love. That's how it was with Renata, the guerilla fighter, and the Norwegian millionaire. He would fall out of love as quickly as he fell into it, but with Ilona it was different. They hated each other at first, later they became lovers, and only afterward, friends. For Julio, Ilona became what no other woman could be before. Even his brother said so."

Everyone was surprised. Nobody at the table knew that Julio had a brother, but before anyone could ask anything about him, Irigandi intervened.

"If Julio loved Ilona so much, why did he betray her?"

And the Captain realized that the questions the girl was asking were also those Ilona would pose herself.

"I can't answer that, and I think no one has the answer. I knew he loved her, and since I heard he had returned, I haven't stopped thinking about that."

Cavafys paused and drank again to wet his throat and think about his answer. "Perhaps he disappeared to get away from the narcs or the Americans who were also looking for him. It is probable that they knew that he was the Condor DEA was desperate to find, but I never understood why Julio didn't tell Ilona of his plans."

The others, who had known him as Don Francisco Lacayo and knew of his affection for Ilona, also didn't understand. Neither did Princess, Hector, or the Colonel. They were all still confused. Neither did La Pajerita, but really in her dementia, she couldn't understand much, nor did she really care to. She was more concerned with the fact that it was the first time she had ever set foot inside a restaurant, and she was just as happy looking at Bebéi, who was watching the others from a distance and curious as to why Irigandi was asking the Greek Captain so many questions.

20

Get out if you can. Life in Santa Clara by the Sea was no longer the same. The narrow streets still held up the old colonial homes, its churches with everlasting grandeur were still present, and the sun brightened up the boardwalk, where the tourists enjoyed the view of the bay and amused themselves with the work of handicraft artists. But now, the residents were afraid.

Ever since the narcs took over, there were no more chairs placed on the sidewalks, and those who did walk out on the street did so hurriedly. No one kept their windows open, and the Cathedral Plaza benches remained empty. They knew that the narcs wouldn't rest until they found Ilona, and all the gangs were cooperating with them.

Silvino asked Rasta Bong to warn Grená to be careful. They already had Ilona's three friends: Doña Cecy, Frida, and Gigi. They also had the Egyptian, and now they wanted the Greek. They will not stop until they find her.

And the narcs weren't the only ones looking for Ilona. The Americans were looking for her too, and that's what Lieutenant Pirilo was telling the Colonel. Their friendship went way back to when Colonel Viera was in the military and Pirilo was a young recruit under his command. Pirilo wasn't ambitious like Rasta or a rebel like Silvino. Pirilo was easygoing, and for him a job at the Mayor's office was a perfect setting. He didn't have much to do other than solving small disputes in the neighborhood and taking care of the Mayor's personal interests.

Pirilo would arrive after his morning workouts and work up until 11 am, when he would sneak out on his escapades over on Pigalle Street. He was smart enough not to let himself be seen partying around there at night, so he would opt to go before lunchtime when the street was still empty. He had many girlfriends there, and, as Lieutenant Pirilo was the leading police authority in the neighborhood, women treated him kindly and respectfully. After his morning encounters, which always left him hungry, he would have lunch in a random restaurant nearby and then focus on playing dominoes. He was one of the best players around, and even when duty called, he always found time to play a round. By 4 pm, he would return to City Hall for his daily meeting with the Mayor. In all honesty, he had little to report since the neighborhood was always relatively calm. By the end of the day, he would meet up with some other cops to play soccer at the small field at the Municipal School. That was the Lieutenant's life, not much ambition and not much to do. He was comfortably single and lived well and at ease.

But that was before.

Ever since they found Julio dead on the street, everything had changed, and that's what he was talking about to the Colonel.

"The narcs control the streets," he said with a disgusted look on his face. "Santa Clara was such an easygoing place that after ten years of working at the City Hall, I never worried about walking out with a loaded gun."

The Colonel looked at him disapprovingly but didn't interrupt.

"Yesterday, a few of them paid a visit to the Mayor, and I suspect that one of them was the one with the mustache and tattoo who kidnapped Bebéi. This morning I sent out the boys to check and load up their guns thoroughly." He vented his anxieties. "Colonel, they are of a different breed. They're not like the criminals we're used to. These guys are violent, without any appreciation for their own life or anyone else's, and worst of all, the Mayor asked us to help them find Ilona."

The Colonel kept listening quietly.

"I'm worried," said the Lieutenant. "If those thugs remain here, our peace will disappear, and the old neighborhood will never be the same. The Americans from the DEA are here as well, with a whole group of investigators asking questions. They're working out of the American Embassy, and they want to find Ilona before the narcs do. Everyone suspects that Ilona never left the country and is hiding out in one of the houses in Pigalle Street. They already interrogated me, and I even had to explain what I do and with whom I talk when I go there."

The lieutenant's disgust grew as he shared the details. And while listening, Colonel Viera wasn't surprised. It was no secret that all women on Pigalle Street respected Ilona, and maybe she could be hiding out there.

That same afternoon what they feared the most happened. The narcs were so determined to find Ilona that they raided Pigalle Street to check each and every house. The confusion and the mess they caused were of a historical magnitude.

Luckily for Pirilo, the invasion took place in the early afternoon when he had already left after an encounter with one of his girlfriends and was having lunch. Most clients at that time were respectable men looking for an early piece of entertainment. Many renowned businessmen and politicians were kicked out on the street with their pants down – literally – and the most remarkable person in that state was the Mayor. He had canceled a meeting with evangelical leaders to hurry without his bodyguards to an unplanned encounter on the street with two Asian masseuses who had recently arrived. The Mayor never imagined he'd be exposed in such a way, in front of the Red Cock, and assisted by the two masseuses. The incident got him in trouble with his wife and also with the Jamaican dancer who was reported to be his first mistress.

Following right behind was Judge Torino, Mrs. Beatriz Almendra's husband, president of the Catholic Women's Association, and a big supporter of religious activities in the neighborhood. Torino thought he was well hidden in the privacy of Madame Mill's home – one of the diplomatic circle's favorite spots – and ended up at the curbside, wearing nothing but his black socks and a red towel. And the most pathetic thing to watch was seeing him trying to explain to the young leftist reporter that his intentions of going there were solely to raise funds to support single mothers.

The next day, the reporter published his version next to Mrs. Almendra's remarks. His wife didn't refrain from using offensive language when referring to her husband and petitioned a nationwide call to action for the expulsion of all prostitutes from Santa Clara – those whom she called vulgar and ambitious and women of ill repute.

Her words, in turn, enraged the residents of Pigalle Street and prompted an outbreak of anonymous gossip, which revealed certain impure secrets of that honorable and pious woman. Among them was her adulterous relationship with Chombo Zen, who always meditated in the streets with a bare torso and, by mere coincidence, was also Mrs. Almendra's yoga instructor.

The narcs didn't find Ilona, and no one wanted to return to Pigalle Street after the brutal invasion, but surprises kept popping up. The Americans, friends of the Lady, were also asking Ling's daughter Kay a few questions. She helped her father at the Chinese store and was also in charge of the accounts for Ilona's restaurant. Because of that, she had to return to the American embassy for three straight days to answer questions about Ilona's business. The Americans seized all documents in her office on the second floor of the store, including files for all Rasta Bong's businesses that she also helped manage. A big mess.

"No one knows what they are looking for, but whatever it is, they consider it very important," commented Hector, the professor and band instructor. And his comment was the starting point of what became a crowded assembly.

First, Rasta Bong, peeved by the seizure of all his marijuana, mentioned that he had received a threat that if he didn't hand over Ilona, they would take him away. Then it was Micky who said that at La Gata Caliente, the drag queen cabaret at the port, they were looking for a Lola Marlene, who, apparently, knew where Ilona was.

Rasta looked at Micky with a disapproving face; the situation was critical, but Micky should not risk revealing publicly Princess' secret.

Colonel Viera showed up, and for some odd reason, seemed happy amid all the chaos. He too had news he wanted to share with everyone while the manicurist started to work on his nails.

"Today, I was visited by a colonel who went to the School of the Americas at the same time I did. He told me that he was here to follow up on Julio Silva. He told me that Julio Silva was a terrorist who had killed a general and, according to his country authorities, had died in a motorcycle accident back in Italy. He said that he spoke with the local police as well as with the Americans, who were after any clue regarding Don Francisco Lacayo, suspecting it was the same person. Apparently, the investigation is getting even more bizarre. The Americans are talking about a Chinese and a Muslim connection. The Chinese filter is with Ling's daughter and the Chinese Doll, who they link up to the Chinese Department of Security, Second Bureau."

Grená immediately interrupted the colonel.

"I told you so! I knew it, but no one believed me! The Chinese Doll is a secret agent, don't you see?" But no one reacted; it was too much news at once.

Regarding the Muslim connection, not even the colonel could explain and warned, "My friend mentioned that they found evidence of a radical Muslim cell in the neighborhood."

By now, everyone was looking at each other with the same look they had when Cavafys started reciting his namesake's poems in Greek. Things were getting seriously out of control, and it wasn't good.

The gathering in front of the barbershop had attracted many passersby, and even the young priest decided to cross the street to find out what was going on. Among the assembled was Bebéi, who kept quiet, busy jotting down notes, the main ideas being discussed.

"It's not fair that mere strangers are making everyone's life hell and the authorities aren't doing a thing," said a man from the Fire Department, faulting the lieutenant. A city counselor from the opposition party criticized the Mayor, "whose main interests were his masseuses."

The fact that everyone talked at once complicated things for Bebéi, who was struggling to take notes and fulfill his end of the bargain with the Lady.

At the door of the barbershop, Pirilo was also listening and thinking. He knew that arguing at the barbershop was not going to get the narcs out of Santa Clara. They needed concrete action, and he had discussed it with Diocles. They both knew that the only way to kick out the narcs and the inquiring Americans was to find out why Julio returned. Without that, there was nothing they could do.

Princess arrived and complicated the discussion further by saying that Julio didn't come back for Ilona but because he was after the El

Dorado. And amid all the absurdities like Chinese espionage and Muslim connections, the search for El Dorado didn't seem far-fetched, which made Lieutenant Pirilo pay attention to Princess's ideas.

Back at the plaza, Diocles was feeding his cats as he watched the four children that were under Doña Cecy's protection, peacefully playing as if nothing had happened. While he watched them, he asked himself how they could be so calm with their guardian gone missing?

21

Searching for El Dorado. "Brave are the men who fear not to follow their destiny." That is how Princess began the presentation to his friends in the old quarter.

From the moment Bebéi gave him the list of Julio's books, Princess had dedicated all his time to understanding the secret behind the deceased's bookshelves. He knew that Julio had never been a bookworm. His life and adventures were more fulfilling than any novel, and he had never had time to read them.

After faking his death, Julio had decided to begin reading, and the books on the shelves were the only clue to discovering what he was looking for. The books, particularly the old ones that had been edited centuries ago and bought at the highest bidding price from collectors, could serve as important clues.

From his analysis emerged a theory, and that is what Princess wanted to explain to his friends. He had divided the titles into five categories: twenty-one on poetry; nineteen on the history of Buddhism (in particular Zen Buddhism); twenty-seven on Colonial America (focusing largely on expeditions in the region of Nueva Granada); twenty-four on the native groups in that area (mostly about the Kuna); and twenty-four on various themes, including cooking and a few novels.

Those books weren't there by coincidence. Julio's interests had been precise, and that's what Princess was confirming now to his friends. Everyone was sitting on bookstore chairs that Princess had for his poetry readings.

Bebéi was sitting on the first row, between Irigandi and her grandfather, who Princess had personally invited. Zoubir was at

Irigandi's feet. On the second row, Diocles was curious to know what Princess had to say. He sat next to Hector, Colonel Viera, and Robespierre, who, despite his dementia, would always stop by when Princess organized readings. Behind them, Henry Moriarty was sitting in the corner with his eyes closed. The old hippie had never been in the bookstore before, but he had surprisingly showed up after he heard Princess was going to talk about the Darien.

Captain Cavafys didn't go; he was focused on reaching the narcs. But Lieutenant Pirilo was there. Not because he was interested in Princess's deliriousness but because he didn't know what else to do. He stood near the door.

Princess's presentation was very elaborate with maps hanging on a chalkboard that had been brought by Hector from the municipal school.

"Brave were those men who ventured out from Europe, crossing the ocean in fragile ships, driven by their wild dreams," started Princess with a slight hesitation. For him, that presentation took much more than any impersonation of Lola Marlene at La Gata Caliente, and he was overacting – not so much in what he was saying, but in his gestures.

"I'm convinced that reading these books, Julio was thinking about the same big dream that moved many adventurers in the sixteenth century: to find El Dorado, the city of gold! The great treasure hid in the jungle that could make its discoverers the richest and most admired in all the world. Julio's interest, or perhaps, his obsession, was Nueva Granada, the region that includes what is today Venezuela, Panama, Ecuador, and Colombia." And with exaggerated gestures, Princess pointed out each country on the map. "And I will go further," he continued. "From what I can gather, the books seem to indicate his special interest in the region of Darien, in present-day Panama." To illustrate, Princess pointed to another map on the left of the chalkboard highlighting the jungle between Panama and Colombia.

Henry Moriarty didn't move in his chair, but Princess observed him and could see the old hippie opening his eyes, curious.

"This is what caught my attention," Princess continued. "Most of the search for El Dorado was primarily focused on Colombia, at other times in Ecuador, and even in the Amazon, however, never in Panama. Did Julio find out something new and unique?"

Bebéi was proud to know all the places Princess was mentioning, since they were part of the Le Breton files. Still, he was worried about Irigandi, who, other than Santa Clara, knew only the islands of Kuna Yala where she was born. But he could see that she was calmly following Princess' words, and her grandfather was too. Both seemed to be enjoying the presentation.

"There weren't many Spanish expeditions carried out in Panamanian territory," Princess clarified, "but those were the ones Julio read about." He stopped, leaving the thought up in the air and placing his hand on Irigandi's shoulder before continuing. "And do you know what puzzles me most? Julio's interest in the Kuna, Irigandi's people." He extended the pause as if waiting for an expression of shock or surprise from the listeners, but as nobody said anything, he continued. "Imagine for a moment, and I need to confess that this is sheer speculation, that Julio found a link between the Kuna and the legend of El Dorado."

Princess insisted on embellishing his pauses to reinforce the suspense.

"A legend that attracted names like Francisco Pizarro, Sir Walter Raleigh, Lope de Aguirre, and many more, which I reiterate, took place primarily in the region of today's Colombia and the Amazon. Not in Panama."

Everyone was attentive to his presentation except for Lieutenant Pirilo who seemed distracted, far away someplace.

"Julio's books show a special interest in the Kuna and some events that took place in Panama, like the British Santa Cruz de Cana Mine, the writings and reports by a Welsh Lionel Wafer, and the expeditions by the Scots, the French, and the Americans into the jungle territory of Darien."

Bebéi began to squirm in his seat, anxious. He knew all about it, but Princess kept talking, not noticing, until he mentioned the name of Richard Marsh.

Bebéi couldn't control himself anymore and exclaimed. "The papers by Le Breton, the ones the Monsieur l' Ambassadeur asked me to file, mention that same man!"

His interruption caused a bit of surprise, but everyone was so dazzled by Princess's words that no one paid much attention to what Bebéi said, and Princess kept on.

"Early on, Europeans had a zealous fascination for Panama, looking for a shorter route to the Pacific, but some historians mentioned a Golden Castle in the Darien, fiercely protected by the native tribes. And it was their hope of finding that treasure, which justified the creation of a new Scottish colony off the Gulf of Caledonia."

Suddenly distressed, Bebéi interrupted again in his Spanish, which got worse when he was anxious, and surprised everyone present by saying, "The Scots arrived at Caledonia, and they savaient that the mines d'or were most likely in the Darien jungle. The French and the English knew this as well. They were the ones who opened up mines in Santa Cruz de Cana."

Princess and everyone else grew silent, looking at Bebéi. Diocles was the first to recover from the initial shock.

"And how do you know all that?" he asked.

Smiling, Bebéi replied, "I already told you that Monsieur l'Ambassadeur asked me to file some papers which he bought from Le Breton's daughter. There are boxes and boxes of papiers which read about everything Princess is talking about. There is a lettre by William Paterson, a Scot, where he tells it all."

Robespierre interrupted him harshly. "What are you saying about the Bretons?"

When Bebéi was about to explain, Princess cut Robespierre off. Robespierre was drunk, and it was important to understand what Bebéi knew about that letter. Princess had read about it and, despite looking for it, he hadn't found it.

"When he was a young boy in Jamaica," Bebéi answered, "Sir William Paterson overheard the pirate Henry Morgan say that there was a great treasure hidden in Darien. That's why years later he convinced the Scots to create the colony in Caledonia, but when they got into the Darien to find the Chateau d'Or, they were swarmed by insects and died. The same thing happened to les Français, who were attacked by the native tribes."

Bebéi grew enthusiastic, proudly showing off his knowledge to his friends. "In the twentieth century the American, Richard Marsh, who Princess mentioned, came close to discovering the Chateau. But he never did, as the jungle and the natives had always protected the secret of d'Or."

Bebéi remained standing while everyone looked at him in silence. He kept surprising them. No one had imagined that he would know things that not even Princess was aware of with all his books.

Princess sensed that it was more important to listen than keep talking and asked Bebéi to carry on talking about the documents he filed for the Ambassador. The roles changed, and Bebéi was now the one answering questions while Princess, sitting on one of the chairs, listened attentively.

Lieutenant Pirilo was not interested and excused himself and left. He was worried about the narcs, and all that talk about legends and Darien didn't make any sense to him.

But for those who stayed, the talk was enlightening. They understood the French Ambassador had asked Bebéi to find clues about the gold's whereabouts, and Bebéi naively confirmed this by saying, "Monsieur l'Ambassadeur never mentions the documents in front of others at the Embassy. He always prefers to talk to me about them when we are alone at his residence."

That morning, Bebéi also mentioned a letter by Sir William Paterson which the ambassador had hired a British expert to translate. In the letter it was written that Sir Francis Drake had joined forces with runaway slaves, who had told him that Darien natives guarded a golden castle.

Princess then confirmed that Sir Francis Drake had been indeed an ally to the runaway slaves to fight against the Spaniards, something that was confirmed by many historians of the region.

Bebéi also mentioned a message written by Sir Francis Drake to the Queen – which was never sent and was lost – informing her of the exact location of the Golden Castle. Princess was excited by the new information and added that the Scots could never establish themselves in Darien because of the natives' resistance.

"It's possible," he pointed out, "that one of the native groups were the Kuna."

Hearing this, Irigandi smiled, trying to hide her surprise. She knew about these events, but she was unaware that the wagas – as the Kuna referred to the white people – also knew these stories.

Bebéi continued speaking, mentioning Francis Borland, author of *History of the Darien in the Eighteenth Century*, a rare book also found on the deceased's bookshelf. Bebéi returned to the subject of Richard Marsh, an American who supported the Kuna at the turn of the last century when they declared their independence.

Relying on his memory, Bebéi kept on describing what he had learned from the documents he had seen. At the end, Diocles summarized it all.

"One can deduce that Julio's interest was the treasure hidden deep in the Darien."

And Princess added, "He wasn't the only one, since His Excellency, the French Ambassador, seems to have the same interest."

Still, they were all confused. If Julio was the Condor, he had plenty of money. Why would he want more if he couldn't leave his hideout?

"He didn't fake his death for a treasure, nor for leaving Ilona. No, I don't believe so," said Colonel Viera, and nobody contested his words. They were confused about Julio's motives too.

Princess insisted on his suspicion that Julio was interested in the Darien and, more specifically, in the Kuna's sacred lands around the Takarkuna mountain.

"Which for the Kuna," explained Princess, "is the birthplace of everything that exists. And do not forget that Julio died in front of a church where he was probably looking for documents."

"Could it be that the Kuna hide a Golden Castle," Hector asked bluntly to Irigandi's grandfather, who didn't answer.

Henry Moriarty stood up from his chair in the corner and sat next to Irigandi's grandfather.

The group kept arguing over those absurd theories, while Bebéi was starting to worry about the amount of new information he would have to report back to the Lady.

Beside him, Irigandi was intrigued. Much of what she heard had already been told to her by her grandfather. He was one of the wise men in the village, and every night he would tell her stories of the father Pap Tunmat and the mother Nam Tunmat and how the first Kuna emerged from the sacred hills of Takarkuna. Her grandfather had told her about their ancestors and the Kuna guardians. Irigandi knew that her parents were guardians and had died protecting the secrets of their people. The Kuna were not rich or powerful like the waga, who came from Europe, but she knew they were chosen to protect Mother Earth's secrets. That was why, when they all left, she suggested to Bebéi and Diocles, whom she trusted, that they speak with her grandfather.

As he was leaving the bookstore, Diocles heard Moriarty whisper to Irigandi's grandfather, "They got close, but they are not there yet. They think it's all about gold."

Those words that Diocles heard were not particularly significant. Moriarty could have been talking about Julio and the gold as his motivation. What caught Diocles' attention was Irigandi's grandfather's reaction. He looked surprised and concerned at Moriarty's words. Why were all those crazy ideas of Princess and Bebéi so significant to him?

Diocles' curiosity was so great that he visited the small room where Irigandi lived with her grandfather that same night. He asked questions but didn't obtain any answers. The grandfather, like him, preferred silence to lies. Diocles left frustrated, and Irigandi was intrigued. She was a Nele, and she knew that her grandfather's silence meant something she would have to understand.

22

The Captain faces the storm. Cavafys knew the cartels, and he was aware that there would be no peace until the narcs found what they were looking for. He knew they had spies all over the place listening to what people said and deciphering their silence. No one was spared, not even him on the *Ithaca*, since there was no corner in the world they couldn't reach.

He had gone through the same nightmare four years before when they sent people to scrutinize Santa Clara to find out if the Condor was really dead. Julio, the Condor, had been responsible for investing the cartels' money. He had been the mastermind behind a complex financial system channeling the cartels' income into a group of legal companies and turning dirty drug money into profitable and clean investments recognized by governments and making it impossible to trace the money's origins.

And Julio was like a brother to him. It was in Gregoria's house, Cavafys' Garifuna girlfriend, where he had hidden Julio back in the days when Julio was still a guerilla fighter. He had been badly hurt, and Cavafys had secretly taken him to Cuba, where they pulled out a bullet from his lung. He was also the first to witness Julio's frustrations with the revolutionary cause when Soviet money stopped pouring in and there were no resources to carry on their fight in Central America.

The Greek Captain was on his side back then when he partnered with narcs to organize cocaine production in the Latin American mountains. Cavafys was probably the only person who never questioned Julio when he discarded the idea of changing the world and plunged into the illegal drug market. He witnessed the full transformation. He saw how Julio began gaining trust among the biggest kingpins, climbing up in the organization, and laundering drug money through lavish investments.

Because of this friendship, the narcs interrogated him for days on end after Julio's plane crash in the Dominican Republic. All of them, at that moment, had doubts. Was it a hoax? Did he fake it to run away with cartels' money?

Now Julio was dead again, and a lot of people were furious. Cavafys didn't have answers, but he wanted to help Ilona. She was missing and he didn't know where to find her. Gigi, Ibrahim, Frida, and even Doña Cecy were also under the narcs' control, and there was no one to help him.

The only suggestion Ilona gave him by phone before vanishing was to speak with Diocles, and he did it. But even more critically, he insisted Diocles go into hiding. Cavafys knew that the narcs would force him to tell them the five names and would never believe he didn't know which of the five Ilona chose. Diocles was a thinker, not a man of action, and before leaving he gave Cavafys a piece of not-so-useful advice. *The only one who knew Julio's thoughts was the dog. We need to make him speak.*

The Greek Captain also knew that Julio's brother was about to show up. He had also met him after Julio's false plane crash in the Dominican Republic. That time the brother showed up in Santa Clara to help Ilona face the mistrust of the kingpins. Those were sad and difficult times. The cartels eventually calmed down after they were convinced Julio was dead and had not betrayed them or stolen from them. But now that Julio had returned to die again, Cavafys knew that an even worse crisis was on the rise.

He had no doubt that the narcs wanted to speak with him, and he would not be able to avoid them. Waiting wasn't going to help, so he decided to take the initiative and go to them. It might well be that nothing could be done for Ilona, but perhaps he could help save Frida, Gigi, and especially Doña Cecy, who was older and in poor health. He decided to face the storm by sailing right into the wind.

He had always kept a good relationship with the cartels, helping now and then with smuggling, hiding some of their men who were excessively hot, and sharing a few contacts he had in Miami. Nothing big to attract attention, but significant enough to keep a friendship with them.

Through his contacts, Cavafys set up a meeting and flew to a small Caribbean island. He didn't want to waste time talking with intermediaries, and set the meeting with top guys who, Cavafys knew, were in direct and permanent contact with the main bosses. And they were all there, Mexicans, Colombians, and even two from the Far East. Ironically in that meeting, Cavafys was the only one not elegantly dressed; his shabby captain's jacket contrasted starkly with the impeccable suits worn by the rest of those present.

Cavafys went straight to the point. "You know better than I that the Condor didn't steal a penny from any of you. Many had confirmed to me after the crash that Julio left everything organized, with the passcodes you needed to recover your investments."

"He must have had a reason to disappear like he did," one of them with an Argentine accent commented. "And you must know Ilona's whereabouts. You are her good friend."

Cavafys said once again that he knew nothing and insisted that the Condor's fake plane crash was a blessing for everyone, especially since the cartels discovered that the American DEA was already at their heels, and close to finding out how he was investing the cartels' money.

"It was the big Russian boss who told me," Cavafys pointed out, convinced that using the Russian's name, would cause an impact among them. "If Julio hadn't faked his death in the Dominican Republic, the DEA would have frozen all your money. Everybody knows that someone had ratted you out back in the United States, and it would be reasonable for the Condor to simulate his death to protect you."

One of the drug kingpins, who looked like a U.S. senator, said sarcastically, "So you mean to tell us that the Condor sacrificed himself for us?"

"I can't prove that, and I don't know why he did it, but I am sure it wasn't to steal from you," Cavafys answered, ignoring any intimidation. "If that had been the case, you would have found out during the last four years. It would have been impossible to cover that up for so long."

Cavafys could see by their expressions that they believed him. Their operations were distributed all over the world, and there had never been any signal that Julio had stolen their money.

"How do you know that Ilona was not in on this?" asked an Italian man who Cavafys had met a few times before.

"You all know very well how much Ilona suffered with his death. Many of you have been to Santa Clara and you know that Ilona lives off the income from her restaurant."

When Cavafys said this, he knew it was not totally true. Julio had left him some money after the faked plane crash, and when he offered to share it with Ilona, she told him that Julio had looked after her as well. But the men at the meeting didn't know it and it was not the right moment to tell them. Besides, the sum Julio had left was peanuts compared to all the drug money he handled as the Condor.

Cavafys noticed that no one asked about Lara, another of Julio's friends, which made him suspect that Lara was on their side and probably helping them with what he knew. He was not surprised. It was no secret that Julio never fully trusted Lara; his heroin addiction made him weak and vulnerable like Gigi.

Cavafys asked them about Ibrahim's whereabouts, and a Japanese man, probably from the Yakuza, confirmed he was with them, adding, "He is answering a few questions."

They all kept asking about Ilona, and the Italian warned him that Gigi had told them what she knew.

"It seems that someone by the name of Diocles prepared a list of five people who could hide Ilona. From what Gigi told us, only Diocles knows the five names, and one of them is hiding Ilona."

Cavafys listened quietly.

"Gigi couldn't stand the withdrawals from her fix. Just by showing her a bit of heroin, she told us everything. We already sent people to get Diocles, and it's only a matter of days before we find out the five names, among which we hope not to find the name of a particular Greek Captain."

Cavafys knew they said this to provoke him, and they knew well that he would never even try to hide Ilona. It would have been suicidal to do so. He also knew that they would not give up until they found her, it didn't matter how long it would take.

Before leaving, Cavafys tried to intercede for Gigi, Frida, and Doña Cecy, but they only agreed to free Gigi. "We'll hand her over to you once you are back in Santa Clara, but not Frida or Doña Cecy. You'll only see those two again once we find Ilona." He flew back to Santa Clara, and while in the small plane that took him back, Cavafys realized that the only way to save Ilona was to understand why Julio had returned to Santa Clara. All he could do was drink, play his bouzouki, and dance until he figured out how to make the black dog talk.

23

Bebéi, the informant. The chaos in Santa Clara worsened upon Theo Cavafys' return. True to the cartels' word, Gigi was freed. She was extremely weak and chose to go to the convent, where she always sought shelter when she tried to overcome her addiction.

Everyone was anxious to hear the news, and Cavafys explained that in exchange for the heroin she needed, Gigi had told the narcs that Diocles had presented to Ilona five names for her to choose who would hide her. And since no one in the neighborhood knew who the five were, everyone was a suspect, except for La Pajerita, who remained sitting quietly next to the door, watching the activity inside the restaurant from a distance.

Diocles, who was the only one who knew, had also disappeared. Grená's son, Silvino, confirmed that the narcs had given strict orders to find him and take him to them.

"At this point, it's most likely that the Americans have him," said Hector, but Colonel Viera disagreed, clarifying that the Americans were still inquiring about him. So now, no one knew Diocles' whereabouts.

Amidst all the chaos, it was interesting to note how calm Irigandi seemed to be with her thoughts far away. She had met the nuns who ran the orphanage, and now, while her grandfather was at the hospital and Bebéi at work, she stayed with the nuns.

"Frida could well be one of them," said Ludmilla and then rephrased, "but it would have been insane leaving Ilona in Frida's care, and probably Ilona would not have accepted."

The main suspects were Hector, the professor and band instructor, and Colonel Viera. One was known to hide the secrets of his revolutionary comrades, and the other knew how to find those who went missing, but they both denied it. Grená suspected her own sons and asked all three of them many times if they were one of the five, and they vehemently denied it.

While all this was going on, more bad news surfaced. First, Micky arrived at the restaurant saying that Diana had been arrested back in the States. She had been accused of breaking and entering and theft. Everyone had an opinion about it. Micky wanted to go to the States, but he didn't even know her address; he only had a phone number. Lieutenant Pirilo said he would look into it further. Bebéi offered to speak with his friend, the Lady, back at the American Embassy. Everyone was giving their own opinions until Cavafys emerged from Ilona's office, which was located way in the back. He had gone there to answer a phone call and now he looked sad. He walked somberly out to the terrace towards the table where Ibrahim always sat to eat and work and asked for a bottle of Black Label and a plate of diced sausage. Ibrahim's favorites. He had heard that Ibrahim's body had been found on the outskirts of Alexandria with all the signs of an execution.

Everyone was frightened. Previously, in Santa Clara, the only known violence were Robespierre's insults to the church ladies at the foot of the Cathedral. But when dealing with the narcs, it was a different story. Now with Ibrahim dead, what would happen to Ilona?

Bebéi was also sad, but he was determined to complete his mission. He needed to keep the Lady happy and well-informed to avoid having Zoubir deported back to the States. That's why he always carried a small notebook in hand, jotting down notes about everything he heard.

With Carmela's help, he prepared a detailed report for the Lady. Carmela decoded his scribbles, gave his notes an organized form, and typed them. She found this work more amusing than the tedious job she had handwriting invitations for the Ambassador.

"Dear Lady, the news I have is that Joseph the Princess explained to us that the books belonging to Don Francisco Lacayo back in his Florida home were evidence that he was interested in the treasure of El Dorado. According to the documents of Mr. Le Breton that my Ambassador asked me

to file, the treasure of El Dorado, or the Golden Castle, by its other name, is not located in the Amazon as the Spaniards previously thought, but instead in the Darien protected by the natives. And I must add, this is strictly confidential as the Ambassador asked me to keep complete secrecy on the matter –Princess doesn't know yet what exactly the deceased had been looking for, but most likely it was a treasure map, which must be hidden in one of the convents in the city. Regarding the three friends whom you could always see eating empanadas at Lais's, I can say that Colonel Viera is still helping out at the restaurant and every day he dons his little Swiss hat and stops by his niece's house. I think he's there to pay a visit, but the funny thing is that before he knocks, he looks around to make sure no one is watching. Ever since the niece returned, or perhaps since he bought that little hat, whichever came first, he seems younger and more upbeat. On the other hand, Hector, the band instructor, has aged and seems very tense ever since people have gone missing. Every day he stops by Saint Joseph Church and kneels before the image of the Virgin. I asked Null-and-void if he knew why Hector did this, and he said that he found it odd as well, especially Hector being a Communist and Communists don't kneel before the Virgin. I don't know what this means, but I'm telling you, just in case you may find it useful. And with regard to the third one, Princess, I know that every Thursday and Saturday after closing up the bookstore, he takes a cab with a suitcase in tow, and he only returns at dawn. No one knows where he goes, but when he leaves, he is always cheerful, and when he returns, he's always exhausted. One day I tried asking him where he had spent the night, and he didn't answer. He's trying very hard to understand exactly what Julio was looking for in the Darien, so I gave him a few letters from the Ambassador's files, which may help. If he finds something out, I'll let you know. Lais, Doña Cecy's sister, is always working. I think she'd rather work than face the reality that her sons and daughters-in-law are always drunk. She still cooks me up *the chicken soup that I love and is looking after Ilona's restaurant. Every night when she heads out, she leaves food at the big house near Saint Joseph Church. Four children live there and rarely play with the others. There is an older sister, called Ishtari, the twins, and a younger sister. They don't go to school, but I did find it odd that in the apartment, there were many books and notebooks on the table. I also noticed that at night some people go to that apartment, and I think they are Gypsies. Ludmilla is Russian and is Ilona's replacement at the restaurant. Her attitude reminds me a lot of yours as well as other ladies I met back in France's Ministry Office, and I can't figure out why someone with such elegance and education can earn a living dancing naked at La Vie en Rose. Ilona's restaurant is still up and running, and it's always full. Late at night, after Ludmilla leaves the restaurant, she almost always meets up with Rasta Bong. They both smoke those tiny cigarettes, which smell funny, and spend the night together. Micky also likes to smoke those cigarettes, but he's with a different woman every night. I think Micky knows all the women who visit Santa Clara, but none of them are as beautiful as Diana, who, according to him, was arrested back in the States. Diana is the one I told you about. She is the one who helped me locate the deceased's house. Maybe you can talk to one of your friends, and explain that she didn't do anything wrong, she was only trying to help me. Null-and-void, who is the dean of the Brethren, is always at the restaurant to talk with Colonel Viera and Lais. Afterward he goes back to La Merced, where he joins up with the bums and drinks until he's smashed. Robespierre, when he's not drunk, insults everyone, especially Princess who, according to him, is a fag, but I don't know why he says that. When he drinks, Robespierre improves a lot; he's cheerful and kind and likes dancing in the plaza. La Pajerita sometimes dances along with him, and when she isn't dancing, she is walking her little bitch all around the city. She walks everywhere. When she reaches a point, she turns around and walks back. All in a hurry, but she really has nothing to do. Another one who doesn't do much is Henry Moriarty. When he is not in a trance, he spends his time reading a book we found back at Julio's hotel. I don't know what is so important about that book. It's a poetry book written by a Portuguese poet by the name of Fernando Pessoa, who, according to Moriarty, is as good as Walt Whitman. He spends all his time reading it over and over again, and cries. The other day I saw him read the book to Cavafys, the Greek Captain who is Ilona's friend. I think there must be something important in that book which should be looked into. The Greek Captain is impatient. He wants to do something but doesn't know what. He went to speak with the narcs to free Frida and Doña Cecy, but he was only able to free Gigi. She told the kidnapers that Diocles chose five persons willing to hide Ilona. Only one of them knows where she's at, and Grená is trying to figure out who they are. Null-and-void told me that he was one of them since he was the one who gave Diocles the idea, but he told me he wasn't the one who ended up hiding Ilona. No one knows who the other four are. Grená thinks that Hector is one of them since he is the leader of a Revolutionary group, just like her late husband, the African Barber. She said that the revolutionaries are always hiding something, and they are very good at it. She also suspects that one of her sons is part of the five, but knowing Diocles, it's not Silvino. He's head of a band of thugs, and Diocles doesn't like thugs. Maybe it's Lieutenant Pirilo, and in truth, he's very uneasy with the narcs having free reign of the old quarter, and I saw him speaking about this to Colonel Viera. Grená thinks that the Chinese Doll is another one on the list, but like I told you before, she thinks that the Chinese is a secret agent, but I think she's jealous of her because she is Silvino's girlfriend, but I'm not sure. What I do know is that Grená doesn't like the Chinese Doll. Chombo Zen walks around in his white pajama pants without a shirt on. He said he showed the temple photo to a few monks, but I don't think he did since he is another one who is all talk. I hope you and your friends can find out the name of the temple that is in the picture I handed over to you, and also find out what Julio was doing there, but in any case, back to Chombo Zen. He goes to the barbershop, then to the Chinese grocer, and afterward he sits on the steps of La Merced, crossing his legs in the lotus pose, and closing his eyes to make people think he's meditating. In the morning, he visits some church ladies, but the odd thing is he always goes through the back entrance. I don't get him. He rarely talks, but one day I saw him speaking to a woman who had a head covering like the one worn by the saints in the church. After speaking to her, he was furious. Frida and Doña Cecy are still missing, and everyone speculates that it was you and your friends at the embassy who were questioning and harassing Ling's daughter, but I'm just telling you to let you know, I know you wouldn't do such a thing. Gigi is recuperating back with the nuns. She was very ill when she returned. Irigandi's grandfather is doing better with his treatment, but he doesn't know anything about the treasure that Princess had told us about. Irigandi still goes with me on our daily walks, and if she's not with me, she's with her grandfather or at the convent with the nuns, where she is learning how to cook and helps prepare the food the nuns distribute. The great news now in the streets is the restoring of the big house, which used to be the old Masonic lodge. No one knows who is restoring it, but everyone thinks once that's done, it will be one of the most beautiful mansions in the old quarter. The Mayor is in trouble and can't go back to his house after they found him at the massage parlor, and to make things worse, he can't go to his mistress's house either; the Jamaican woman was as peeved as his wife. Hereabouts they talk negatively about the Mayor. Grená thinks he has some deal with the narcs, and when she asks Pirilo, who works at the City Hall, he doesn't answer. Another one who is disliked around here is the archbishop. I don't know him, but they say he is very arrogant and according to Princess, he likes young boys, but I don't understand much what that means.*

Zoubir is doing fine, in good health and well fed, and I can bet he is better off with me than if he were back in the States. Oh, and I almost forgot, Cavafys told me that Don Francisco Lacayo has a brother who lives in the States and is coming to Santa Clara very soon."

24

La Pajerita helps. Chaos reigned across the old neighborhood, but for many, it was business as usual. Those who worked did their jobs, and others filled their time with whatever they wanted. Some entertained themselves in gossiping, others dumped their woes, and yet others lost themselves in their fears, but not La Pajerita; she knew very well how to be busy, despite having absolutely nothing to do.

La Pajerita never strolled in search of new discoveries like Bebéi, nor did she meditate on everything she saw like Diocles. She didn't escape from her frustrations through getting drunk as Null and Frida did, nor did she hide behind her dreams like Moriarty. She didn't know how to cook like Lais, sell books like Princess, or teach like Hector. Nor did she understand why Grená loved to listen and rehash stories. Despite all that, La Pajerita never had a minute to lose and was always in a hurry.

At the first ray of light, she would wake up on her bench on the boardwalk and, with her little bitch at her heels, she would hike across the city towards the convent to get her cup of coffee and piece of bread with jam which would keep her going all morning.

She had to eat hastily because she liked to be the first to arrive at La Merced Church and help the priest pass out the religious cards with prayers to the Virgin to everyone who attended Mass. From whatever money she collected from the cards, she kept only what she needed to pay for the few things she must buy at the Chinese store, and the rest she would deposit in the donation box near the church door.

As soon as Mass began, La Pajerita would swiftly leave and hike across the city towards the fish market, where she would pass in front of each stand and greet each and every fish vendor. That was her duty. No one really noticed the importance of what she did, especially because she was always in a rush and her greeting was almost inaudible. Still, La Pajerita knew very well how essential her morning visits were to assure a peaceful and profitable day at the market. This was why she always went above and beyond not to forget anyone and greet them all. It was hard for La Pajerita to imagine how a day at the market would turn out without her encouraging visits to boost their spirits. Too bad she had to do it in such haste, but it was also crucial that she return to the boardwalk to greet tourists and hand out fliers of neighborhood events that she regularly collected from the City Hall.

The residents of Santa Clara were used to La Pajerita. There were times she would get confused and hand out religious prayers at the boardwalk, and the fliers for the next salsa concert to churchgoers, but the important thing was that everyone received a piece of paper from her own hands.

And she had to do the work at the boardwalk so hurriedly because it was a must for her to then pass by the City Hall to say hello to Lieutenant Pirilo before he left for his tour of Pigalle Street. She had to be on time to then distribute religious cards for those attending the noon mass. And all of this had to be done before she had to rush off to the school to make sure all mothers were positioned waiting for their kids, and then she had to run over to Lais' place to pick up the chicken soup and bring it, while still hot, to the French Embassy for Bebéi's lunch.

La Pajerita hated the rain. Not because it made her uncomfortable – she actually loved walking and showering at the same time – but because she knew that other people didn't understand this, and they looked at her disapprovingly while she walked around completely drenched.

That day, however, was very special; she had done something really important, something that would make Bebéi happy. She had always mistrusted Arcadio. He was evil, and she knew it. On the day of the parade, La Pajerita saw how Arcadio stood by the dead man's body, and she knew he wasn't there to revive anyone. It was most likely he was there to steal. This became obvious to her when he showed up a few days later with a new pair of shoes, but she couldn't prove they came from the dead man. Besides, if she had said anything, Arcadio would call her a liar and beat her as he had done so many times before.

That was why she had sneaked underneath the steps of the hut, where he usually slept, and searched through his things. But she hadn't found anything.

She had decided to follow him. As Arcadio mistrusted everyone, it took her a while to discover his secret hideout. It was inside the ruins of the Spanish Fort where waves broke on windy days; a refuge only accessible when the low tide revealed a narrow rocky path.

When she had reached the end of the path, she came across those things he was hiding: a passport, an empty wallet, and a few documents revealing important things.

After she had left the hideout, La Pajerita went to tell Bebéi at the Embassy. And she wasn't worried about what Arcadio might do to her. What was important was Bebéi's happiness, and happy he was when he saw what she gave him. Along with the stolen wallet, Arcadio had kept the passport with the date of Julio's arrival in Santa Clara and plane tickets to Darien and Kuna Yala.

As soon as Bebéi opened the passport, he saw that the name on it was not the one they knew. The picture was the same and resembled the deceased, but the name was different.

Followed by the proud Pajerita, he walked to Irigandi's house. Bebéi knew that the plane tickets confirmed Princess' theory that Julio was looking for the El Dorado in the jungles of Darien. They confirmed Princess' theories and were consistent with the notes Bebéi had seen at Julio's Florida house, mentioning Takarkuna and Paya, both places well known to Irigandi. Takarkuna was the sacred mountain, and Paya was the township where her grandfather learned his ancestors' traditions. But, curiously, when Bebéi asked her, Irigandi didn't say anything. Her grandfather had constantly reminded her that secrets taught by Mother Earth to the Kuna should never be shared with wagas.

Since Diocles was still missing and Bebéi and Irigandi didn't know what to do, they decided to talk to Princess. He could help them understand why Julio flew to Paya and Kuna Yala. La Pajerita went along with them, and as soon as they arrived, they noticed the bookstore door was open, but no one was inside.

"Could it be that Princess went missing too?" Irigandi asked, and Bebéi didn't know what to say.

The three kept walking to the corner of La Merced, and the first person they saw was Grená, who got frightened after learning that Princess was not at the bookstore.

"Could it be that they took him?"

That morning, Robespierre was particularly eloquent, standing apart on the top of the steps, yelling that those missing just proved that the monkeys were invading Santa Clara.

"They are going to take us one by one, and soon they'll come from the mansion's rooftops."

Grená ignored his madness, and when he saw the passport, she yelled to Rasta.

"Call Pirilo and tell him to come here right now."

In less than ten minutes, Pirilo was there, as well as Rasta Bong, and a small crowd, all of them curious to know what La Pajerita had found.

The Lieutenant studied the passport carefully – page by page – and then shared his thoughts.

"We can see here that this wasn't the first visit he made to Santa Clara. He was here three months before. So, this was his second visit, and when he died on Saturday, he had already been here for a few days."

Pirilo also mentioned that the passport had a different name and clarified something that was puzzling the Lady and the Americans. They had found out that the deceased had been registered at the same hotel three months before, but they could never find his entries to the country.

The Americans of the Embassy didn't know Julio had a second passport with a different identity, and La Pajerita, who found it, was now a local heroine. Bebéi insisted that it would be best to take it personally to the Americans, which would earn him some points and increase his chances of keeping Zoubir. Lieutenant Pirilo didn't object, but before handing it over to Bebéi, he spoke.

"This passport and the papers La Pajerita found confirmed Julio keen interest in the Darien. In his first visit to Santa Clara, he had also chartered a light aircraft to fly to Paya."

"And what about Princess?" Grená asked. "Do you think the Americans took him too?"

"No," said Pirilo. "The Americans have Ling's daughter and Diana, who is in jail in the US. Frida and Doña Cecy are with the narcs, and if anyone took Princess or Diocles, I think it must also be the cartels."

At that moment, Cavafys arrived, attracted by the hustle and bustle, and warned them that it would be best to make a photocopy of the passport and give a copy to the narcs so they wouldn't think they were hiding information. Everyone agreed to this except for Grená who snatched the passport from Pirilo's hands.

"This passport stays with me! If the Americans want it, let them release Kay and Diana; and if the narcs want it, they must release Doña Cecy and Frida and also Princess!"

A unanimous silence surrounded her, but everyone's thoughts were boiling, and Pirilo thought to himself, how strange! Why didn't she mention Diocles? Could it be that Grená knows where he is?

25

A family high reunion. Grená's three sons called for a family meeting; they believed that their mother was in grave danger. Grená was stubborn, they knew it too well, and the situation was worsening. The narcs had run out of patience and wanted to find Ilona soon, with no negotiation, much less for a passport. Silvino suggested the meeting to make Grená understand why the narcs wanted to clarify, once and for all, why Julio faked his death back in the Dominican Republic.

The meeting took place in Grená's house after Rasta closed the barbershop. And since it was a serious matter, Rasta postponed his early evening ganja.

Lieutenant Pirilo was the first to speak and went to great lengths in his description.

"A few years ago, the U.S. State Department launched a full-fledged operation called Isla Grande. It involved many American government organizations in finding out how the cartels laundered money. This was a vast effort that took many years of investigation and cost millions of dollars. They discovered that most of the cartels had merged their laundering operations, channeling all their drug income under one single code name: Condor. And it was a must for them to dismantle it. Thanks to a mole, they could relate the Condor to a name: Don Francisco Lacayo. They closely traced his steps, analyzing each financial transaction, and when they were ready to expose the Condor and the whole operation, his plane crashed."

Rasta and Silvino were standing a little away, staring at the floor, but their ears were tuned to what Pirilo was saying.

"The Americans first thought that the accident was staged to sidetrack the investigation. That's why all those agents came around here asking about Don Francisco. A huge effort and years of investigation had collapsed with his death, and the only Operation Isla Grande outcome was a large and useless report."

Grená had heard part of this story before, and now Pirilo was filling in a few missing links. She was happy. For the first time in a while, she had all three sons together in her house.

"Julio had given the narcs a secure and efficient way to launder their money," Pirilo continued. "They all trusted him, not only the Mexicans and South Americans, but also the Europeans, Russians, and Japanese. All of them. Thanks to the Condor, millions and millions of dollars were directly laundered by them. Julio allowed the cartels to bypass the international bankers who were getting almost half of what they were laundering. And his death brought questions. Was Julio robbing them? Did the bankers kill him? Or was he killed by one of the cartels trying to steal the others? Without him, the union disappeared, and a war started between the cartels."

Trusting the happy expression on Grená's face and thinking that standing removed from the main living room made him invisible, Rasta gave in to his craving and lit a joint as a reward for having resisted for so long.

Pirilo continued. "It took a long time for the cartels to calm down, but they proved that the Condor's death had left no beneficiaries."

Noticing Rasta was smoking, Silvino decided to do the same. He reached into his sock and pulled out a joint the size of a firecracker. He had prepared it for special occasions and being with his mom and brothers all together was definitely a reasonable justification. As he inhaled the first long drag, Pirilo stared straight at him, and Silvino realized that Pirilo wanted him to talk too. So, he handed the joint over to Pirilo, who, after studying it closely, decided to wait a little bit before inhaling.

"The narcs didn't lose any money," said Silvino. "Despite sniffing here and there, they didn't find any money missing and were convinced that the Condor had dealt a clean hand."

As if it was burning through his hand, Pirilo gave the joint back to Silvino, who quickly returned to his spot by the door, enveloped by the cloud that Rasta had puffed up.

Pirilo resumed talking. "The Condor's plan was so brilliant and efficient that also included a mechanism to have all resources returning to the original investors in case he died."

At this point, Rasta stepped in, already high as a kite. "The Condor is a legend. He was the Bob Marley of money laundering."

Pirilo hardly resisted smoking, but as he had only smoked a little, he was the only one who was able to keep talking with Grená. He watched as Silvino approached their mother with arms open wide, speaking in a sweet, melodious tone, chuckling between phrases.

"Mother, I think you can now understand what happened the day of the parade. Everyone thought that Julio had died and that Saturday, while you were parading so beautifully with Bebéi and Princess, that belief was shattered. The problem resurrected suddenly, but how were you to imagine all of this, Mother dear?"

"Mom is the best!" exclaimed Rasta with a cackle while Silvino tried to continue talking, stifling his laughter.

"The fact that Julio reappeared," continued Pirilo, "brought back the suspicion that his death was planned to hide something, and the narcs think that he wasn't alone. They want to find out who was with him. Nowadays, everyone distrusts everyone. And knowing that the Condor was alive and right under their noses made the Americans and particularly the DEA look ridiculous. How could a single man have halted a huge operation and made them lose loads of money? They are pissed off, and they want to know everything."

Grená understood that she had to be careful. Julio's death wasn't just a neighborhood dispute that could be solved with the help of her sons and some bums.

Silvino, skyrocketing with his powerful joint, told them something that neither Rasta nor Pirilo were aware of.

"The cartels are not together anymore. The Mexicans had Gigi and let her go, but the Colombians have Frida, and the Russians have Doña Cecy. And there's yet another group which is rising, the worst of them, the Venezuelans. The same ones who kidnaped and beat Bebéi. You can't negotiate with them peacefully. They all know about the five names and want to find Diocles."

Silvino was hardly speaking, but he tried to finish what he had begun.

"There's one thing they are all sure about: Ilona knew all along. According to them, Julio would have never betrayed her. If Julio was able to leave behind the life of wild parties and women, including the Norwegian millionaire, for her, no one believes he would have left her like that."

Lieutenant Pirilo finally inhaled the last tiny bit of Rasta's joint and explained to Grená.

"The Americans and that woman, who Bebéi call the Lady and is the boss, want to find out what Julio did, but they believe that both Ilona and the narcs were framed."

When he said that, Rasta and Silvino came off their high with a crash landing.

"What? What you talking about, brother?" Rasta asked, his words flowing like liquid smoke.

"Are you sure, my brother?" Silvino added and then laughed as if it were all a joke.

"You see, the Americans know about Julio's past fighting with the Latin American guerrillas. He was in Chile during Allende's Socialist regime and later supported many revolutionary causes. Always under direct instruction from Havana. That's why the Americans believe that he faked his death to remove himself from the world of drug trafficking and resurrect with a load of money for new revolutionary causes."

Grená was proud of seeing her sons working together.

"But," Pirilo continued, "they knew Julio had broken ties with Fidel a long time back. The Americans now feared that Julio would re-emerge as the head of a regional group supporting radical Islamists or maybe even the Chinese."

Now Grená understood what Pirilo, and Colonel Viera had been secretly talking about. The Lieutenant always scoped out the Colonel when he needed a better understanding of how things ran in the world. That's probably what drove the Colonel to believe there was a connection between the Chinese and the Muslims.

"The Americans have Ling's daughter, and they're looking for the Chinese Doll," said Pirilo. "And they're also surveilling every Chinese person in Santa Clara. They also took Chombo, and they're trying to find out Clara, his ex-wife's, whereabouts. She's a Muslim activist who showed up in Santa Clara a few days ago. They believe that the Black Caribbean Muslims are involved. They realized Frida is an ex-terrorist and are planning to deport her back to Germany to pay for her crimes. They are even looking into Null-and-void's background since it seems that he was involved with a pyramid scheme that scammed many. And amidst all that, I have the Mayor buddy-buddy with the Venezuelan narcs letting them freely walk inside the City Hall," he vented. "I don't know how all this is going to end."

Grená kept quiet, thinking, trying to make sense of everything she heard.

"What does all this have to do with what Princess spoke about?" asked Rasta, who, despite smoking all those joints, was able to keep a level head. "Was Julio looking for a hidden treasure up in the Darien?" And after he said that he smiled but then grew serious again. "We can't forget that the passport and the notes about the aircraft confirmed that Julio was looking for something up in the jungles before he died."

26

Grená is in full control. At her shaved ice stand in front of the church, Grená spends her days listening and spreading news, but there are days when she gets infuriated, and when that happens, be careful. She might be good at gossiping but has always been even better at fighting.

She was wife and long-time companion of African Barber, the founder of the Socialist Revolutionary Party in Santa Clara, and her husband turned into a barber not out of vocation but out of necessity. No one wanted to give him a job, since he was a strong union supporter and a fearless fighter against any injustice or oppression. He became famous for the strikes and protest marches he led, paralyzing the city. Back then, Grená was by his side in all confrontations.

Then came the dark times. It started with a group of young colonels willing to oust corrupt politicians to clean the country. Still, as it often happens when democracy is overturned, the patriotic colonels were replaced by older and more corrupt generals, anxious to fill their pockets and smashing any opposition to their regime. Back then, Colonel Viera was a leader among the young colonels and was forced into premature retirement. It was a time when the streets were kept quiet, and government rats were going around delving for the slightest rumor of civil unrest. Anyone who defied the ruling power was met with fiery resistance, and the African Barber was one of them.

He was arrested, beaten, and tortured more than once. But he never resigned and kept fighting. That's when he and Grená opted for her to stay out of the political struggle and take care of their sons. Life was impossible for them, and the barbershop was closed. Grená started to sell shaved ice refreshments to make ends meet.

Hard times for everyone, but as always happens, democracy prevailed, and the dictators were repudiated. But then Grená faced a new storm. The African Barber died, and she struggled to convince Rasta to reopen his father's business.

Finally, a break came. Rasta successfully ran the barbershop, Pirilo got a job at City Hall, and the family had all money they needed. Her sons even proposed that she stopped working, but she didn't accept. Selling refreshments gave her a unique opportunity to listen to and share gossip. And that was what she liked to do. That was, until Julio's second death happened, followed by the arrival of all those thugs, asking questions, spreading fear, and kidnapping her friends.

"Enough! I'm fed up with this mess. If the police can't do their job, and our authorities shake hands with narcs, I'm going to challenge whoever is threatening us."

She thanked her sons for their concern, opened the windows to air out the smoke from the joints, and looking determinedly into their eyes she repeated: "If they want the passport, they'll have to free our own."

Silvino looked at her in surprise and Pirilo in admiration, but Rasta was worried.

"Yes," Grená reaffirmed. "We have plenty of problems to choose from, but from now on, it's going to be me running the ruckus, not them!"

She was enraged but completely confident.

"Your father taught me that we should never allow anyone to lead our destiny. Problems always exist but let them be our problems and not those brought on by others. Now they'll have to play by my rules! I will hide the passport and be the only one to know where to find it. When they release our friends, I'll give it to them, and that's all. End of story!"

The next day when she opened her stand in front of the steps of La Merced, the word had spread, and everyone in the old quarter passed by to support her determination.

"They want to know? Well, me too! If they want the passport, let them come and talk to me!" she kept repeating.

And in front of Robespierre, who looked on with fear, she began giving out orders. Even Henry Moriarty opened his eyes to listen. The only one still drunkenly sleeping was Null.

"From Diocles' five, the only one we know about is Null. In his good old days, he was a powerful man, but it's hard to imagine that today he would be capable of hiding Ilona, or that Ilona would have chosen him as her protector. Null is out! Then who are the other four?"

She scanned the crowd gathered to listen to her and shot looking at Rasta Bong.

"I already asked them, and I was assured that none of my sons are on the list. So, if it's not one of my sons, then I'm sure that either Colonel Viera or Hector is there. We must find and protect them. And discover who the others are."

As a final word and showing her genuine feathers as the woman who had led protest marches next to her husband, Grená announced a measure that had never before been attempted.

"Let me be very clear, no one is allowed to get drunk here at La Merced until we find out who are the five chosen by Diocles!"

Moriarty looked at Robespierre, dumbstruck. They both looked at Null-and-void sleeping off his drunken stupor. He didn't move, but a loud fart reassured everyone that he was alive, and that his last meal had been the chickpea stew from the Asturian Association.

The narcs were powerful, but women of Santa Clara respected Grená, and they all committed to taking turns to stay on her side.

It worked. Her strong posture sent a message and that same afternoon, the Lady from the American Embassy arrived in her limousine with an elegantly dressed chauffeur and two bodyguards.

The Lady was in a generous mood and paid for ice creams for the kids who were playing in front of La Merced, while her driver unfolded a chair and an umbrella and placed them beside the stand. The Lady, with her elegant attire, sat next to Grená, who was dressed in white since it was the twelfth of the month. Above them were two large umbrellas, Grená's yellow one and another with North American colors for the Lady.

The Lady started by saying how happy she was with everyone's attitude, notably Bebéi's, and added that Zoubir would probably remain in Santa Clara.

Grená listened but didn't play along and went straight to the point.

"Diana must be released from prison, and the Americans should stop harassing Ling's daughter."

She also asked where the Chinese Doll was, even though Grená didn't like her. The Chinese Doll was part of the old neighborhood, and her return was needed to get things back to normal.

With finesse and polite diplomacy, the Lady said there was nothing she could do for Diana since she was already under American jurisprudence in Florida.

Grená, however, not caring a rat's ass about diplomacy, interrupted her bluntly.

"Then you're wasting your time sunbathing here. Either you hand over Diana, or you don't get the passport, period. And the same goes for the two Chinese women."

The Lady paused for an instant and looked at the crowd before her as if she was pondering her next words, and then she whispered to Grená, "You know very well that the Chinese Doll is a spy for the Chinese Government. You were the first one to figure it out. They are probably the ones who got her out of the country,"

Grená looked surprised and asked, "Did she leave the country?"

The Lady nodded, confirming.

While Grená was considering where the Chinese Doll could be, the Lady asked Grená a question loud enough for everyone to hear.

"By the way, where is Diocles nowadays? No one knows if he was kidnapped or is in hiding. Do you know anything?"

Grená denied it, but her face wasn't too convincing. She insisted that the Americans stop harassing Ling's daughter, and the Lady replied that she would do whatever she could, but she had heard that they were investigating the accounts of the companies for which Ling's daughter worked as an accountant. Among them, some Chinese, in which interesting things were found.

Grená pretended she was not listening and insisted that Diana and the two Chinese women had to be freed, and there was not too much for them to discuss. Still, when she stood up to leave, the Lady stopped and, as if remembering something at the last minute, she mentioned trying to look casual.

"The other day, I heard friends talking about an armed robbery that took place a while back when the African Barber was still alive.

They say it was a big heist, but it was never known how it ended, and the arms and the explosives were never recovered." Looking deep into Grená's eyes, she asked, "Since you and your husband knew a lot of people, I wonder if by any chance you ever heard about the robbery?"

Grená kept motionless for a few seconds. Then, making it seem as if it had nothing to do with her, she said that she knew nothing about it, and the Lady spoke with a mischievous look.

"How odd, with all the contacts you had."

The Lady left leaving Grená lost in her thoughts. That incident happened many years ago, before Don Francisco Lacayo's plane crash. The African Barber and some sympathizers of the Revolutionary Party assaulted a truckload of arms. They got them but never used, nor returned, them. The African Barber was the only person who knew where they were hidden, and he hadn't shared with anyone.

It wasn't until later, on his deathbed, that he gave Grená a letter to be forwarded to whoever would succeed him as party leader. A year later, she handed it to Hector. She knew the letter had information that could be used to find the weapons, but she never read it. Hector also never found a valid reason to use them, and Grená, worried, had asked Rasta to find Hector as soon as possible. The two truckloads of weapons were still hidden; could it be that the Lady knew something about them?

After the Lady's visit, it was the narcs' turn to approach Grená. First, the Colombians, through Cavafys, proposed to her that they had Frida and would agree to hand her over in exchange for the passport. In Cavafys' opinion, they realized that they wouldn't get anything out of Frida; she was used to rough methods to extract information, and she would never tell them a thing.

Later, Silvino spoke with the Russians and returned with bad news.

"They could care less about the passport, and they will only return Doña Cecy in exchange for Ilona; that was the deal."

And they had also told him to be quick since Doña Cecy's health was deteriorating.

By afternoon it rained, and with it came the other bad news. Four men stood at the La Merced Church's entrance, staring at Grená. By their gestures and style of clothing, she assumed that they were Princess's friends, and one of them signaled to her they wanted to talk.

Grená never liked to abandon her stall, but as they didn't budge, and she was curious, she crossed the street.

"Let's go inside the church," she told them. "Even though the priest may not be able to forgive our sins, we can stay dry."

They followed her inside, and she noticed that two of them had bruises.

"Ever since Lola Marlene disappeared, La Gata Caliente has turned into hell," the youngest one said. "The cops made it clear that the club would remain closed until she returns."

Then, one by one, the four men shared details; the night before, the Mayor's bodyguards raided the place and beat everyone there, including Judge Almendra's son. Jonas, Pirilo's assistant, was injured. Not even the archbishop's assistant was let off easy.

They also mentioned that Princess was in a secret hideout, but before leaving, he asked them to ask Grená to speak with Hector and see if it were possible for him to keep the bookstore running.

Grená kept listening, but she didn't know what to say. All she had were questions to which there were no answers. She wanted to bring peace to the neighborhood, but she didn't know how. If the bodyguards raided La Gata Caliente, they were following the Mayor's orders; Pirilo, who supposedly was the security chief, was not even aware since he had spent the night before with her and his brothers.

At least this mess helped reunite my sons, she thought. This made her smile, but only briefly.

Princess had gone into hiding. Doña Cecy was sick and far away from home. The Chinese Doll was out of the country – although in her case, it would be good if she never returned. But that was not true for Ling's daughter, and she and Frida were still being interrogated, one by the Americans and the other by the narcs. Grená was also unsure about Hector, who had been displaying weird behavior lately. Diocles was far away, but Grená was not worried about him, since at least she knew where he was. And now there was the story of the weapons too.

While thinking, Grená watched Null and Robespierre arguing on the steps of La Merced, and she sensed that they too were engulfed in fear.

She also saw Irigandi walking with Zoubir and the priest. It seemed that the priest was also enchanted with Irigandi's smile and he took her to the convent every day.

Irigandi seemed at ease, and Grená didn't notice that the little Kuna was also lost in thought. She couldn't figure out why her grandfather remained silent when Diocles asked about the Darien. He was the one who taught her about the sacredness of the Kuna land, about Mother Earth's great treasure hidden far from the Spaniards' greed and all other wagas. He had also told her about the gold and things even more beautiful than gold.

Irigandi didn't understand her grandfather's silence, but she trusted him. He was also a Nele and told her how important it was to defend the Kuna.

Irigandi sensed Theo Cavafys' and Pirilo's doubts. The Greek Captain wished he knew how to make the dog speak, and the Lieutenant was concerned with the Venezuelans' gang controlling Santa Clara and giving orders to the Mayor. He knew that his life and that of the residents of the neighborhood were at risk.

At the American Embassy, the Lady was sure that Julio had fooled the narcs. She had to find out who Julio's new partners were – the Chinese or the Muslims?

And far away from there, Diocles was safe but unable to think, and still he could not understand why Julio had returned.

Everyone was asking all sorts of questions, but no one knew the answers, and that same night, while strolling with his dog, Bebéi noticed the Lady's limousine parked in front of Grená's house, and he eavesdropped on what they were saying.

"I decided to accept your offer... If you give me the passport, Diana will be released, and no one will ever bother Ling's daughter again, I promise."

Bebéi smiled. The two women were very different, but he admired them both.

27

The brother arrives. Now that Lais was cooking at Ilona's restaurant the window where she sold empanadas remained closed, and her regular customers were addressing more crucial matters. Frida was with the Narcs, Diocles, and Princess had vanished, as well as Hector, who seemed oddly nervous and, according to his wife, hadn't slept at home. Among her usual clients, only Colonel Vieira was around, and he was surprisingly calm and a little bit distracted.

"I'm not sure what's going on with him," Grená said, keeping to herself the suspicion that the Colonel's mood was somewhat related to the regular visits he was paying to his niece.

The *Ithaca* sailed off with its crew – there was cargo to be delivered – but Captain Cavafys remained in Santa Clara. He was trying to negotiate the release of Doña Cecy, and, as Ilona was missing, he was staying at her house. What intrigued him was that he saw the four children who were under Doña Cecy's care playing with Irigandi, and when he asked the little Kuna if the kids were not worried about Doña Cecy's absence, she gave him an unexpected reply.

"No, they know she's fine."

Bebéi kept walking his dog, seemingly unaffected by all the anxiety in the air; he was focused. He knew that Julio had gone to Paya, which meant he was searching for the El Dorado secret, but no one else seemed to pay much attention to Princess' theory.

Bebéi even tried to speak with the Ambassador, but he noticed that his single interest seemed to be in locating the treasure.

That's when Bebéi came across an unlikely discovery. Robespierre, the crazy bum, was the grandson of Le Breton, author of all the documents bought by the Ambassador. It was true that

Robespierre was a different breed of Le Breton. Indeed, his grandfather had been a well-respected historian, while Robespierre was a madman. But the silver lining for Bebéi was that between the first swig and drinking up the bottle, Robespierre had moments of clarity which Bebéi could take advantage of to better understand why Robespierre's ancestor was looking for in the Darien. It wasn't much, but it was all he had.

Robespierre had often shared that when he was a boy, he would hear fantastic stories about his grandfather. Still, the problem was that Robespierre couldn't talk about the Darien without mentioning the monkeys ready to invade the city. It wasn't an easy task, but Bebéi knew that nothing came easy in Santa Clara, and, without anyone else to rely on, he decided to try with Robespierre.

The first thing he did was to bring it up to the Ambassador. He knew that it was risky, but it was the only option. He explained to the Ambassador that the grandson of Le Breton lived in Santa Clara and could possibly help them.

One morning when Robespierre had begun drinking and lost his bitterness, Bebéi took him to the Embassy. The conversation with the Ambassador started well, and Robespierre explained that his grandfather believed that there was much gold in the Darien and the Kuna protected the site, making it a living hell for anyone who tried to come near it. It was then, out of courtesy, that the Ambassador offered him some Pastis. Robespierre accepted and kept narrating that his grandfather had known the intentions of the French, the Scots, and the English, but none of them ever found where El Dorado was located.

The Ambassador listened attentively and was kept entertained by what Robespierre was saying. As he knew that the drinks were soothing his interlocutor, he made sure that his glass remained full. A tricky maneuver since as soon as the Pastis hit the glass, Robespierre would swig it in one go.

Robespierre insisted that the gold was not in Cana, where the English had looked, but near Paya. And he explained that something would squash his efforts every time his grandfather tried to visit the region.

"At times, it was the accidents, other times disease, and yet others, attacks by the natives. Each time the expedition had to be called off."

Robespierre kept on drinking and said that his grandfather believed that the Kuna were the ones protecting the secret. He later added that his grandfather suspected it wasn't just gold that was being hidden, which the Ambassador found interesting.

Robespierre clarified that the castle wasn't made of gold exactly, but instead of a yellow material, which was much stronger than gold, so strong not even fire could destroy it. At this point, the Ambassador sensed that the Pastis was confusing Robespierre's words.

After another glass, Robespierre explained that the Golden Castle was the monkeys' hideout, the ones who controlled the jungle and that they wouldn't allow anyone to get near it. He also warned the Ambassador that the monkeys had instructed the Kuna to attack anyone with poisonous deadly arrows.

The Ambassador realized that his guest was getting out of control and cut the conversation short. But when he walked his guest to the garden, Robespierre surprised him by shouting that the monkeys' king was on the Embassy's rooftop and started to scream. Hearing the row, the security guards approached, and Robespierre climbed up a tree, jumping onto the roof, where he kept shouting that the monkeys were taking Santa Clara.

It took two hours to get him down. They had to call the police, and even the firefighters, while Robespierre kept singing "La Marseillaise" from the rooftop. It wasn't easy, and unfortunately, no one paid attention to Bebéi's suggestion of giving Robespierre more Pastis to calm him down.

Later that day, the archivist, frustrated by his failed efforts, told Grená what had happened, and she rolled in laughter.

"That wasn't the only crazy event of the day," she said, still laughing. "The Americans are now interested in Chombo Zen. Can you believe it? They came up with the idea that he has connections with terrorists. Since no one knows the truth, everyone makes up whatever they want to believe."

It was in the midst of those crazy events that Julio's brother finally showed up. It was his first visit to Santa Clara after Don

Francisco Lacayo's plane crashed in the Dominican Republic. Cavafys was anxiously waiting for his arrival. The Captain could not make the dog talk, and now he hoped that the brother would help him understand what Julio did.

Ilona and Julio always agreed that whatever had happened in the past didn't matter, and this is why neither she nor anyone else who lived in Santa Clara knew much about Julio's previous life. Cavafys knew he was a revolutionary fighter and had seen a photo of Julio when he was known as Comandante Indio taken in Nicaragua, where Julio held a guitar in one hand and a rifle in the other.

Captain Cavafys secretly took Julio's brother to Ilona's house. Bebéi was still taking notes to the Lady, and Cavafys didn't want her to know about the brother. Actually, the brother was not the only secret Cavafys was keeping there. Since the day before, Hector had also been hiding at Ilona's house.

He only invited Pirilo to the conversation. The Lieutenant knew Santa Clara like no one else. and could help. But first, he had to know the real Julio's story.

They sat in the living room, once shared by Julio and Ilona, and were going to start talking when the bell rang, and Irigandi was at the door with the priest.

She was a Nele and knew that the brother was there and wanted to listen to what he had to say, and the priest was her eyes to walk in the cobblestone streets when Bebéi was not with her.

Cavafys tried to suggest that the conversation would be boring, but it was pointless. Irigandi wanted to be part of it. They invited her in.

"We were orphans," started the brother, "raised by two different families, but we always stay in contact. And if you are confused with just two of his deaths, I know of four of them, and I arranged the very first one."

After he said that, Cavafys opened a bottle of a Guatemalan rum, and they all got comfortable in their seats ready for a long talk.

"As students, we would go together to anti-government marches and spend time visiting the laborers' neighborhoods, getting to know them and listening to their problems."

Hector lowered his gaze; that was also how he started out.

"But then Julio met Mariana. She was a student and deeply involved in politics. Despite her youth, she was already a commander of a revolutionary urban cell. They met at a student congress, an encounter that quickly developed into a passionate love affair. It was summertime, and right after they met, they vanished for two weeks to go to a beach. Upon their return, Julio was dumbstruck and told me that Mariana was the woman of his dreams, but their love affair was cut short when we found out she had been detained.

"The military repression was getting tougher, and we heard that she was being tortured. Julio suffered a lot, and he lost his mind. We didn't know anyone in the police or the leftist organizations. We only knew that she was still being tortured, and Julio was going insane with rage. One day he disappeared. He just left me a message saying he would solve matters his way.

"After a few weeks, Mariana was released without any explanation and sent into exile. Much later, I found out that he had sent a list of ten military generals' names and an anonymous note to a local reporter, threatening that he would kill them one by one until Mariana was released.

"We always loved guns; Julio was an excellent marksman. His intensity was stoked by being madly in love. He killed the first one, and he didn't need to kill the second. The other generals were terrified and put pressure to have her exiled. Afterward, the military began a search to find the unknown sniper, but Julio was never found. They never suspected Julio since, other than me, nobody else was aware Julio knew Mariana."

Cavafys was following and drinking his rum. He knew most of the story, but it was important for Hector, and mainly Pirilo, to know it.

"Mariana was exiled to France and admitted to a hospital in Paris. It took her six months to fully recover from the torture she went through in prison. Worried, Julio went into hiding. The military were set on finding the sniper, and he was conscious they would retaliate if he got near her. It wasn't until a year later that he finally went to Paris to find out that Mariana had married one of the doctors who had tended her at the hospital. Can you imagine how he took this?"

Cavafys knew about Julio's heartache; he had heard it many times with rum and a cigar aboard the *Ithaca*.

"After finding out that Mariana was married, Julio set off for Chile. It was the Seventies, and Allende's Socialist regime had just been put into power. He did a lot of work and became the contact between Chileans and La Habana, working closely with Commander Manuel Piñeiro, better known as Barbarroja."

And when he said the name of Barbarroja, Hector moved in his seat as if trying to better hear about the legendary revolutionary who handled all ties between Fidel and the revolutionary groups of Latin America.

The brother continued: "Julio kept working under Barbarroja well into the early '80s. But Chile opened up another chapter inside Julio's heart. Monica, a young Chilean teacher who was also active in the political movement and was kidnapped on the tragic September 11, 1973, when Allende was killed. Once again, generals took away the woman he loved. Monica disappeared along with Allende's Socialist dream, and she was never found again."

The brother stopped to serve himself another glass and settle his thoughts.

"From Chile, Julio went to Ecuador, holding on to the false hope that Monica was still alive. He kept working for Barbarroja, helping the revolutionary movements in Ecuador and Colombia, until Barbarroja sent him off to Angola and Mozambique as part of a team of military consultants that Havana sent to those two African countries."

Hector, the Socialist professor, had learned about all this while on his college days back in the old Soviet Union at the Patrice Lumumba University.

"Around that same time, he became sick from a kidney infection. His condition worsened, and they sent him to Paris, where he spent several weeks in a hospital. He ended up losing one of his kidneys. In fact, Julio left bit and pieces of his body everywhere he went: two toes from his right foot in Chile, a kidney in Angola, and later on, when he almost died, half of his lung in Guatemala."

After a pause, he continued speaking.

157

"When he was in Paris, I was interrogated by the Army, and I realized they suspected Julio could be the sniper. I immediately traveled to France to meet Sonia. She was a good friend of Julio; something between a muse and a counselor. It was with her that we came up with a plan to protect him. The best option we could come up with was to kill him."

The brother said this with a smile, knowing that this statement could sound strange, but then he remembered that when it came to Julio and his many deaths, a fake killing wasn't farfetched. He continued speaking.

"With the help of a few Italian friends, we staged his death by a motorcycle accident near Bagni de Lucca in Italy."

Hector interrupted to remind Pirilo that this death was the one mentioned by the two agents who visited Bebéi, trying to identify the corpse's fingerprints.

"With a new identity, which he got in Paraguay," the brother continued, "Julio went back to work in Latin America, always under Barbarroja, supporting the revolutionary fight in Central America, and particularly, the Sandinistas. It was them I took that photo that Ilona has of Julio as Comandante Indio. We always kept in contact. Julio strength wasn't so much in fighting, but instead in gathering resources and channeling them for the revolution. He was a money man, and it was also around the time he met you, Cavafys."

The Captain nodded with a nostalgic smile.

"Afterward, with Reagan as president in the U.S., the fall of the Soviet Union, and China's disinterest in Latin America, the scenery changed completely. The irony is that all this happened when the revolution had reached its height in Nicaragua, and the fight was taking shape in El Salvador and Guatemala. But the international financial support was vital for their success, and they needed money. It was then Julio and Lara developed the idea of an alliance with the narcs. They knew it was a rash decision, but it was the only viable one. Without it, the counterrevolution would destroy them."

Cavafys interrupted to reminisce about the night aboard *Ithaca* when Julio and Lara spoke for the first time about an alliance between the narcs and the revolution.

"I watched Julio, thinking to myself, how just a man, alone, aboard my ship, could dream of destroying the American Empire, but he was like that, a crazy adventurer."

Cavafys raised his glass in Julio's honor.

"Some leftists got enthusiastic," continued the brother, "but the head in Havana didn't accept it. Julio had a lot of arguments with Communist Party leaders. He insisted that it would be the only way to maintain what had already been won. Still, the Party didn't agree, claiming that the image of the revolution would be at stake. Frustrated, Julio went through a period of self-doubt. It was around that time that he almost got killed in an ambush in Guatemala. His doubts only grew while he was recovering, and he finally decided to break ties with Havana and go on his own with his plan. He was alone, and his only support was Renata, his companion during that time in Central America. But she decided to return to her native Peru to fight alongside the Sendero Luminoso, an organization that did see his proposal of alliance with the narcs in good terms. Julio was not the same; he was depressed, with no enthusiasm or plan. He couldn't live a normal life, and was no longer welcomed in Havana, but he would never give up. Thus, Julio had to find a new way to rise from the ashes."

28

The secrets behind the Altar. The conversation in Ilona's living room continued. Hector seemed to have forgotten the stress from the last few days, and Pirilo followed each word of Julio's story attentively. Next to them was Irigandi, and she was not interested in the details. She had a clear mission – to understand why Julio had faked his death.

"In those days, some South American traffickers approached him to help with cocaine and marijuana production in the Andean countries. The demand was booming in the United States. The cartels' main problem was how to better organize poor Andean farmers, and Julio knew how to work with them. At that moment, he really didn't have many options left. Julio always dreamed big, and he was not going to conform to a common life with a nine-to-five job.

"He had burnt his bridges and had no plans of looking back. No more political strife, no more revolutions. The world of drug trafficking became his new challenge. But for that to happen, he had to die as a revolutionary. He owed it to his ex-comrades and all of his past. When he heard about Renata's death in an explosion in Arequipa alongside others from the Sendero, Julio jumped on the opportunity, and with help of some Peruvian friends, they altered the report, including his name among the dead in Arequipa. There was even a flash in the Granma praising his virtues as Comandante Indio defending the revolution in Latin America."

While the brother spoke, Pirilo wondered how faking death, and keeping it secret, had never been a problem for Julio.

"After that, we completely lost contact. Years later, I was in Milan, and I received a mysterious invitation to a get-together in

Positano. Curiosity got the best of me, and to my surprise, it was Julio who had invited me. He was aboard a big yacht, sporting elegant attire and living the life of a jetsetter. I knew Julio was a different man now, yet he still had the same twinkle in his eyes. After that meeting, I never saw him again, but we spoke over the phone a few times, and he talked a lot about Ilona. Later, when the plane crashed in the Dominican Republic, I came here for a couple of weeks, helping Ilona to put things in order. That's all I know."

Everyone was quiet. Julio's life was a kaleidoscope of surprises. There was something new popping up at every corner. What they had heard didn't help those listening to understand why Julio had staged his death in the Dominican Republic and why he had never told Ilona.

Cavafys broke the silence, commenting that he was sure that Julio hadn't staged his death to rob the narcs.

"I always had doubts about Julio's death," his brother added, "I knew him. If he faked his death, he had a purpose, and if he didn't tell Ilona, Cavafys, and me, it's because it was something big. What I think…"

Irigandi perceived the brother was about to elaborate on his doubts, but the conversation was halted by screams coming off the street. Alarmed, they went to the door to see La Pajerita, desperately running towards them. It was almost night. No one could understand what was going on, and neither was La Pajerita able to explain herself.

Then they saw a woman running in the middle of the street, telling everyone that the cops were at Saint Joseph Church tearing down the Virgin's Altar.

"The end of the world is here! The end of the world is upon us!" the woman shouted.

Hector went out onto the street holding his head with a dazed expression. His words were barely comprehensible and what could be understood made no sense.

Pirilo tried to calm him, and Hector kept repeating: "Oh my God, they know! Now what? What will happen to Doña Lourdes?" Nobody understood.

They ran toward the church and saw the chaos. Sirens were blaring, all kinds of lights shining from police cars and fire truckers, and the streets surrounding the church were packed with cops and military personnel.

Robespierre was up in a tree nearby, yelling, "It's them! The monkeys! The monkeys are here to destroy our city. No one will get out alive! They were just waiting for the right moment to invade, and that moment is now!"

People were running back and forth between the church and the mad man in the tree, all watching in disbelief.

Desperately, Hector looked at Pirilo and pleaded, "Promise me that you will look after Doña Lourdes?"

Pirilo just nodded, not clear on what he meant.

Half an hour later, the entire neighborhood seemed to be assembled in front of the church, witnessing the unimaginable. Except for Null-and-void, who was wasted, and Henry Moriarty besides him, engrossed in deep meditation.

The cops had torn up the main entrance of Saint Joseph's Church to give way to heavy machinery to bring down the interior walls.

"The Virgin's Altar!" cried the devotees in desperation. "They're destroying the Virgin's Altar!"

Then some police dressed in special gear showed up as if expecting a fire or explosion, and this only agitated Robespierre even more.

"You can run, but it's too late. The monkeys will take over the city!" he yelled.

A team of anti-riot police dispersed the onlookers, backing them away from the church. Nobody knew what was going on, but the whole city was there.

Pirilo was still trying to calm down Hector, who kept talking non-stop. It wasn't until late that explanations that actually made any sense started to be spread.

"They found a hideout full of ammunition and explosives camouflaged within the church. It's believed that they were the ones stolen years ago."

The weapons had been hidden beneath the altar where many devotees knelt to pray day after day. Late at night, an arrest warrant was issued for Hector, the professor. That's when Grená figured out what had happened. Those were the weapons that African Barber had stolen. In those days, he had worked at the reconstruction of Saint Joseph Church. When he and his group had attacked the military convoy, they never planned to find so much loot. Not knowing what to do with it, her husband had decided to bury it underneath the west wing of the church, the site upon which the Virgin's Altar was later built.

Hector had his hands tied when he read the letter with the location. If he alerted the authorities, they would know that the African masterminded the heist, harming Grená and her children. So, the arms remained almost forgotten. It was only after the persecutions began in Santa Clara that Hector felt that someone would be able to find them, which prompted him to pass by the church every day to see if he noticed anyone suspicious looking at the altar. This was when Bebéi noticed him and reported it to the Lady at the American Embassy.

The Americans investigated and then informed the Army, who ordered some engineers to inspect the walls and flooring, finding the grenades, pistols, rifles, and ammunition lying there almost entirely corroded by the seawater that seeped through the walls from the sea nearby.

Hector was detained together with other members of the Revolutionary Party, but he immediately attested that he was the only one who knew about the arms. Such a selfless act – like others he carried out in his life – gained him respect in the old quarter, and the nickname "Dinosaur'" given to him by Princess.

When the news of his detainment spread through the neighborhood, there was an immediate outcry. The first one to arrive was Colonel Viera, who approached the official in charge of the operation, claiming that he had known Hector for many years and knew that he would never plan or partake in any armed action.

Lieutenant Pirilo tried to convince him that it would be best to wait until the investigations were conclusive, but the Colonel didn't bat an eyelid, and made a pronouncement.

"Hector is a dignified man. What you are doing is a horrible mistake and goes against all the fundamental norms of the Law."

The second one to show up and who caused a major commotion at the station was Princess, who had emerged from hiding when he found out that his friend had been detained. He was calm and ready to hand himself over to the police.

"It doesn't matter what happens to me! I came to tell you that I have known Hector for many years, and I know that he is a decent man, incapable of any violence." He added, theatrically, "I came here, with open arms, to plead for his release."

After Princess, the teachers from the school showed up, confirming that Hector was an exemplary teacher and friend. They were followed by the student's parents, and old students themselves, who could attest that Hector never mixed politics with his work as a teacher. Later, old band students also showed up, many of whom had become famous musicians, thanks to their beloved instructor.

Then Grená showed up at the City Hall along with Rasta Bong and Lais, to say that Hector was kind to all residents, and from there, she went to the American Embassy to tell the same thing to the Lady. By mid-afternoon, the young priest arrived along with a delegation of devotees to say that Hector was one of the main contributors in all events organized to collect funds for works related to the church. Then came the nuns, not just one, but all of them, claiming that Hector was always ready to help when they needed to fix or move something at the children's home. And they added that for the last ten years, Hector had taught music lessons there, free of charge.

One by one, everyone from the old quarter showed up to speak for Hector. Whether he was a Socialist or not, he was a good man.

Upon seeing so many people present, the officers decided to accept the priest's proposal and freed him on the condition that he wouldn't leave the city until the investigations had concluded.

Finally, after an evening of surprises at the church, and a morning in jail, Hector could go home and hug his wife of many years, and the cause of great anguish, Doña Lourdes.

The one who didn't get off the hook, however, was Princess. Pirilo pulled Rasta aside to tell him in private, "Don't ask me why, but you need to get Princess out of here and now! Bring the Gypsy van to the back of City Hall, and I will be there with him."

Seeing Rasta's confused look, Pirilo was more explicit. "Ask Mom to come with you and take him to the American Embassy."

Still clueless, Rasta did what Pirilo wanted, and could only understand later, when Silvino explained that one of the narc groups, the Venezuelans, wanted Princess for themselves, and the Mayor was at their call.

"That is why Pirilo chose to send him to the Americans."

Seeing that everything was calm again, Colonel Viera put on his Swiss hat and, with a smile on his face, went off in the direction of his niece's house, happy that the streets were deserted. He had known wars and battles, but naively thought that the empty streets were a sure sign that his secret would remain hidden and protected. Obviously, he didn't realize that behind half-opened windows, eyes followed him, and he was oblivious to the comments whispered from the second floor of the bakery.

"There he goes again, that pervert, with his stupid hat and his ass perked and ready to meet up with his niece."

Far from there, in her little room, Irigandi, lay unable to sleep. She was thinking about what Julio's brother would say when La Pajerita showed up screaming. She wanted to ask him because Sister Eugenia, the nun she knew back at the convent, was keenly interested in learning as well.

29

Keeping up with the news. There's always something new happening in the old quarter. Everyone was still on edge and not trusting anyone or anything. Outside of the church, the ladies were gossiping about Colonel Viera's escapades, the general surprise of the arms hidden by the austere Professor Hector, and the latest about Princess. Now everyone knew that the bookshop owner was also Lola Marlene.

People were talking about Chombo Zen too. The one who would meditate on the streets, with a bare torso and white cotton pants barely hanging on to his waist. Most considered him handsome but lazy. According to Grená, he had never worked a day in his life, and he lived off of the help of some older ladies. If you take into account Princess's wagging tongue then, they divide their time between the crucified Christ, the words of the young priest, and Chombo's potent cock. But it's best not to pay any attention to idle gossip.

Chombo's real name was Walter Simpson the seventh, the same name his great-great-great Ashanti grandfather was forced to adopt when he was bought as merchandise in Jamaica. Since them, Chombo Zen sought spiritual comfort, first as a Catholic, then as an Evangelical, later as a Black Muslim when he married Clara, his strong-willed Muslim wife, and finally as a Zen Buddhist.

With time, his wife Clara got tired of nagging her husband every day to do something productive, and she traveled to Trinidad, where she accepted a position as a university professor and kept leading the Black Muslim Community. Chombo stayed behind in Santa Clara, pursuing his monk-like meditating, giving a few yoga classes, and comforting older ladies. The authorities were interrogating him, and no one knew why, just like no one knew where Diocles had gone, or who was hiding Ilona.

In the city, there was also a brand-new rumor that the Chinese were restoring the big house, which used to be the old Masonic Lodge, for their new Ambassador. But the Chinese Doll was still missing, and, according to Grená, the farther away the better – God willing never to return.

Nobody had news from Doña Cecy, but Irigandi kept insisting that she was all right.

"How could a blind girl know more than all city eyes?" Null asked.

Grená was still in a foul mood because of all the chaos, while Cavafys kept negotiations with the narcs to free Frida. Many times, the narcs would talk about releasing her but then would change their mind, and Cavafys couldn't figure out why.

As the days passed, worry grew into fear, especially when unknown armed young men started patrolling the streets. They were probably working for the narcs. Few left their homes, and the anxiety led to sadness. The streets of Santa Clara were not the same, but Ilona's restaurant was still open and running under Ludmilla.

"I think that there is nothing left to surprise us," Cavafys said to Colonel Viera, right when two men arrived at the restaurant to take Ludmilla away.

According to Lieutenant Pirilo, the narcs thought Ludmilla could very well be the fourth person on Diocles' list, and the Americans discovered that she was a fugitive from Swiss authorities, linked with an international group who stole artwork.

"And there's more," Pirilo continued. "It looks like her father is Russian, and one of the kingpins in the international drug trade."

Everything sounded so absurd that no one could think what would happen next. Across the old quarter, the only one that seemed to be focused was Bebéi; he knew he had to keep the Lady happy and figure out what Julio was looking for in the Darien. Like Diocles had said, this would be the only way to save Ilona. For him, prison, kidnapping, invasion of churches, and the discovery of the weapons, none of those mattered. His sole focus was to keep the Lady happy with the reports that Carmela helped him to type. They were about to finish the latest one right when Ludmilla was picked up.

"Dear Lady, within this past week, the latest happening in Santa Clara by the Sea was the discovery of arms and explosives underneath the Altar of the Virgin of Saint Joseph Church. Who would have imagined! They took Professor Hector handcuffed as a suspect due to him going to the altar to pray every day. Rumor has it that this isn't true because when the weapons were stolen, Hector was abroad studying in the Soviet Union. People say that your friends at the American Embassy found out where the arms were hidden, but that's something you would know better than I. What is being said is that Hector is a good man. Everyone here wants to know who were the five chosen by Diocles. We know that Null-and-void is one of them, and possibly Princess could be the other. He showed up at the City Hall, and someone is interrogating him to find out if he knows of Ilona's whereabouts, but I'm sure you know more about that than me, especially since it's said he is at your Embassy. I heard that he used to work at a nightclub near the port called La Gata Caliente and that he would dress as a woman with the stage name of Lola Marlene. When the police raided the club, they also found the archbishop's assistant, but all priests during their sermon on Sunday said that no one from the clergy was at that place of sin and damnation. Although I'm not sure what that means, I'll tell you since it may interest you. Everyone thinks that Colonel Viera and Hector are the other two on the list of five, but nobody knows for sure. Also, they say that Colonel Viera is having an affair with his niece and that he visits her every day, but I am surprised since I always see him going to the early morning mass at La Merced with his wife. The Colonel thinks no one knows about his affair, but Grená told me that his niece never got the government scholarship she told her family about, and instead, she was in Miami living off older men like the Colonel. Everyone is

waiting for the day Otilia, his wife, will find out all he's been doing. Nobody likes her, and she can get pretty violent when she argues with him. But that's not exactly my problem. What concerns me most is that no one wants to talk to me about El Dorado. Joseph the Princess already told us that Julio was looking for the treasure of El Dorado, which was proven by his plane ticket to Paya. Still, if we don't find out why he went there and later to the Islands of Kuna Yala, we'll never know why he was here in Santa Clara when he died. That's what Diocles said, and I'm sure he's right. Robespierre is the only one who helps me in rare moments when he's not sober but not yet drunk. According to him, his grandfather came close to the Golden Castle. And now I'll tell you in detail what Princess told me: Back in the sixteenth century, there was a pirate by the name of Francis Drake. He came to Panama, and the runaway slaves told him the native tribes who lived in the Darien sport gold ornaments, and I can confirm since I saw the illustrations, which were among Le Breton's documents. For the slaves the gold wasn't important since they didn't wear necklaces or earrings as it reminded them of the chains which were used to enslave them. Drake learned where the natives got the gold, and before dying, he wrote a letter to the Queen of England telling her about its location. This letter ended up in the hands of a Spanish priest, and according to some letters, which Le Breton got back in England, Captain Henry Morgan, another pirate, found this letter when he burnt the city to the ground in 1670. He found the letter, but not the map since the priests hid it in a different unknown location. What makes more it interesting is the fact that Don Francisco Lacayo, who was also Julio, died in front of the ruins of the Dominican Convent. That's what led the Princess to believe that he was looking for the treasure map here in Santa Clara. The Princess also told me that Captain Henry Morgan, another pirate, told the story of the map to a friend in the Bahamas without noticing that a young Scottish boy named William Paterson was eavesdropping. Morgan forgot about the treasure, but not Paterson. Many years later, then a grown man, and renowned in Scotland, he convinced the government to send out a Scottish expedition to colonize the Darien. There's a letter on our files that old Le Breton collected, which clearly shows that for Paterson, the real reason for the Scottish colonization was to find the secret of El Dorado, but when Paterson and the Scots tried to get close, they were held back. According to Robespierre, it was the indigenous people who attacked the Scots, but he explained to me that, in reality, the Kuna do whatever the monkeys tell them to do. I know this story seems absurd, and Carmela, my friend typing out this report, doesn't want me to talk about the monkeys, but Robespierre speaks about them with such conviction that I thought it best to tell you. According to him, the monkeys told the Kuna that if they continued to live in the jungle, the Spaniards would keep coming back and find the treasure, and that's why Irigandi's Kuna ancestors decided to move to the islands of Kuna Yala. Leaving behind the guardians to protect the secret. Irigandi knows about this very well since her parents died defending the sacred lands of their people. An American like you by the name of Marsh came close to it. He suspected that their sacred site was Paya, the city that Julio visited before his death, and that the Golden Castle was somewhere between Paya and the sacred Takarkuna Mountain. But now I will tell you another version of that story, and this one nobody knows about it. It's what Henry Moriarty told me and is almost as absurd and confusing as the monkeys' story, but as you asked me to tell you everything I knew, here is what Moriarty believes. And I insist, that this one is highly confidential, and not even Grená knows about it. According to Moriarty, some extraterrestrials visited our planet a little after the year one thousand. Their knowledge was a thousand years more advanced than ours will be in a thousand years from now. I asked him how he knew all that if he had never read or talked to anyone, and he told me that it was through telepathy. He even confessed that *sometimes, when people think he is stoned, he is listening to information floating in his mind. Anyway, back to the aliens, Moriarty explained they wanted to share what they knew with earth people but couldn't find anyone with enough knowledge to absorb it. And as they knew that they would only be able to come back in a thousand years. And Moriarty explained why, but it was too complicated for me to understand. It's something related to the routes of the stars that, like comets, only come close to the earth from time to time. At that time, the only thing the aliens could do was to talk with some people in what today is Iran but was Persia in the year one thousand. It seems Persians had, at that time, the most advanced knowledge on earth. Still, even so, the aliens could only teach them some basic things, such as mathematics and the functioning of the human body, and even help them to write the first basic encyclopedia. They left all other things they knew and wanted to share in some kind of files, to be opened in the future when earth people would be able to understand. They also left similar files in other parts of the planet where they believed our civilization would develop; one in Europe, another in the Far East, and one in the Americas. But as you know, at that time, America didn't have cities, and they didn't know where civilization would develop, and they chose a midpoint between North and South America to leave the files. Do you get it? According to Moriarty, the Kuna are protecting the alien's files, which they call the Mother Earth Secrets. And the guardians, like Irigandi's parents, try to protect the secrets with their lives. The files become even more important since all others in Europe, Iran, and China were destroyed. I told all of this to the Ambassador, but he refused to talk about it, which I don't get, since before he was very interested, and I think he still is. The other day I overheard him speaking with some Chinese people who were at the Embassy, and who are looking into buying mining concessions across the region. But he doesn't want to talk anymore with me, and he even told me that I should wrap up my job here and go back to Paris. I'm worried. I don't want ever to leave Santa Clara. I also wanted to add that Julio's brother is in Santa Clara and staying with Captain Cavafys, back in Ilona's house. From what I heard, the Greek Captain is still negotiating with the narcs about the release of Doña Cecy and Frida. Another one who I can see walking around worried is Lieutenant Pirilo. He stopped playing soccer and doesn't visit his girlfriends on Pigalle Street so often. Last week he didn't show up two days in a row for his round of dominoes, which had all his friends worried. According to Colonel Viera, there are a lot of thugs around. In fact, the other day the bank's general manager was held up as well as a Jewish shopkeeper whose clothing store is off of Central Avenue. And lastly, I'd like to ask you a favor, there's a real bad man in the neighborhood by the name of Arcadio, and he's very angry with La Pajerita, the one who found the wallet and the passport that belonged to Julio, which that bad man stole. The other day, in revenge, he hit her with such vengeance across her face. Would you please send one of your friends to warn him that if he does that again, he'll get a beating? Don't worry, he's a coward. If you go ahead and tell him that, you won't have to carry out the beating. He will become fearful, and he won't touch La Pajerita ever again. She's a good woman, as is Carmela, who types out what I say on a clean sheet. They are the two women who help me the most in figuring things out and setting up these reports I send you. Oh! I almost forgot, next week I'll get the cast off my arm."*

That same evening, while the city slept after days of turbulence, Bebéi set out to walk Zoubir carrying Julio's ashes that he hoped to return to Ilona. It had been a while since he took the ashes for a walk, and while on his stroll, he saw Irigandi at the Cathedral Plaza with the four children that Doña Cecy took care of. They were all listening to a Gypsy who played the violin.

30

Sister Eugenia's prayers. At the convent, all the nuns were asleep, except for Sister Eugenia. She was still awake, inside the chapel, staring at the altar candles. The flames moving in the dark made her thoughts spin around. She didn't speak. From the first day of her vocation, she took a vow of silence. That way, no one would know her past.

She worked in the kitchen, preparing food for the children who lived there and anyone else who cared to show up at the convent doors hungry. There she had no bills to pay, errands to run, or problems to solve. She didn't even have to smile at those who spoke to her.

When she arrived, and for many days afterwards, the only thing she did was sleep. The more she did it, the more she wanted to keep sleeping. She slept until she got rid of all of her sleep deprivation accumulated over time.

Sister Eugenia no longer carried sadness inside. Floating within a dark cloud, she was hopeful that one day she would appease her tightened chest, but not yet. Now, all she needed was strength to cope with her anxiety.

Sister Eugenia knew that Doña Cecy was fine, the Gypsies had confirmed it to her, but she sure missed the food the old witch must now have been cooking up to the delight of her kidnappers.

If Theo knew Doña Cecy was fine, he wouldn't be worried, but she couldn't reach him safely. He was trying everything humanly possible to help her figure out why Julio betrayed them, but she couldn't tell him her whereabouts. Theo Cavafys was even questioning the dog who couldn't answer his questions.

By now, everyone knew that Princess was also Lola Marlene. Sister Eugenia had always known that Princess tried to keep Lola Marlene apart from his bookstore, but the wall came tumbling down, and they could no longer ignore each other's presence.

She was also sure that Julio didn't betray her. She felt that when she petted the dog, but she still couldn't understand. Diocles said that it was to protect her, but from what? She sensed that even Theo had his doubts. Money could be an obsession, but not for Julio. Did he want it to finance his revolutionary dreams? Maybe, but he would have told her.

Sister Eugenia watched the dancing flames, reminding herself that after chasing so many dreams, Julio found peace and fulfillment next to her.

The only thing that made her uneasy was spending her days and nights alone. Mother Superior didn't allow any contact. She was completely cloistered, and her presence inside the convent was a well-kept secret. Those were the rigorous instructions given by the priest.

She was lucky that they allowed Irigandi to visit her.

"She can't see anyway, so let her in," Mother Superior said, and Irigandi was the light that brightened her days, bringing news about her friends.

Julio's brother had arrived in Santa Clara. Sister Eugenia knew all too well why he once came and never again returned. A woman always knows when a man has fallen for her, and she knew that he had gone, so as not to see her again. She was grateful. For her, there would always be only one love.

She was up to date with everything that Julio did: how he organized his businesses, where the accounts were located, and who his partners were. She knew about the Zurich account. *Keep these numbers, and if one day I go missing and you need money, just go there, and give the bank these numbers. You'll have everything you need.* She never touched it. She didn't need it, and whatever she needed, she had in Santa Clara. That was enough for her to live. He was the only thing she missed. Why had he left her?

Before the plane crash, they dreamt about leaving everything behind and moving to a far-away place, but they knew it was impossible.

He was involved with the cartels, and not just one or two, but all of them, and he would never be able to convince them to let him quit peacefully. His success had become his prison.

Julio's brother said that he knew why, but what did he know? Even Ibrahim, who had shared all of Julio's secrets, hadn't known that Julio was alive. The memory of the dear Egyptian and the thought of his death saddened her.

She knew that her brother, El Nacho, was obsessed with destroying her, and now he was powerful, using Julio's betrayal to turn the cartels against her.

In the dead of night, Sister Eugenia could listen to the Gypsy violin. She knew how important Santa Clara was for the Gypsies. They were there raising their princess, Ishtari, the oldest of the four children who lived in the abandoned house protected by the band members who were always playing around her, reminding the young princess of her Gypsy roots.

Sister Eugenia knew Ilona's whereabouts, and she remembered the Colombian author who, in *Cartagena de las Indias*, told her lovely stories about a woman who showed up with the rain. He was the first to give her the name of Ilona, which she adopted to break with her past, just as Don Francisco Lacayo had done to overcome Julio's.

For her, Santa Clara didn't have secrets. She knew that the Chinese Doll was about to return, much more powerful than before, and from the nuns, she found out that Gigi was fine and ready to return to a healthy life, until, of course, another crisis would make her fall again. She wasn't surprised about Ludmilla; with her elegance and charm, she kept the restaurant running. Her father was a great friend to Julio, and one of his most significant partners in the businesses Julio carried out with Ibrahim.

She wasn't worried about Frida either; the German was able to stand anything. She was worried, however, about Ling's daughter, and couldn't figure out why they had detained her. Thanks to Grená's, she was free again, but could it be true, as Bebéi thought, that the Lady up at the American Embassy was indeed a good person?

Sister Eugenia also felt pity for Diocles, who had to go into hiding to protect her. But she knew that he was fine. She wasn't worried at all about Bebéi's reports since he didn't know who the nun in the convent was.

She was very grateful to the priest, whom she had met at the restaurant, and little by little, she noticed that behind all the righteous talk he had learned from the Vatican, he was beginning to think for himself. Gigi had foretold that *Santa Clara will make the young priest as good as Brother Bernardo, the former priest who worked for the poor and went out to live up in the mountains.*

The young priest was growing weary of the wealthy ladies' hypocrisy and each day he would enjoy, more and more, his conversations with Null-and-void. That's why Diocles chose him to hide her. A secret no one knew, except for Irigandi, from whom it was impossible to hide anything. That night, as Sister Eugenia left the chapel, she thought she saw a monkey atop the roof.

31

The Lady tells them all. With Ludmilla detained, Colonel Viera faced a new problem: who would welcome customers at the restaurant? Lais was running the kitchen. He was in charge of groceries. Null – when sober – helped with the finances. But the restaurant needed someone to manage the waiting staff, supervise, and greet customers. Gigi was barely recovering from rehab, and she was too weak to handle any task. The crisis quicky and unexpectedly resolved itself when Frida finally showed up.

After negotiations back and forth with the narcs, Cavafys finally got them to release her. No matter how hard they tried to intimidate, mistreat, and torture her, Frida hadn't uttered a word. In any case, she couldn't have told them what they wanted to know because she didn't know Ilona's whereabouts. The only reason the narcs hadn't released her sooner was her rage. On two separate occasions, when they got distracted, she violently mistreated them with her powerful arms. It took Cavafys a lot of talking to convince them that it was far better to hand her over and let her get drunk on the steps of La Merced.

Her new attitude, however, took everyone by surprise. When they told her they needed backup for Ludmilla, she immediately replied, "Now that I've been sober for so many days, I can wait a little longer. This mess will come to a close one day, and by then, I'll take up my bottle. But for now, the best way to screw those sons of bitches is to make sure that Ilona's restaurant stays open."

It sounded absurd to think of Frida greeting customers, but there was no other option. The Colonel's niece was in charge of taking her to the beauty salon and she deeply enjoyed watching Frida sitting amidst elegant ladies with styled hair and manicured nails. Everyone at the salon that day would never forget the image of that strong Germanic woman beautifying herself – especially when she got a chin wax.

Another big problem was finding clothes that fit her. She was tall, strong, and robust – an unusual feminine physique. It was Cavafys, who always favored big women, who reminded them that the Mayor's wife had somewhat the same shape.

"And it can't be just any old dress. To transform Frida into a hostess, the dress must be special," the Colonel's niece told the dame who agreed to help with evident curiosity and a desire to watch the entire spectacle.

That night, when Frida walked into the restaurant all dolled up like a lady (or almost one) and sober as could be, Cavafys remembered the good times they spent together when she used to work at Cloud Castle.

Aside from the restaurant, life in Santa Clara was deteriorating fast. In the surrounding neighborhoods, the narcs and gangs began to have spats amongst themselves where innocent people got hurt. It was no different in the nightclubs and cabarets of Pigalle Street. On what was supposed to be a peaceful Friday night, one of the narcs, who had recently arrived, hit a Gypsy accordionist, starting a brawl that completely destroyed the whole second floor of a cabaret. And it was not only that. On the same night, a dispute at a Rastafarian reggae bar ended up with Micky injured. This is what Lieutenant Pirilo was telling Cavafys while Frida greeted the restaurant's customers, struggling to walk in her tight shoes, which she later discarded to go on barefoot.

Pirilo wanted to get the narcs out of Santa Clara, and it was becoming an obsession. He missed soccer games, ignored his girlfriends, and even domino games. And that is why that night he was talking with the Greek Captain. They were both waiting for Julio's brother, who had promised to tell them his theory about Julio's fake plane crash. The same one he had started, and was interrupted, when La Pajerita showed up screaming. Despite of the late hour, Irigandi was also there. She was anxious to hear what the brother had to say.

As soon as he arrived, they chose a table in the terrace, and he started to talk. From the beginning, it was clear that the brother believed Julio faked his airplane death to protect Ilona.

"The Americans were about to find out that Julio and the Condor were the same person. And if detained, everyone close to him would have suffered, especially Ilona. Julio knew very well that death could be a path to a new rebirth, but in the Dominican Republic, he didn't do it for himself but for others, and greatly suffered for it."

Cavafys and Pirilo were all ears, but not as much as Irigandi. She had to understand everything to be able to repeat it to Sister Eugenia. Frida, however, had no time to listen to them; she had to focus all her senses on keeping her abstinence while serving vodka drinks to the customers.

"Now that time has passed, I have learned that it was all part of a chain of events originating at a basketball game in Miami."

And he told a story that he had never told them before.

"A few days before the plane crash, I went to watch an NBA Championship Finals game. There were four of us. A doctor friend had gotten the tickets. After the game, we went out for some beers and ended up smoking a joint. It was a pleasant evening. Aside from the doctor and me, we were with two more acquaintances – a golf player and his brother who worked at the State Department on something that he didn't want to say. We were parked in front of the Arena, enjoying the joint and listening to Simon and Garfunkel on the radio, and a voice mentioned the name of the song: "El condor pasa". Our buddy from the State Department began to laugh uncontrollably and said something like, *No way, even here the Condor is at my heels.* Finally, when he regained his composure, he added, *Guys, don't worry, the Condor's days are numbered.* That caught my attention. I did't know exactly what his job was, and I didn't understand why he had laughed so hard, but I knew that Julio was the Condor, so I called him that same night to share what had happened."

The brother paused to check that everyone, especially Irigandi, was listening and understanding. Then he continued.

"I know this can sound weird, and it could have been a mere coincidence. But the accident off the Dominican Republic took place four days after I called Julio. And my first thought, when I heard about the crash, was that Julio faked it, but I was not sure." He looked at Cavafys. "I didn't mention it to you or Ilona because it could give you false hopes. I had lived this before, and I knew if his death were staged, Julio would come back, and I chose to wait. Later, as he never returned, I thought it was for real, but now we know it wasn't. For me, the only explanation that makes sense is that he did it to protect Ilona. The Americans were about to capture him, and he didn't want to bring Ilona and others down with him. Everything happened so fast, that he didn't have time to prepare or even warn. He just vanished. And that also explains why he never returned. If anyone found out he was alive, either the narcs or the Americans from the DEA, they would be furious, and take revenge on him and even Ilona. And he only came to Santa Clara to see Ilona for one last time before dying."

They all remained silent; the fake plane crash could have been to protect Ilona, but no one believed Julio returned to see Ilona.

And Irigandi, who was there to know the truth, asked, "Why then, did he go to Paya and Kuna Yala?"

No one knew the answer. Things were not all clear, but at least they had something to tell the narcs and the Americans. It would probably not be enough to calm them, but it might buy them some time.

The next step would be to share the brother's theory with narcs and Americans. Cavafys volunteered to talk with the narcs and proposed Pirilo would speak to the Lady, but the Lieutenant immediately declined. The Mayor and his new Venezuelan buddies were keeping a close watch on his every move, and if he attempted to approach the Lady, they would know. Cavafys had no choice, he would have to handle both talks.

They all left, and Irigandi went straight to the convent. She had promised the priest she would help the nuns. At least, that is what she said.

Early next morning, the Greek Captain went to the American Embassy, and Grená joined him. Pirilo had suggested that Grená knew the Lady, respected her, and perhaps her presence would make things smoother. Cavafys agreed.

The Lady greeted them in a friendly manner and took them to a small interior meeting room inside the Embassy, with a beautiful view of an internal garden. She was alone and listened to the whole story that Cavafys told her.

When he finished, the Lady spoke with a resigned expression.

"You mean to tell me that the Condor escaped, and the entire Operation Isla Grande collapsed, thanks to a night of pot smoking after a basketball game?"

Cavafys nodded, and what the Lady said afterwards, surprised him.

"It might be true and helps me to fill some blanks on the investigation, and I can tell you exactly what happened with Julio."

Grená and Cavafys looked at each other with smiles on their faces.

"We have always been sure that the plane crash in the Dominican Republic was not staged. The entire investigation following the event proved that the light aircraft fell by mechanical failure and bad weather and was not planned by anyone. Thanks to the British Passport that La Pajerita found, and Grená so kindly handed over to me, we know that Julio had a second identity he used for traveling. We could now retrace all flights he did before and after the plane crash. We already knew that he hadn't fabricated his disappearance, and now we know that at the same time the private plane left for the Dominican Republic, Julio was on a commercial flight to Miami. We couldn't understand why, but what you just told me explains why he changed his plans at the last minute; he knew we were close to catching him."

Grená was still struggling to understand, and the Lady continued with her story.

"The plane crash happened without him planning it, and he took advantage of the opportunity. Something similar to what he did to kill his Comandante Indio identity in Peru. While the accident took place, he was flying, and he also had a reservation to fly out to the Dominican Republic the following day, which he never used. We figure that he might have found out about the accident while in Miami, and it was then that he decided to disappear – a point of no return. After his faked death, and with his American I.D. – the same one that Bebéi found at the hotel – he purchased the house in Florida. He kept using his bank account in Grand Cayman, with enough money to last a lifetime. With his other passport, the British one, he traveled to many countries. Apparently, Julio loved the mountains. He visited the Pyrenees, the Alps, and the Asian mountains. He also spent a long time in Kyoto, living in a Zen monastery, the one in the picture Bebéi found at his house; and during the summer, he traveled throughout Tibet.

Grená was speechless, trying to imagine how far were those places the Lady was talking about, and wondering if they would have shaved ice refreshments there.

"From what we could learn from his British passport, we know that he returned to Santa Clara every year, never for more than a few days, perhaps to see Ilona from a distance, when she walked down the street or was working at the restaurant. We also discovered some old videos of a man who would watch the terrace of the restaurant with binoculars from the boardwalk that could have been Julio. He had a lot of money in an account in Zurich under his British identity. From this account, a lawyer withdrew funds to send to a friend he had in Greece."

Having said this, she smiled at Captain Cavafys, who kept a stern poker expression.

"We also found out," continued the Lady, "that he did have another account in Zurich, controlled by a secret code, but this one was never touched, which leads us to believe that this one has been kept for someone else. Ilona maybe, who knows? There is enough money on that account to safeguard someone but not enough to fund a revolution. The dog, Zoubir, he purchased on one of his trips through Australia, and later, he lived with him in Kyoto. There are many pictures with both of them traveling through Tibet."

The Lady seemed happy to share what she knew with Grená.

"He also traveled a lot to Paris, where he visited someone very dear to him, a woman," and looking at Cavafys, she added: "Just like he had left some money for you, he also left some for that woman by the name of Sonia, who still lives in Paris."

Cavafys nodded and clarified to Grená that Julio's brother had talked about her, and the Lady continued.

"When he found out about his illness, he returned to Florida, where he went through a cancer treatment. Ironically, Sonia, his French friend, was battling the same disease. Julio knew that death was knocking at his door. The brain tumor kept growing, which makes us think that he knew that this would be his last trip.

"I agree it's intriguing why he visited Paya, but we know by informants in the area that he never contacted the FARC Colombian guerrillas. We don't know what Julio's interest in Paya was, but since he wasn't interested in the guerrillas, it stopped being our concern. We also know that he visited some islands of San Blas, but we didn't delve further. Since we now know that he wasn't planning anything against the United States, his life and secrets are no longer a matter to us."

And to Grená's delight, the good news kept coming.

"We know that Ling's daughter and Chombo have nothing to do with Julio, but we found some interesting news." She smiled to Grená since she knew that she disliked the Chinese Doll. "The Chinese are buying up the port of Santa Clara: banks, hotels, and a lot of urban property and even mining concessions in the surrounding area. The appalling thing is that it's not only Chinese businesspeople who are involved but the Chinese Government as well. It seems they are promoting the construction of an entire base in Santa Clara to conduct business all across the Caribbean. They purchased the old Masonic Lodge and are now restoring it into a mansion for the new Ambassador who is soon to arrive. From what we know he is an important member of the Party. This is why we kept Ling's daughter for so long; we discovered that the Chinese Doll had asked her to handle the accounting for some Chinese friends, and it was based on that information that we were able to unveil their vast array of investments."

Grená listened, satisfied that she had been right all along, The Chinese Doll could be whatever she wanted, but she was not a simple hooker.

"We also found out that Chombo Zen is not a Muslim terrorist, although someone had indeed used his passport to smuggle people from Ethiopia and Somalia into this country. And this is what has me concerned now. We want to know what these Muslims are planning. And, after you told me that interesting story, I also would very much want to know who that special agent was who brought down the biggest fraud investigation in American history after smoking a couple of joints?" This last part, she said with a particular smile before going further.

"Regarding Ludmilla, we weren't the ones who detained her. With all the investigations, we discovered that the Swiss Police had been looking for her all along. We had to report what we found to them, and they informed the Interpol, but they don't have any proof, and I believe they will release her. Diana, as you know, is free. Julio and all his deaths are no longer of interest to us, so now our problems are focused elsewhere. Chinese expansionism and radical Muslims are our concerns."

Meanwhile, Grená was pondering what a radical Muslim would look like? Certainly not like Chombo Zen.

"We don't know where your friend Ilona is, and I can assure you that no one in Santa Clara has a clue either. I can tell you that Null was one of the five, and the other three were Princess, Ludmilla, and Hector. And none knows Ilona's whereabouts. We don't know who the fifth one is, and the only person who can tell us is Mr. Diocles, but we don't know where he's hiding out either. Rumor has it that his hideout is not a secret to some people. Are we right Grená?"

Grená kept quiet.

"You can be at ease now. I'll tell Bebéi that we no longer need his reports, which can now give him some free time to find out about the monkeys who hide out in the Golden Castle and who sooner or later will invade Santa Clara."

Then, after a quick pause to ponder a new thought, the Lady turned to Grená and said: "Better yet, his reports are quite entertaining, and if you agree, we can just let him continue to report to me, and I'll pass them on to you."

Grená knew that Bebéi was an excellent source of the latest gossip, so she nodded in agreement and smiled.

"You can tell him that he can keep his dog from now on, and finally, but not least, we'll leave Princess a few more days with us. We know the Venezuelan cartel is looking for him, and the problem is that the Mayor owes them a lot of favors. And by the way, don't worry, we looked into your son Pirilo, and rest assured, he is an honest man, and he's not involved in the Mayor's dealings with the Venezuelans."

Cavafys listened quietly, but there was still something missing. He still couldn't figure out what Julio was looking for in the Darien, and while he thought about it, he realized that he felt a certain type of admiration for the Lady. Too bad she is so petite, he thought.

Before leaving, the Lady said something else that astonished Cavafys and Grená.

"Julio's reasons for being in Santa Clara are no longer my concern, but there is something that may be important to you which my agents found out. They were in Kyoto and spoke with some of the monks at the monastery where he had stayed. They said that Julio had found out about a son and was keen to find him before he died."

Now that was a big surprise! Captain Cavafys never knew that Julio had any children.

32

More mysteries to unveil. Cavafys needed a drink; his mind was unused to so much news. He was a man of the sea where days of lonely navigation would go by between the hustle and bustle of ports. Even awful storms would come and go but in Santa Clara, the storms seemed endless. The wind constantly changed direction, and the compass spun without finding the North. Julio had a son, and he never bothered to tell him. How could anyone understand him if no one ever knew his true identity?

"At least the Americans were appeased and are no longer looking for Ilona," he told Pirilo. "They now want to know what Chinese and Muslims from Pakistan, Ethiopia, and maybe even the Caribbean are up to. But our problem is to convince the narcs. They don't have all that information the Americans do. The Lady knows everything. When and where Julio traveled, what he ate, and even how many times he farted before taking a shit in Kyoto. The narcs don't know any of this. They only want to know how much he stole and who is the son of bitch who helped him."

Pirilo also needed a drink. Americans appeased were not necessarily good news; without them, the narcs would have free range. Pirilo wanted to kick the cartels out of Santa Clara to regain his peaceful life, but how?

Lieutenant Pirilo and Theo Cavafys shared some rounds and sorrows from the restaurant terrace, watching from afar the boardwalk, where Zoubir, Irigandi, and Bebéi were strolling. They had learned to respect the little Kuna. Sometimes she seemed to float in the air, but she could sense and think better than many grown-ups.

Irigandi's grandfather had told her stories of their ancestors, which were not so different than what Bebéi and Princess had discovered. Her grandfather had refused to speak with Diocles about the Kuna's tradition, and she understood. A lot of what they learned from their ancestors should remain among the Kuna, and Bebéi and the others were wagas, not part of her people. But something there made her chest ache, and she didn't know what.

Her grandfather had told her that within Takarkuna Mountain, Mother Earth's secrets are hidden, and the Kuna are their protectors.

She was there when her grandfather told Diocles he didn't know anything about Paya, and she knew well that Paya was where her grandfather learned the secrets of their ancestors. She understood his silence, but there was something else. Her grandfather was also puzzled. "There is something that isn't clear to me, and until I figure it out, it's best not to speak," he said.

Bebéi was a waga, but she felt that Bebéi's questions had triggered strong emotions. Something she didn't understand, nor could her grandfather explain.

Her grandfather told her that what Mother Earth was hiding inside Takarkuna was not gold, and it was a gift Nana and Baba, the mother and father of all gods, had given to the Kuna people. "Something that enlightens and brings forth the full knowledge of the ancestors."

If it was more precious than gold, what could it be? Irigandi asked her friends. Captain Cavafys said it could be the fountain of youth. Grená that it would be to see the African Barber again. Frida, now sober, told her that it was to be reborn again as a child on the first day of school. For Null everything was more precious than gold, and for Bebéi, it was the friendship they had.

Irigandi could only sense emotions, and as for gold, she didn't know what to make of it. But she knew that in Julio's story and Bebéi's findings, there was something that touched her deep inside. She didn't know what it was, but she could feel it.

She knew that far away, Diocles was sad. His hideout offered all splendor that nature could give, and the people around him lived in harmony with the sea, the wind, and the sun.

Irigandi's family had welcomed Diocles to their island in San Blas as one of their own, and that was the big secret only she and Grená shared.

Diocles was hiding out, surrounded by a turquoise sea, in the same little island where Irigandi was raised.

Irigandi's parents had died young. Her father's family lived on another island and were the guardians of the Kuna people. Her parents met during college, fell in love, and married. Soon after, they moved to the Darien, as all guardians must, leaving her behind. She never saw them again. since both died protecting Mother Earth's secrets.

Her family cared for Diocles, but he never got an answer when asking about Irigandi's parents.

Meanwhile, while strolling on the Santa Clara boardwalk with Irigandi and Zoubir, Bebéi was thinking about the Kuna. He remembered the papers he saw at Julio's desk, mentioning Takarkuna, Paya, and the guardians of the Darien. Was that what Julio was looking for?

Back on the restaurant's terrace, Lieutenant Pirilo and Cavafys kept on drinking, watching the three walking by, and they weren't thinking about Kuna or the secrets of Darien. Their concern was to bring Ilona back home and kick the narcs out of Santa Clara, but there was something new. Julio had a son. Was he looking for him?

"The only person who could know would be Sonia," the brother said. He knew Sonia was Julio's friend and confidante. If he told his secret to anybody, it would be her.

Sonia was a well-respected professor at the University of Paris. She was a psychologist, and author who wrote on feminist issues. To her, Julio had even confessed his identity as the sniper who killed the general, and it was alongside Julio that she celebrated the launch of her book, *Lilith: Adam's First Wife*. They had always been friends but never lovers. When it came to sex, Sonia preferred women. Julio was also the best person at her wedding with Tsehai, a beautiful Ethiopian Muslim, which had surprised some who knew her, since Sonia was Jewish.

Sonia lived through the angst when Julio lost his revolutionary passion and supported him when he decided to change his life and join the drug trade.

"Why not?" she told him. "Who can tell you what is right or not? Follow your guts. There's a reason they're inside of you."

It hadn't been easy getting hold of her. Sonia was going through treatment at a hospital, but Julio's brother spoke with Tsehai, and early the following morning, he talked over the phone with her, and she shared the little she knew.

"Julio never told me he had a son, but once when we were talking about children, he told me, jokingly, that he had a hunch that the indigenous woman who saved him from the ambush bore a child by him."

Sonia hadn't said much, but everyone in Santa Clara was so anxious for news that Julio's son's story spread like wildfire. The rumors were so many that a conversation that began under Grená's umbrella ended up as a public gathering in front of Rasta's barbershop.

All wanted to listen to Julio's brother except those who had been kidnapped or were hiding, and even the bums of the Brethren showed up just slightly drunk, which helped the meeting flow better. Hector, the professor, decided to show up. The whole event of the arms apprehension depressed him, but his wife, Doña Lourdes, insisted he needed a new start. Colonel Viera was with him, balancing his friend's sadness by happily smiling at everyone.

He doesn't miss a beat, Grená thought.

The Greek Captain was there, and also Lieutenant Pirilo. Gigi, Ilona's friend, came, along with the priest. She looked better but was still weak. Even Ludmilla showed up with Rasta Bong. They had been able to negotiate with the police for her release under the condition that she wouldn't leave Santa Clara.

As soon as Bebéi saw the crowd and heard what they were talking about, he went in a hurry to get Irigandi.

"They're talking about Julio and Paya. You must come!"

He dragged her to the barbershop, and Grená was sharing what the Lady had told her when they arrived.

Grená patiently answered all questions, and the brother shared what he knew and what he had spoken with Sonia.

"Everything began in the Seventies, during an ambush close to the Colombian border. Julio was traveling in a small aircraft with other guerrilla fighters, transporting arms from Havana to Colombia. They were attacked while the plane was refueling on an airstrip within the Darien. He later found out that a mole within the Cuban Communist Party who knew about the flight had ratted them out. Julio only escaped death thanks to an indigenous woman, who was cleaning the small hangar at the airstrip, and for some reason, had realized that they were going to kill him and hid him. When the attack began, she showed him a large woven basket, and he jumped in without knowing who she was. He waited quietly until the weapons were silenced, long into the night, until she returned to the hangar to take him. All his comrades had died, but Julio survived, thanks to her help."

While the brother spoke, Irigandi's eyes seemed to sparkle, and she felt an overwhelming sensation in her chest as she listened to that story.

"He hadn't a clue where he was and only knew it was an airstrip near the border between Panama and Colombia. There wasn't much she could do to help him since she didn't speak Spanish, and they could barely communicate. After realizing that Julio wasn't among the dead, those who had planned the ambush kept looking for him through the jungle. Many weeks passed, and he remained hiding in her small hut until he could reach a radio transmitter and contact his comrades in Cuba."

This was the version the brother knew. He remembered that a few times Julio had said that the woman was mysterious, maybe an enchantress, and for some reason, she decided to live alone, away from everyone. "If Julio told Sonia that he could have sired a child with her, it might be true. Julio had always been a man with good instincts."

Bebéi intervened, confirming that he saw a note mentioning the woman-guardian at Julio's desk in Florida, and Cavafys added that Julio could have been looking for that woman.

Rasta disagreed, mentioning the ambush had happened thirty years before.

"That native woman would now be older than Grená and would not be living in the middle of the jungle."

At that point, Robespierre, sitting near the shoeshine box, got up and, very confidently as if having solved the mystery, retorted, "I know! She worked for the monkeys, and they were the ones who saved Julio."

No one commented, but they kept sharing every hypothesis, from the least reasonable to the most absurd.

"Perhaps the idea of having a child never seemed important to him," Cavafys insisted, "but when he cloistered up in the Japanese monastery, he decided to find his son. That's why he made the trip to Paya. Maybe the ambush took place there, and Julio was looking for someone who could tell him the whereabouts of that woman."

Theories kept popping up.

"Perhaps the answer was in the books, and that is why Julio bought all those expensive old books about the Darien and the Kuna," said Bebéi.

But the only person who could back him was Princess, who wasn't around.

Irigandi was silent. She was sure the indigenous woman was a guardian. Only the Kuna guardians still lived in the jungle, and she would ask her grandfather, but without the presence of any waga.

And since no one else had anything interesting to add, Null closed the meeting. "There's no more to say, and we could care less if it's true or not. This is what Cavafys is going to tell the narcs. Julio disappeared to protect Ilona and went to Paya to find his son. The narcs should give us back Ilona. After that, they can go straight to hell." Considering his mission accomplished, he left the barbershop.

Robespierre followed him, making an equally firm statement. "Now we can go back to what is really important."

Cavafys and Lieutenant Pirilo walked toward the restaurant talking about the next steps. It was a full moon, and Cavafys sensed that Pirilo was not himself. Cavafys didn't know how to make a dog talk, but he was good at helping friends vent their sorrows. He invited Pirilo to share a bottle of Caribbean rum. They sat at the restaurant's terrace, and Cavafys took his bouzouki out of the bag and started to play. No secrets could resist a good rum, a full moon, and old Greek songs.

"I'm only telling you because I know you want to help Ilona," said Pirilo, "but what I'm about to say is better no one else finds out. We are in deep shit. Behind the search for Ilona, there's a rivalry among the narcs for control over Santa Clara. It's a rivalry between Latin American cartels."

While Pirilo talked, Cavafys kept playing and only paused to fill up the empty glasses.

"The Chinese cartels that the Condor also helped out in money laundering seem to have a pact with their government that Santa Clara must be a drug-free zone. I don't know what the Chinese are up to, but the truth is they're all over the place. The Russians also don't want the narcs here; to my knowledge, a Russian owns most of the ships that operate from the port of Santa Clara. I suspect that he is together with the Chinese and don't want the Americans to think that Santa Clara is a drug gateway, and from what I heard, the Russian has a lot of influence over the drug cartels."

Captain Cavafys listened quietly. He knew the Russian was one of Julio's best friends from way back and a former KGB agent. He had helped him with the arms trade for the Sandinista revolution. And the Captain also knew that after the fall of the USSR, the Big Russian Boss, as he was now known, began trafficking drugs, and had laundered narcs' resources from which he made a large fortune, and invested in banks and created one of the biggest shipping lines in the world. But he didn't mention anything of that to Pirilo. Cavafys knew who the Big Russian's daughter was, and there was no need to share her name with Pirilo yet.

Meanwhile, the Lieutenant kept on talking. "The Colombians and the Mexicans have always operated the Caribbean and never had issues over the routes. Their rivalry is about distribution points inside the United States. That's why Santa Clara has always been a quiet place. The drugs would pass through, and the cartels didn't have to get involved in the city. But things have changed. The Venezuelans are putting pressure on the Mayor now, they want to run the place, and they're dangerous and violent. Ilona is just an excuse to detonate a conflict that was already coming anyway."

Anyone who didn't know Cavafys would think that he wasn't paying attention to what Pirilo was saying but this wasn't so. He kept playing his bouzouki with his eyes closed, but each and every word was carefully registered in his brain.

"The American Lady seemed to have a liking for the Mexicans, and don't ask me why. I have no idea how those big things work, but the fact is the Americans are working with the Mexican narcs in exchange for information about terrorists."

Pirilo knew the Mayor had daily covert meetings with the Venezuelans, giving them information that he shouldn't. Pirilo lost all authority over his people. Now the narcs determined which investigation to carry through or not; they even took some people out of prison. Local merchants now had to pay a tax to keep their business running and "protected." Pirilo also found out that the Mayor had ordered new arms and equipment. All under the narcs' orders.

"That is why I sent Princess to the Americans. The Mayor would release him to the narcs, and those guys would torture him to find Ilona's hideout."

Cavafys kept playing his bouzouki.

"The others are calmer," Pirilo concluded. "You can negotiate with them, especially the Russians. They're the ones who have Doña Cecy, and I don't think they would have a problem letting her go, but the Venezuelans are using Julio's betrayal and the excuse to find Ilona to control the city."

Little by little, the Condor's story was unfolding, and it was clear that there wasn't much that the two of them could do. But at the restaurant's terrace with the moon shining brightly over the sea, the two kept enjoying songs until dawn, and even the Gypsies silenced their instruments to listen to Cavafy's bouzouki.

33

An unusual assembly. The following morning Cavafys woke up with his spirit recharged. The sky was still gray, but he could finally see the sun beginning to shine between the clouds. Ilona, her restaurant, and all his friends in Santa Clara by the Sea were an essential part to his life. He could be sailing anywhere around the world, but the Caribbean was his home. There he had access to the most important things in his life: the rum he liked to drink, good cigars to smoke, the women he loved, and the freedom to sail the *Ithaca* wherever he wanted. Cavafys always missed Julio, but if Julio was not physically present, his memories were so powerful that Cavafys could still feel him by his side. Julio never believed he was better than others, and never wasted his time. Julio and Ilona were like him; they loved to live and enjoy every moment by focusing on it, all senses, thoughts, and emotions.

Captain Cavafys knew how to read maps, understand sea currents, respect the winds, and adjust to changes. That is how he survived with his *Ithaca*; making concessions when needed but proudly preserving his independence. And he could see the storm was passing. Pirilo made him see that the cartels were not united anymore, and Cavafys knew which ones mattered, which did not, and how to split them apart. The Venezuelans were powerful in Santa Clara, and like the heavy clouds in the sky, they were scary, but Cavafys knew that there was a whole world behind them, and winds coming from Asia were blowing as never before.

He knew what route to take, and he called Lara, his contact with the narcs. The message was straightforward. *Tell the cartels that Captain Cavafys has important things to say, and wants to meet them to negotiate the release of Doña Cecy and a truce for Ilona to return peacefully to Santa Clara.*

Lara consulted with them and came back with their answer. "There will only be a meeting if you bring Ilona with you or all of the five who were on Diocles' list."

Cavafys agreed. He didn't know who the fifth person was, but at least they knew four of the five, and that should be enough. Not all cartels wanted the same, and the Greek Captain was sure that he could play with that. The challenge was to convince the four to attend.

First, he talked with Ludmilla. Cavafys knew that no cartel would dare to harm her. She might be mad with her father, but her father was not with her. Ludmilla knew it and accepted to join him. Then he talked to Null, who agreed with no hesitation, and made clear that he would go anywhere provided there were bottles of rum waiting for him.

The third was Hector, and he was depressed. The old teacher had dedicated his entire life to the revolution and was frustrated.

"Julio at least chose a new path while I kept doing the same thing all my life. I wanted to change the world, and the world had been changing without me."

But despite it all, he felt he was obliged to help bring their friends back to the neighborhood, and after venting his sorrows, he accepted.

The only one left was Princess. Cavafys was willing to ask the Lady at the American Embassy to let him go, but he knew it was risky. If Princess showed up, the narcs might not let him go.

He tried first speaking with Lara telling him that he could bring three of them. Lara reported back clearly stating that they didn't accept the deal, and one of them, the Venezuelan, was very clear, "If the Captain wants to speak with us, the fag must come with him."

Cavafys spoke with Grená and then with Pirilo, and the three of them went to talk with Princess, who surprised them with his calm response, "Of course, I will. I can't stay in this clean and boring hole for the rest of my life. I miss the smell of sweat and dust, and here I feel dead. If they want to talk, what are we waiting for? I have no idea where Ilona is, and I do not have anything to hide."

Lieutenant Pirilo was the most reluctant to accept, but Grená pressured him, and he suggested a compromise.

"Since they're all nearby, let's have the meeting here. In Santa Clara, we can at least try to protect Princess."

So that was what Cavafys informed Lara. Not what the narcs wanted, but all they could offer, especially since no one knew who the fifth person on Diocles' list was.

Lara went with the offer and came back with an amazing reply. "They accepted, but it needs to take place at Ilona's restaurant."

Cavafys didn't understand, but in any case, there was so much that wasn't clear to him that he decided to carry on with the meeting, and off he went along with Grená to ask the Lady for Princess's release. She accepted, but not before saying, "Our sources tell us that the cartels are more toned down, but the one who requested Princess to show up at this meeting is the Venezuelan, who is bent on the idea that Princess knows Ilona's whereabouts. If the meeting takes place at the restaurant, it's okay, we can help Lieutenant Pirilo so that no one will lay a hand on him."

Cavafys confirmed with Lara, and they scheduled the meeting to take place the following day. When everything was set, Grená came with an unexpected proposal.

"You asked me to take you to the Lady, and I complied. Now, I want you to take me to the meeting."

Grená couldn't take it anymore. She was fed up with all that was going on in the neighborhood.

Captain Cavafys felt that the meeting was slipping out of his control. A meeting with so many guests seemed counterproductive, especially taking place at the restaurant, where the real bosses wouldn't expose themselves. Still, he had nothing left to do, so he decided to go ahead with it. When he thought that everything was up and ready, Irigandi also insisted on being present.

"All of you can see and hear them, but I'm the only one who can sense what they're feeling," she argued irrefutably.

Cavafys thought the meeting now looked more like a hoe-down, but he had agreed already to Grená's presence, and one more guest would not make a difference.

No one said a word to Bebéi. The Greek Captain asked to leave him out of this. Cavafys didn't want him rattling off about the treasure in the Darien, which would only confuse things more than they already were, so Bebéi and Zoubir were not invited.

Chuckling, Cavafys counted heads in such a peculiar gathering. The kingpins on one side, and on the other: a shaved ice vendor, a revolutionary professor and band instructor, a Russian acrobat who danced nude, a drag performing bookshop owner, a little Kuna, a bum who could never keep his pants on, and a sea captain far away from his boat.

It was an odd lot, not to mention Pirilo's people surrounding the restaurant backed up by American Embassy agents. Later on, Cavafys added Frida to the list; she could greet guests and sit behind Princess as an extra protection in case anyone tried to harm him.

On the narcs' side, there were three lawyers: one representing the Russians, another for the Japanese, and a third for the Latins. All were impeccably dressed in name-brand suits with pleasant smiles and clean-shaven faces. When the meeting was about to begin, another man arrived. This one had an intimidating and unpleasant expression. Cavafys immediately recognized him as El Nacho, Ilona's brother, but he didn't share this with his Santa Clara friends.

Cavafys had seen him once, many years before, when he threatened him because of his friendship with Ilona. Time had definitely hardened his face with bitterness, besides the row of gold teeth and the numerous tattoos covering every inch of visible skin.

Without any introduction, the newcomer sat at the table and said, "It looks to me that there's one missing. Where is that idiot with the broken arm."

With his thoughts running a mile a minute, Cavafys remembered what Lieutenant Pirilo had said about a violent Venezuelan, and he did not doubt that this was the despicable character sitting at the restaurant, behaving as if he owned the place.

"So, this is Ilona's famous restaurant," exclaimed El Nacho, scoping the place out.

Cavafys understood why he had accepted to hold the meeting at that place. Ilona would never have allowed him to come inside, and that gathering was the opportunity for him to come to the spot where she worked. No one from Santa Clara knew who he was, but Cavafys realized that Irigandi had sensed something since she stood up and pulled a chair to sit behind El Nacho.

At this point, Null-and-void skipped all formalities, and, using his previous executive skills, opened the meeting.

"This meeting has begun. Cavafys will explain why Julio staged his death and what he did before returning to Santa Clara. Then you can ask questions. Theo, you have the floor."

Cavafys told them everything that had been discovered in the last weeks, and while he was speaking, one of the lawyers interrupted.

"Now I know where I've seen this bum." He placed a finger on his forehead as if checking for old memories, then mentioned a name that no one recognized. "He used to work for a prestigious investment bank on Wall Street."

Null cast his eyes and acted as if he wasn't talking about him. Cavafys intervened and said this was not the issue to be discussed. Null might have done other things before, but he was there as one of the five in Diocles' list.

Relieved by the Greek's defense, Null regained his composure as moderator and continued speaking.

"Now that the irrelevant issue is resolved, let's get back to business. Theo, please continue – we don't have all day."

After Cavafys' speech, the representatives of the Latins posed a few questions. Hector and Colonel Viera answered them, and Ludmilla and Grená remained silent, looking with mistrust at El Nacho, who held his arrogant expression. Null-and-void, despite a few chickpea shells in his beard, managed the meeting with exact precision, giving each enough time to speak but preventing anyone to overtake the floor or diverge from the central theme.

El Nacho hounded Princess with all sorts of questions. It was quite evident that he thought Princess was Ilona's custodian, but the bookshop owner stood firm.

"Those here present might not know details of my life, but you have the means to find out who my friends are, and from what I gather, you have done a fine job in harassing them. With that said, you know very well that at this point, even if I wanted, I wouldn't have the means to hide her."

Cavafys insisted on the theory that Julio's reason for staging his death was to protect Ilona and the entire Condor scheme, and that Julio had not returned for Ilona but instead to find the son he never met at Paya.

Apparently, this version was convincing, or at least the narcs' suspicions were allayed. Then, one of them, who had been staring at Ludmilla the whole time, asked to take the stand. He was a Croatian who was working with the Russians and represented the group that had Doña Cecy. He said very little, but what he said was welcomed with joy.

"As a token of our willingness to cooperate, we will free Doña Cecy."

The meeting began to bear fruit, but as Lieutenant Pirilo had warned, the problem was El Nacho, the Venezuelan, and Cavafys was not sure if the Venezuelan wanted to control Santa Clara or just to take revenge on Ilona.

A few questions later, Null, in his unique style, interrupted: "What was important was said and done, now what's left is silly talk. I'd much rather go and drink than listen to all of you. Therefore, this draws the meeting to a close. The one with the yellow tie will release our Cecy, next week Ilona will return to Santa Clara, and the rest of you can go fuck somewhere else. Meeting adjourned."

And without further ado, he got up and went back to join his Brethren at La Merced. The others stayed behind, but there was nothing left to say. The lawyers left. El Nacho also left, along with his bodyguards, and from his car window, he kept staring at Princess with an arrogantly threatening expression.

"They're not all convinced," Grená said, "but at least they seem calmer."

Irigandi finally intervened, a little bit frightened. "The man sitting next to me is evil, full of hate. He has a lot of bitterness towards Ilona. Each time her name was mentioned, I could sense his evilness."

"That would be El Nacho, Ilona's brother," Cavafys clarified.

Frida, who overheard them, quickly ran out the door to see if she could still catch him up and returned screaming to Cavafys, blaming him for not telling her that it was Ilona's brother. She kept swearing that she would kill El Nacho without remorse, but luckily for everyone's well-being, she couldn't catch him.

"While he's around Ilona can't come back," Irigandi insisted.

Cavafys knew it, but despite his initial doubts, the meeting was a success. El Nacho did not kidnap Princess, nor did Frida kill him, but he did agree that it was too soon to bring Ilona back. It was best if she kept hiding, and being on the safe side, they decided to take Princess to the Lady and keep him under her protection. What they needed to do now was wait until Doña Cecy was released, which didn't pan out as easily as they had expected.

She had indeed been kidnapped, but they didn't know that her captors were treating her like a queen. In return, she cooked for them. Rumor had it that during the first days she was captive, Doña Cecy, noticing that her captors only ate pizza and drank coffee, proposed to cook them a healthy meal. The idea was so well accepted that within days, the number of narcs doubled, and all the misfits who recently arrived in Santa Clara looking for Ilona started to gather there for their meals.

When Theo arrived at the indicated hideout, he had to wait until Doña Cecy wrapped up cooking dinner for all of them. Even Cavafys shared in the last meal amidst heated and emotional speeches by the captors, thanking her and bidding her farewell.

Back to Ilona's restaurant, late at night with Doña Cecy, Theo heard the happy sounds of violins as if celebrating from afar. Just then, he understood it was the Gypsy way to celebrate the safe return of Doña Cecy, who had never been harmed, and was always protected by them.

Lieutenant Pirilo hadn't joined in the celebration. He deemed it too soon to celebrate, especially with El Nacho wanting to take control of the city. If that happened, Santa Clara by the Sea would never find peace again.

34

The Grand Chinese Circus. The Chinese are coming! At least that's what everybody was talking about in Santa Clara. They had bought the house where the Old Masonic Lodge used to be, and the word on the street was that it would be the new Chinese Ambassador's residence.

The Masonic Lodge was erected near the Cathedral Plaza, and it was one of the most beautiful pieces of architecture in the city. It had been abandoned for a long time; too big to be used as a family house, and given its poor condition, and all restrictions imposed by historic conservation, a considerable amount of money would have been needed to restore it to its value. One day, however, the eternal For Sale sign disappeared, and contractors showed up to start the project.

Initially, there was much doubt. There were workers from all over: Chinese, Russians, and Africans. No one had a clue who the new owners were up until the Masonic symbol was replaced by the red star of the Chinese Communist Party. The irony was that other than Ling's grocery, no one knew at that time how important a role the Chinese were playing in Santa Clara.

Chinese investors bought the port and the big fenced-in lots where large, modern warehouses were being built. Next to the city, they built factories where an array of products would be assembled, and farther out, they engaged in mining activities. Banks, hotels, casinos, and several other businesses were now part of their portfolio. Rumor had it that from Santa Clara, they would control an entire network in production, inventory, and transport across the Caribbean, giving China a definite presence all along the Atlantic. Something like Ling's store, where everything was sold, but on a bigger scale. And all the property-buying and investments went almost unnoticed. They arrived discreetly, and nobody, including the Americans, noticed the extent of the Chinese presence until the old Masonic Lodge was turned into a luxurious residency for their Ambassador.

For the inauguration, Beijing sent one of their best and most experienced diplomats. Before arriving in Santa Clara, he was a prominent member of the Political Bureau responsible for foreign relations. A fascinating character, and his wife was a wonderful surprise too.

The Ambassador's wife was an intelligent and lively woman, who spoke better Spanish than most of those who were born and raised in Santa Clara. She was beautiful, happy, and pleasant and had a doll-like height.

No one within the diplomatic circle had heard of her before. The only thing they knew was that she had just married the Ambassador, but back in the old city, it didn't take them long to figure it out. She was the Chinese Doll, the former Master of Ceremonies to *La Vie en Rose*, the most upbeat and visited cabaret on Pigalle Street.

The good news was welcomed with festive energy. The Chinese Doll told her friends that she was back, and all were invited to the grand occasion, and she even sent a special message to Grená: *You are my guest of honor.*

The invitations were delivered in wax-sealed envelopes made of matte rice paper with fancy Chinese decorations, which read: *The Ambassador Lee Woon Wey and his wife request the honor of your presence at the inauguration of their humble residence.*

For Bebéi, it was the first invitation he had ever received. He spent a night staring at the envelope, and, because of its importance, he placed it next to the pot with Julio's ashes in front of the mirror at the entrance of his apartment.

The event couldn't have come at a better time. Things were beginning to settle in Santa Clara. The Americans were at ease, and, for some odd reason, the Lady started to treat Julio's brother very kindly. Out of the blue, he became her favorite. The gossip at La Merced said it had something to do with a joint smoked after a basketball game in Miami. It seems the Lady wanted to make the brother forget the whole story. At least that's what Grená was saying.

The narcs were more toned down as well. But their mistrust towards Julio was still in the air, and reflected in their abandoning Ilona, who had to remain hidden from her brother.

Doña Cecy returned home to the dismay of all narcs who now had to go to Ilona's restaurant to eat her home-cooked food. And she didn't want to take even a day's rest. As soon as she arrived, she went straight to the restaurant.

"Lais, you can go back and take care of your grandchildren. I'm back now and will look over the restaurant."

Lais returned to work at home, where she found a truck unloading a stove, a refrigerator, and a few other appliances for her apartment. And a note that read: *Kisses from your big Sis. Thanks for everything.*

In truth, this was a gift from the narcs for all kindness Doña Cecy had rendered them. She had accepted but asked for the goods to be delivered to Lais's home. Doña Cecy always had everything she needed, but not Lais.

On the new Embassy's inauguration day, the town woke up in a cheerful mood. Starting at the Cathedral Plaza, from Ling's store all the way up to the Chinese Ambassador's new residence the streets were full of colorful flags and Chinese jugglers. Bebéi was delighted, and it wasn't only because of the party; Diana had returned to Santa Clara, and as soon as she saw him, she ran up and kissed him on the cheek.

"The best kiss I ever had!" he said to everyone he met.

In the early afternoon, there was a Chinese drum show inside the Cathedral that almost deafened the whole city, and a Chinese dragon ran across the streets, followed by barking dogs and hundreds of squealing children.

"Santa Clara is now a big Chinatown," commented Lieutenant Pirilo to Colonel Vieira while they were shaved at the barbershop.

Pirilo was all smiles. He had been offered a part-time job as a security consultant to the Chinese Embassy, something that had peeved the Mayor. Still, the way things were running back in the City Hall, Pirilo was considering whether to quit his job, and the Chinese Doll's proposal meant he had options.

The Embassy guards were responsible for security, and Pirilo, as a special consultant, would guide them with their integration into the new cultural environment. It was a laidback job, which wasn't too demanding, very much Pirilo's style.

The enthusiasm was felt in every corner, except for with old Grená. When Rasta Bong asked if she needed something to wear to the party, she made a face. "I'm not going. I don't like Chinese people," and that was all she said about it.

On her invitation was handwritten: *Come in what you feel comfortable wearing – the party will be all night long.* But Grená wouldn't budge.

Bebéi, on the other hand, received two invitations, one for him and one for Zoubir, and they were both ready. Bebéi bought a new suit with the help of Carmela, who was also invited. But he wasn't the only one who needed help. Ludmilla and the colonel's niece were in charge of dressing the Brethren members: Ludmilla was responsible for Null and Moriarty, and the niece for Robespierre.

There was an array of activities in front of the old Masonic Lodge, with trucks and containers coming and going one after the other. The entire house was decorated with furniture and artifacts brought directly from China and all revolving around one central theme: the Chinese Circus.

In early evening the jugglers performing on the streets entered the Ambassador's house, and the dragon, followed by fireworks, arrived at the house entrance at the same time that the corps of diplomats had formed a line to get inside.

Everyone wanted to be the first to greet the new Ambassador and his wife first, but no one outsmarted La Pajerita. She arrived two hours before with her bitch on a leach, appropriately clean and with a pink ribbon on her neck. La Pajerita got there, stood patiently at the start of the line, waiting for Bebéi, who arrived fifteen minutes before the doors opened.

At six o'clock sharp, the Ambassador and his minute wife, dressed in elegant revolutionary Chinese attire, showed up at the top of the steps, ready to receive their guests. The Ambassador was wise in his expression, and the Chinese Doll was smiling joyfully, something she learned from Ilona when greeting her customers back at the restaurant.

Bebéi and La Pajerita went up the steps, and their stress was obvious. La Pajerita's invitation had been given to her by an Embassy employee, who also helped her find an appropriate dress for the occasion. Her face, as always, expressed her utter state of dementia, but thanks to her discreet dress, one could say that there was an air of elegance about her. The two were the first to enter. The Chinese Doll kissed Bebéi just like she did on the day she helped him find the construction worker who knew the deceased. La Pajerita stood almost frozen. She was carrying in her hands some holy cards of the Virgin and some flyers of an upcoming music concert to pass out during the party. At least with papers to deliver, she felt more confident.

Their two dogs were escorted to the kitchen where the Ambassador's Chinese dogs were waiting. There they had food and toys to play with, and as soon as the Chinese bitch, adorned with small jewelry, tried to approach Bebéi's dog, La Pajerita's bitch quickly got in between and let it be known Zoubir already had company.

Following Bebéi, the rest of the diplomatic corps, one by one, entered the house. The first was the Japanese Ambassador and his wife, then the German and the Spanish. All invited ambassadors, government officials, heads of international organizations, members of national and foreign businesses, artists, and writers were present to show their respects to the Chinese.

Bebéi stayed back by the door, waiting for the French Ambassador, and took the opportunity to introduce La Pajerita to his boss's wife. The couple were very diplomatic and greeted La Pajerita respectfully.

The house and its rooms were all enormous, each one decorated for the occasion. At the center, there was a large interior garden topped by a glass sky ceiling of huge proportions, rising four stories.

Bebéi visited all rooms and greeted all waiting staff, the circus artists, the guests, and even the security guards. All with no exception. He and La Pajerita were thrilled.

In the lobby, jugglers with unicycles did somersaults, while in other rooms, contortionists were performing above tables. In the main hallway, tightrope walkers dangerously exhibited their skills while in the interior garden, dancers were throwing batons and Chinese flags in the air.

Irigandi was also one of the first to arrive; the priest accompanied her. She was more beautiful than ever, dressed in her native Kuna attire and a colorful mola across her waist.

"The mola is an essential piece to a Kuna woman's attire," Irigandi explained.

That particular one belonged to Ilona; Julio had commissioned Kuna artisans to embroider it with gold, and she had framed it and placed it in the main living room in her house. Doña Cecy had also borrowed a pair of Ilona's golden earrings and a necklace to adorn Irigandi's beauty.

Right after the young Kuna, Captain Cavafys showed up, dressed in his uniform, a white jacket, and a black tie. He looked handsome, not for the beauty of his face since the Greek Captain never had that, but more by the captain's uniform, his sailor's look, and the attitude of a fearless man. From the entryway, many ambassadors' wives smiled back at the Greek, and the Captain soon became the star of the party by reciting verses by Konstantinos Cavafys and flirting with many. Even before he pulled out his bouzouki, he had already at least ten admirers in search of a private moment with him.

Chombo Zen, who was no longer detained, also came. He didn't understand why they had interrogated him, and he was glad to be free. He hadn't wanted to attend the party but had been convinced by his ex-wife Clara who had recently returned to Santa Clara and had begged him to go with her.

Chombo had conceded and arrived with Clara by his side. He was barely recognizable without his bare torso, but she was dazzling in a colorful dress and an exquisite cream scarf covering her head, combining Muslim elegance with her Afro-Caribbean charm. Clara immediately caught everyone's attention, especially Lieutenant Pirilo's.

Pirilo followed the party's every move through the Embassy security cameras. His primary role, as the Chinese Doll had explained, was to explain to Chinese agents some local peculiarities, such as having Silvino, the head of a gang responsible for robberies in the area, as a special guest to the event.

For some reason, the Chinese Doll held a particular liking for Silvino, and he arrived very discreetly. After him came Gigi, who was showing signs of a full recovery. She was still thin, but her face was less pale, and the curves of her body showed signs of life again. Gigi wasn't dressed like the wives of the diplomats; instead, she wore a fitted black leather dress, with a sensual, modern look. No woman drew more attention at the party than Gigi. Her black hair and blue eyes stole the limelight from the best cabaret dancers, who showed up dressed so formally that no one would even guess their profession.

There was, however, a guest whose entrance caused a ruckus, and that was Rasta Bong. He showed up wearing an outfit inspired by Prince Selassie, the Lion of Judah, and he sported it radiantly. Rasta decided that if his good friend the Chinese Doll was the Ambassador's wife, he would celebrate it by showing his best. He asked the old quarter tailor to make him a tunic like the one shown in a famous photo of Selassie. The tunic was a dark, somber green made of silk. With it, he wore a brilliant white shirt embroidered at the collar. His dreads were down and shining, almost touching the floor. Rasta didn't enter walking like the rest of the mortals; instead, he levitated above a cloud of all the ganja he smoked, engulfed in the One Love spirit.

Rasta Bong was Black and proud, a descendant of the Lion of Judah, parading amidst worldwide ambassadors and authorities without fear. He owed nothing to no one. Rasta was the master of his destiny, a stunning Black man, proud of his dreads and the marijuana he planted, which raised him above all pettiness from the wealthy and powerful.

35

Partying under a sky ceiling. The guests kept arriving. The Mayor climbed the entrance steps with his wife at the same time as the Jamaican dancer. Everyone knew that the latter spent more time with the Mayor than his wife. Between the three, they kept civil appearances and greeted each other respectfully, showing some improvement since the scandal when the Mayor was found with the Asian masseuses.

Colonel Viera came with his wife, but his eyes searched hungrily for his niece and her bosom. But he was worried. Oddly enough, his niece had asked for a loan to repay an old debt and now wanted more to pay her credit card. By this point, the Colonel didn't know where else to get money without his wife finding out.

The Chinese Doll kept welcoming guests with a smile. The Lady showed up, escorted by a newly arrived friend from Washington, and a guest of honor got there right after her. He was a Russian tycoon, owner of a large merchant fleet, who was closing on a joint venture with Chinese investors to build a Chinese-Russian shipyard in Santa Clara by the Sea. It was a surprise for many to see him in Santa Clara. He was renowned, and rumor had it that he was one of Julio's best friends, which was evident when he came across Cavafys and greeted the Captain warmly with a long hug.

Cavafys was surprised to see him there, but whatever the reason was, the Russian was an influential figure who could help him to solve Ilona's situation.

The lawyers who participated in the restaurant's meeting arrived together, all in elegant attire with their wives dressed in exquisite taste. The Church clergy and all the priests and pastors of the old neighborhood were also there. The Gypsy band played in the main hall, while Colonel Viera charmed everyone with his dancing abilities.

Frida arrived a tad late. She had to make sure that everything was running smoothly at the restaurant. Frida was glad that her Chinese friend was back, and they had both talked extensively that morning.

Null went thanks to Frida's persistence, but he just came in, walked from one side to the other, and walked out. For him, the party and all the hoopla brought back unpleasant memories.

Frida was particularly concerned about Robespierre. He was unpredictable, and Frida had recommended strict surveillance. Before arriving, she gave him a dose of rum, necessary to ward off the bitterness and rage, putting him in a docile mood. Still, as soon as he entered, Robespierre started to drink up the champagne and it was impossible to control with all those waiters passing around.

Henry Moriarty was also meandering about through the halls in a white tunic and a hippie-like vest with flowers that Ludmilla bought him with Chinese Doll's money. He spent most of the night next to the Italian Ambassador's wife, comparing poems of Walt Whitman, Fernando Pessoa, and Giuseppe Ungaretti. It was such a pleasant debate that when the Italian Ambassador was ready to leave, his wife decided to stay and continue talking about poetry over champagne. This would be something she would regret the following day when she woke up on the steps of La Merced with such a hangover that she couldn't get up and found herself in a vomit state, being licked by the dogs and Grená staring at her in surprise trying to figure out who the new Brethren member was.

Micky and Diana were joyful. That afternoon Rasta had helped them to get them the money they needed to open up a hostel for backpackers in an old house that Diana wanted to revamp. Bebéi was delighted to see her, and every chance he got, he would smile at Diana from a distance.

Bebéi was enthusiastically circulating all over the place, making sure everything was in perfect order. In one hour, he had memorized the names of all staff, and when a waiter would pass by with a full tray, he would quickly give a hand.

Ludmilla was the first big star of the night. She didn't enter through the main entrance like others. She came floating from the sky ceiling hanging from a rope over the interior garden of the house. Rasta Bong watched his Russian love with admiration as she pirouetted above the room.

Ludmilla showed herself off with pride, and she knew that Rasta was not the only one admiring her. Another one was also there. The Chinese Doll had told her that he would be, and that's what prompted them to plan the performance from above to impress him. That other person was her father who had abandoned her. Ludmilla wanted to make him suffer, but she wanted him also to respect her. Her man Rasta watched on as her accomplice, eyes red from the weed and his Rastafarian grandeur, while the Russian tycoon looked back at both of them, embarrassed.

Hector, the professor, was one of the few who wasn't having fun; he was still depressed. His dreams of changing the world had come to an abrupt end. On his side, Doña Lourdes, a loyal friend, and partner, kept reminding him that he had friends who put their lives on the line to take him out of jail. But even knowing this, he was still bitter.

After Ludmilla, the tightrope walkers performed, followed by an Indian dancer, the latest act at La Vie en Rose. She amazed everyone with an exotic and sensual dance, moving her hands and eyes as no one had ever seen before in Santa Clara. The Mayor stared at her without a blink.

Last but not least came the main performance. Thanks to the Lady of the American Embassy, who encouraged him to perform, Lola Marlene showed up. Why not? Now everyone knew her secret, and it was time to introduce himself to his friends as she really was.

Lola Marlene was spectacular, with the grace of a diva, singing French songs that wooed all present, and especially excited the French Ambassador. They had discussed the Darien secrets many times in the bookstore, and the Ambassador could not believe his friend was such a seducing woman.

Earlier, at the beginning of the party, the French Ambassador had met up in private with the Chinese Ambassador. They both confirmed their interest as partners in mining concessions in the Darien, but after Lola Marlene's performance, the Ambassador was rattled.

In one of the side rooms, Lais served her empanadas, and even amidst all those Chinese dishes, a whole line of people were waiting to taste her delicacies.

Clara, Chombo's ex, spent the night talking to members of the diplomatic corps. No one knew much about her after she divorced Chombo Zen and went to live in Trinidad. At the party, Chombo watched her from afar and felt she had changed. She seemed much more committed to her religion and politics. He was surprised that she had wanted to go to the party. According to what she said, she was trying to get funding to build a new mosque and was making valuable contacts. That's what she had said, but Chombo didn't trust her.

The Colonel's niece recognized Clara from a lecture she attended in Miami about runaway slaves, but the niece spent most of the night beside Ling's daughter. They seemed to get along very well. But it wasn't all fun and games. In the Ambassador's new home, some were having fun while others worked, and while Lola Marlene sang, many conspired in the hallways, or at least that's what Lieutenant Pirilo noticed as he watched through the cameras the actors of the Great Chinese Circus.

36

A tiny mishap solves a big problem. Lola Marlene, the French chanteuse, continued to awe everyone on stage with the lights flashing and changing colors, adding magic to her songs. The guests were bewitched, but Lieutenant Pirilo was concerned. He knew Ilona was still in danger, and El Nacho was the crucial problem. Ilona's brother kept insisting that Julio betrayed the cartels, and that Ilona knew all along. Without the cartels' blessing, it would not be safe for Ilona to return.

Lieutenant Pirilo didn't know where Ilona was hiding, and it seemed that no one did. Maybe Diocles, who was the only person to know the fifth person on the list, but Pirilo didn't know where he was. How could anyone vanish entirely in such a small neighborhood?

That evening, Princess could sing to his heart's content as Lola Marlene, but at the end of the night, he would have to return to the American Embassy. Pirilo knew he couldn't stay there forever, but now, if it was not for the Lady's protection, Joseph the Princess and Lola Marlene, no matter which one he chose, would be at the mercy of El Nacho. While watching all the town's critical players through the screens, Pirilo couldn't stop wondering what he could do.

Little Irigandi sitting on the first row, next to the stage, was at ease. She knew Ilona's hideout, but she was also a little intrigued about what else was going on. When she shared with her grandfather what she heard about Julio and Paya, he replied with puzzling words.

"There is something that pertains to you back in Paya, but only you will figure it out. No need for anyone, not even me, to help you."

She felt the same kindness as ever in him, but his behavior was intriguing her. Until now, she could sense his anxiety, but not anymore. The old man seemed to have found answers to his doubts.

Bebéi was captivated by Lola's songs and took advantage of that magical moment to memorize every detail of the party. He had always been impressed by big street celebrations, and while still living in Paris, on the eve of July the fourteenth, everyone would go out on the street to dance. Bebéi loved it. But he had never been to a party such as this one. It's like July the fourteenth, but inside a large home, he thought.

Bebéi was sure there was a treasure in the Darien and was intrigued that no one wanted to talk about it. He understood that Irigandi or her grandfather kept the secret. It was best to keep the treasure with the Kuna, rather than let the French Ambassador or a crazy family like Le Breton to take it. But what about the others? Why they were not curious? Julio went to Paya before he died. Why? And to distract his mind from these doubts, he helped waiters pick up empty glasses. He watched Robespierre, who had finally realized his dream of dancing with birds; a Chinese magician placed three doves on a baton that Robespierre was holding while spinning across the salon.

La Pajerita was behaving remarkably well handing over cards to the guests. When she realized there were more guests than cards, she bestowed some colorful pamphlets she found stuffed in a box in one of the empty rooms. They were promoting the Techie Festival in Shanghai, and it was a pity that almost no one could understand a word written on them since they had been sent by mistake to Santa Clara and were composed in Mandarin and Turkish.

Pirilo was following every move from the security room, and not only with cameras. He had now learned to use the directional microphones the Chinese had, and he could listen to any conversation he wanted. He just had to point out the camera, direct the microphone and be part of any conversation as if he were sitting on people's shoulders.

"Don't worry about us," the Chinese Doll was saying to the Lady when they talked in the library. "From our end, we won't do anything to threaten your country. We wanted our niche here in the Caribbean, and have it now. We never had anything to do with the Condor. Some Asian narcs still have doubts about his faked death, but they're fine now. From what we know, there was never any contact between the Condor and radical Muslims, but there is something strange going on in Santa Clara, so we had best stay alert."

The two of them agreed, and the Lady added: "That good-looking woman, the one named Clara, arrived in Santa Clara a few weeks ago with a group of people who don't fit the usual profile of this city's visitors. We've been tracing their moves, and we suspect they plan to do something on this end of the world. We think their target might be the Panama Canal, and if that's the case, it's a major concern to us both."

The Chinese Doll told her that they didn't know Ilona's whereabouts nor why Julio returned to the city to die, but they felt comfortable that he wasn't a threat. She and the Lady agreed that they also had a particular liking for Bebéi, and the Chinese Doll made an additional comment, "I see you keep a constant dialogue with a few narcs."

The Lady kept quiet, which in diplomatic lingo meant that it would neither be confirmed nor denied.

"As I told you," added the Chinese Doll, "our narcs are at ease, and so are the Russians, but perhaps a good word from you to the right people may help resolve this conflict between the Latin cartels. Thugs controlling Santa Clara is a headache that none of us want."

The Lady listened but remained quiet. The American Embassy's relationship with cartels was highly confidential, and she agreed that El Nacho was a problem. Still, as a very disciplined professional, she cut the conversation short with a smile.

Pirilo kept following the Lady when she was approached by Irigandi, asking what she knew about Julio's visit to Paya. The Lady was pleased to talk with the little Kuna and repeated what she had already told. She said, "After speaking with Grená and Cavafys, I asked my friends if they knew anything else, and it seems that the Condor was looking for a woman who lived in Paya many years ago."

Irigandi smiled, pleased to hear that Julio was looking for the mother of his child. But Pirilo gave a close-up of Irigandi's face and could sense that she still had doubts.

The Lady then joined the man she had come with; a friend that Pirilo knew was the man who shared some joints with Julio's brother four years earlier after a basketball game in Miami. Julio's brother had recognized him, and they were chatting. The Lady approached them with a worried expression. Her friend was explaining to the brother that it would be best to forget the past and that what happened in Miami should stay in Miami. He even suggested that his government could drop all accusations against Bebéi and Diana if Julio's brother could forget the unpleasant incident.

At that moment, Frida crossed in front of Pirilo's camera, and he followed her. She was going to the ladies' room and Pirilo realized that he also had cameras inside it.

Frida met the Chinese Doll who was refreshing her makeup.

"So, the one who spilled the beans to Julio's brother about who was after the Condor is a friend of the Lady?"

"No, that's not her friend. It's her boss," the Chinese Doll immediately corrected her.

"I don't get it," Frida insisted.

"Today, the pot smoker is one of the heads of the CIA and the Lady's boss," said the Chinese Doll, grinning from ear to ear. "He is being considered for a top position. But they are worried. If the story of the joint spreads, he and his team, which includes our lovely Lady, are screwed."

Back in the main room, Pirilo watched Cavafys spreading his charm toward the ladies. Or at least toward the strongly built ladies. But Pirilo knew the Greek Captain would never forget Ilona was in danger, so he closed up when Cavafys approached the special Russian guest. He mentioned that Ilona was still hiding, and the Russian answered gravely.

"As much as I'd love to, I can't help you. Anything I do would make others think I was aware of Julio's staged death. It cost me a lot to appease the other cartels' doubts about my participation in the plane crash. Now I must be very careful."

At that moment, Cavafys felt his last and best of cards slip out of his hands and pursed his lips in frustration.

Then the Russian added, "But as I told you, Julio left all accounts well organized, and everyone, including the Chinese and the Mexicans, are appeased. It is the Venezuelan who is making all the fuss."

Cavafys told him that El Nacho was Ilona's brother and the trouble he was causing had nothing to do with Julio's death.

The Russian listened, thought a bit, and then replied, "Whatever the reason may be, your troubles start and end with him. The Venezuelan is tough and doesn't respect anyone. There's no other option for you. Either you take him down, or he won't stop until he gets what he wants. I can't do anything about it. They'll suspect I'm trying to protect myself."

Bebéi then approached them, telling the Lady was asking to be introduced to the Russian, and the three walked towards her. Pirilo realized that the Russian was charmed by the American and chose to follow Cavafys and Bebéi, who kept talking about El Nacho. Cavafys told Bebéi what the Russian said, and Pirilo was delighted with Bebéi's suggestion.

"I had an issue with Arcadio after he hit La Pajerita," said Bebéi. "What I did was to ask the Lady to threaten Arcadio, telling him that if he dared put a hand on La Pajerita again, she would make him wish he were never born. She was very kind and asked one of her friends back at the Embassy to have a little talk with Arcadio. Now, when Arcadio comes across La Pajerita, he crosses the street to avoid her. The Lady is very good at scaring people. Why don't we ask her to help us with the Venezuelan?"

Bebéi could be naive, but he was right. Only the Americans could scare El Nacho, but it was not so simple. Pirilo knew El Nacho should be eliminated, but his hands were tied. The Mayor owed the Venezuelan favors and would never allow Pirilo to confront him. And even if he could, what would he do? The Lady was the answer, but why would she do it?

While thinking, Pirilo kept watching the party through the cameras. He saw Colonel Viera, with his little Swiss hat and ass in the air, dancing salsa and merengue with all women present except his niece. She was, apparently, more interested in chatting with Ling's daughter.

Pirilo followed Clara for a while. She was extremely attractive, but her main interest seemed to be to contact as many Ambassadors as possible to talk about her Islamic Foundation. It was boring for him to watch.

The other woman catching the eye of all the men, whether married or single, was Gigi, dressed in a tight black leather dress, with a sensual cleavage. She remained seated the whole night next to the priest, showing off her legs like two elegant classic columns delighting the eyes of everyone who passed by that room.

The Russian and the Lady didn't talk for a long time. No doubt the Russian liked her, and quite probably she liked him too, but their conversation was very formal since the Lady was worried about her boss's problem.

Pirilo noticed that the Russian seemed interested in Ludmilla, and finally approached her.

Ludmila's reply surprised Pirilo. "Why don't you go to hell." And she added with a firm expression, "Now, it's too late to get to know me."

Pirilo was puzzled by her attitude and got even more appalled when he watched Frida commenting to Cavafys not far from where the Russian and Ludmilla were.

"Don't even dare get involved in family feuds," said Frida to the Captain. "Those two have a long history. He never acknowledged her as his daughter when she was a little girl, and now I understand why she is pushing him away."

It was only then that Pirilo found out Ludmilla was the daughter of the Russian tycoon. This one will surprise my mom, he thought, laughing.

For the first time ever, he would tell Grená something she didn't already know. And Pirilo kept listening to Frida.

"Do you see, Theo? When Julio joined the drug trade to achieve his revolutionary goals, the Americans called it an evil alliance. Still, in the name of anti-terrorism, this elegant Lady here, from the alliance of the good, had chatted with an old Russian narc and shared a drink with her Mexican buddy, the biggest cocaine smuggler, who is flocked by the women from *La Vie en Rose*. Do you see now why I get wasted?"

At this point, Cavafys thought it best to forget his woes and have some fun, and that's exactly what he did. He went dancing with the Austrian Ambassador's wife – a strong lady – who had passed by him many times, smiling. The night was for celebrations, and Cavafys drank, danced, and wooed the robust woman by playing the bouzouki. Even the young priest got up to dance hasapiko with Gigi, and while everyone was entertained with dancing, champagne, and music, Lieutenant Pirilo left his bunker to chat with Julio's brother.

Pirilo knew the cameras could follow him, so he chose a dark corner and whispered in Julio's brother's ear. He talked about El Nacho, Ilona, and the Lady and her boss's concern about what happened in Miami.

Julio's brother listened and nodded, agreeing.

Pirilo returned to the bunker in time to see Julio's brother approaching the Lady and her friend, mentioning that everybody would be grateful if the Americans could help them get rid of Ilona's brother. He added that by doing so, he would never mention the joints story to anyone again.

The Lady listened silently. Still, even in her silence, it was impossible to deny that Santa Clara's problems would never get resolved with El Nacho running the city.

Lieutenant Pirilo kept following her through the cameras and didn't know what she could do to kick El Nacho out of the neighborhood, but he knew her well enough to know that when she wanted something done, the Lady knew how to do it.

The party continued until dawn, and many were about to fall over in their drunkenness when Pirilo saw the Lady approaching the kingpin of the Mexican cartel and turned the microphones towards, to hear their conversation. The Lady seemed excessively relaxed – as if pretending she was drunk, Pirilo thought.

"Now that we are partners, I want to give you a friend's advice," said the Lady, and the Mexican straightened up in the chair to better listen her.

"Be careful with those Venezuelans."

The Mexican, although drunk, opened his eyes, interested.

"Do you remember asking me if I knew who had ratted the Condor out during Operation Isla Grande four years ago?"

The Mexican nodded.

"Perhaps this is no longer important to you, but it was El Nacho who kept us informed. He's Ilona's brother, and he did so to take revenge on Julio."

After she said that, the Lady went off to keep dancing. There was nothing else left to do. The Gypsy band kept playing and no one was left sitting. Even Pirilo left his bunker and danced, sure that Santa Clara would again be a peaceful place. Too bad that as everyone left the party, with the sun already shinning, Frida disappeared. No one followed her, but according to one of the Gypsies, she was back to her old self with two bottles in her hands.

37

The holy day of hangovers. The old city of Santa Clara by the Sea was awakened by the bells of La Merced calling all to the 7 a.m. mass, but unlike previous Sundays many were still asleep and didn't show up. The few churchgoers who did turn up were surprised to see the disheveled appearance of the young priest who didn't feel like talking that morning, blaming it on a "terrible migraine." But he couldn't fool anybody – many had seen him at five in the morning dancing hasapiko in front of the Cathedral with Gigi, Theo Cavafys, and the honorable wife of the Austrian Ambassador. A taller and more robust woman than Frida, who that same day kissed her diplomatic career goodbye to go sail with the Greek Captain of the *Ithaca*. Which made Doña Cecy wonder about Gregoria, his Garífuna girlfriend back in Livingston and what would happen the day he showed up with an extra Austrian crew member on board at Santo Tomás de Castilla. But it may not be a problem, she said to herself. Many of Theo's love affairs ended as soon as his hangover wore off.

Grená was one of the few who woke up early; she was the only person invited who didn't show up at the Chinese party. She noticed all the streets were empty, and, as was her custom every time she showed up at La Merced, she checked out who was sleeping on the steps of the church. She was happy to see Frida with a bottle of vodka in her hand, a good sign that things were returning to normal. Next to her, Null was farting and sleeping, and not too far off, Moriarty was wrapped up around the Italian Ambassador's wife with a beatified look on his face.

Grená wasn't yet updated with news from the party, but it didn't faze her. She could bet that all information would start to pour even before the mass ended.

The first one to arrive was Ludmilla. She was with the Rastafarian, all high and still celebrating. Rasta was with her but was not in the capacity to speak, and when he did speak, no one could understand a word he was saying. He kept smiling with his eyes as if he had received a divine revelation.

Ludmilla stopped to tell Grená about the tightrope walkers, acrobats, and Lola Marlene's show. Grená egged her on for more details; she wanted to know everything – who, what, and when. And the two talked for almost an hour. Ludmilla was tired but knew she couldn't go home before telling Grená everything.

While the two chatted, others started showing up, and when Bebéi arrived with Zoubir, there were already more than twenty people trying to huddle underneath the yellow umbrella. Some shared their stories, and others listened to the latest gossip about the party.

Princess was the star of the evening, singing as Lola Marlene for the first time in front of his friends. No one could stop talking about him.

"He is way better than those singers one sees on TV," said the Chinese, Ling, who had left his son to man the store, and had walked over to Grená's to catch up on the news.

They also mentioned Gigi, who had been dressed like a slut! according to one of the churchgoers. She spent the whole night chatting with the priest. How disrespectful of her!

They said that Colonel barely danced with his wife, and that Clara, Chombo's ex-wife, had been elegantly dressed and had spent the entire night approaching foreigners. Then they gossiped about the Lady's friend, who was actually her boss, and they all agreed that he looked like a goober.

People were also saying that the Chinese Ambassador was too old and sat the whole time, while the Chinese Doll ran back and forth talking to guests. And it was Lieutenant Pirilo, in a relaxed tone, who related the embarrassing moment when the Mayor had confused the Vietnamese Ambassador's wife with one of the Asian masseuses from Pigalle Street.

"Thank goodness, neither the Ambassador nor his wife understood what he was saying. The only one who got it was the Japanese

Ambassador standing nearby, who kept quiet because he was also a regular client of Madame Mills' cabaret."

Grená listened to all of the gossip patiently, and later, when she had heard it all, she called Bebéi to join her and rest a bit from the sun inside the church. Grená knew that there were more things that only Bebéi could have noticed.

"Now that I know everything that happened at the party tell me exactly what you saw."

Bebéi began sharing something that worried him. Almost at the end of the party, he noticed that Colonel Viera was peeved with his niece.

"I thought it was because she had spent the whole night talking to Ling's daughter, ignoring him, but it wasn't that. They were talking about some money she owed. I didn't understand it, but I sensed the Colonel wasn't happy."

Grená listened quietly; she knew that sooner than later, the niece would blackmail the Colonel, which wasn't a bad idea. And it was the least the bastard deserved for betraying his wife.

Bebéi also told her that Frida couldn't keep her eyes off Cavafys the entire evening and that the Greek Captain talked with the Russian tycoon who Ludmilla disliked.

"Many times, the Russian tried to approach her, but she brushed him off every time."

Grená, who didn't know yet that the Russian was Ludmilla's father, kept listening, thinking that the Russian was just another old, perverted fart like the Colonel.

Bebéi also described the heated discussion the young priest had with the Archbishop.

"I'm not sure why, but I think the archbishop doesn't like our priest very much. He is so stern with him! A complete opposite in how he treats the other young men in the neighborhood – always smiling and pleasant."

He also mentioned that the Lady and her American friend went out of their way to butter up Julio's brother. But Bebéi couldn't explain why. He also said that the Chinese Doll talked to the Lady in a separate seating area, and they seemed like old friends. He also mentioned that the Chinese looked very fond of Silvino, and when the two were alone, she couldn't stop patting down his pants.

"As if she was making sure he had his wallet in place."

He later said that he had given Pirilo and Cavafys the idea to speak with the Lady to see if she could help them get rid of El Nacho. Finally, he said something which had seemed odd to him. "Monsieur l'Ambassadeur tried to touch Lola Marlene's breasts," and Bebéi added, confused, "I would never have thought that Joseph had boobs."

Grená went on listening and smiled. The only thing that still struck her was that Pirilo was in a chipper mood after the party. How could that be possible if Ilona was still missing, El Nacho was free, and all the thugs were doing whatever they wanted in the neighborhood?

Once Bebéi finished talking to Grená, he continued walking Zoubir, but he was displeased. No one wanted to help him find the treasure of El Dorado, and the only one who seemed remotely interested was the Lady's new friend, who had asked him about documents belonging to the French Ambassador. He even went as far as to mention to the Lady that she should help Bebéi in the search, and he was not even from around here. Everyone else in Santa Clara could care less about it.

He passed by to pick up Irigandi. Her grandfather was on his way to Rasta Bong's barbershop. Rasta had discovered that the grandfather was an expert in native healing plants and opened for him a space in the barbershop to prescribe natural and organic medicine.

Bebéi and Irigandi walked with him, and her grandfather said something unexpected and unusual.

"When coming here, I knew I had other grandchildren who could see, and help me more easily, but my ancestors told me that I should take Irigandi. It took me a long time to understand, and now I know why." He didn't say anything else. He just kept walking, leaving Bebéi and Irigandi puzzled.

Nothing else happened that Sunday morning in Santa Clara, just the general hangover, but the evening was a whole different story. Santa Clara had a big shoot-out. The first in the ever-peaceful old quarter.

The gunshots rang out across the city. First, only a few, then a few more, and soon after that, a deafening roar of continuous rounds of ammunition, heard by all for the very first time in their lives. It looked like a war had broken out. After the shots, there was dead silence, only interrupted by the sound of speeding cars. About fifteen minutes later, one could hear police sirens arriving at the scene.

Everyone stayed indoors, not daring to go outside. It wasn't until the following morning that residents started talking. There were many versions. The radio and television mentioned nothing.

Nacho was ambushed, definitely drug-related was the first information. The big house where he would stay got surrounded, and they were trying to kill him was confirmed soon after. He was able to get away, but everyone in his gang had to hand over their guns was the welcome news spreading out the streets.

Lieutenant Pirilo arrived at Grená's stand, and with the same calm expression he had when he played dominoes, he explained what he knew.

"First, a car with four men showed up at City Hall telling us that we should stay calm and what was about to happen had nothing to do with us. The same kind of message the narcs relayed a few weeks before, which could only mean that they would carry out something big. We waited, and after we heard shots, and we noticed ten black vans firing projectiles. Three of Nacho's men died. It seems the cartels banded against him and crashed his gang, but El Nacho got away."

Everyone was scared, except for Bebéi. When he came upon Grená, he mentioned with a big grin, "You see how the Lady always solves our problems? She fixed the problem between Arcadio and La Pajerita, and now the Venezuelan won't bother us anymore."

Later that night, the Lady brought Princess to Ilona's restaurant. Many showed up anxious to hear the news, including Cavafys and his new girlfriend, the Austrian ambassador's wife—who, according to Null, who also went to the restaurant, didn't understand a rat's ass what they were talking about.

The Lady explained that the cartels found out that El Nacho was the snitch providing information to DEA at the time of Operation Isla Grande – the one who ratted out that Julio was the Condor – and the narcs banded together to wipe him out and avenge themselves.

Lieutenant Pirilo stayed quiet while Bebéi listened, smiling, and winking at him.

"From what we know," the Lady continued, "he was able to get away, but everyone in his gang handed over their weapons, and El Nacho is now on the cartels' target list."

Everybody was relieved, and Captain Cavafys was the first to ask if Ilona could come back. The Lady looked at Lieutenant Pirilo and they both coincided in confirming.

"We did our inquiries, and Ilona, Princess, and Diocles can now come back," said the Lieutenant.

At that moment, Bebéi surprised everyone, including Irigandi, with an unexpected question.

"Can I go get Ilona?" he asked.

It was unimaginable that Bebéi was aware of Ilona's secret hideout, but he proved it.

"I can pick her up at the convent where Irigandi sees her every day."

Cavafys, wrinkling his brow, still skeptical, said, "You mean to say that all this time, the only people who knew where Ilona was hiding were Bebéi and Irigandi?"

Irigandi, sitting next to Bebéi, clarified shyly, "The fifth one on Diocles' list was the priest. It was he who Ilona chose to hide her, but I didn't know that Bebéi also knew the secret."

And Bebéi explained, "I got suspicious when Irigandi told me that I couldn't mention about Ilona or the priest on my reports to the Lady, and I figured Irigandi was always happy when I would go pick her up at the convent. I could even feel a set of eyes watching us from a second-floor window, and it wasn't hard to realize it was Ilona."

Null then interrupted to close the discussion.

"All these theories are fascinating, all of which I could care a damn about. Let's free Ilona at once. The Greek should go with the Argelian and the girl to the convent and bring her back. The rest of us will wait here while Doña Cecy cooks the risotto we missed so much."

Lieutenant Pirilo then asked Irigandi, smiling as if knowing she had the answer. "And Diocles? How do we find out where he is?"

"Today. I'll send out the message," Irigandi promptly replied with smile, and while walking to the door, she clarified. "My grandmother's house in San Blas was the best option, I can assure you. And it was Grená's idea to send Diocles there."

Grená, who had also arrived, nodded quietly.

Ilona's return was great news, and everyone except Colonel Viera showed up at the restaurant. No one had seen him since the party, but the night was one of celebration, and people forgot about him.

The restaurant that night was full of friends, with Doña Cecy in charge of the food and the Gypsy band of the music. Ilona arrived radiant and enjoyed being updated with all that took place in her absence. She was surprised when they told her about the five names on Diocles' list.

"He mentioned the five names to me, but he told me that only one person would be able to hide me." And as she said this, she looked thankful to the young priest.

That night, Ilona also met the Lady, who told her about the stranger who watched her from the boardwalk with binoculars, making Ilona smile with tears.

"Tonight, I want to drink till I fall over drunk and erase every bad memory from my head. Many times, I cried, thinking I would never come back and sit on this terrace again, but tomorrow I'll disinfect the entire restaurant and burn the chair that my son-of-a-bitch of a brother sat on."

38

The secret is revealed. The next day, the old city of Santa Clara by the Sea awoke relieved as it hadn't been in a long time. El Nacho was now running from the cartels, and his gang had scampered out. People began opening their windows and putting back chairs at the curbside to chat with neighbors. The streets' fear had dissipated, and the dogs were back chasing pigeons at the plazas, and children ran behind La Pajerita's son's ice cream cart. He was still wearing his clown costume and had upgraded his cart by raising the seat two notches, which made him look as if he was pedaling from the second floor, adding a music box playing a carousel tune.

A festive mood spread on the streets, and Robespierre was the most enthusiastic, dancing happily around. Amid all this excitement, Princess re-opened the bookstore. Now that he had nothing to hide he was anxious to return to his books. His only concern was crossing paths with the French ambassador, who seemed to be a tad confused about Lola Marlene and the nostalgic songs that stirred up his heart.

Julio was dead, true, but at least now it was clear he hadn't betrayed anyone. Ilona was back home, and at any moment, Diocles would show up and walk around with his ex-presidential, philosophical flair.

Cavafys sailed off to the *Ithaca* with his Austrian girlfriend, tugging along a blue sack filled with their belongings. To Doña Cecy and Ilona's surprise, his love for the Austrian had held up for three long nights of partying and drunkenness.

And while Doña Cecy watched Cavafys and his girlfriend sail away, she noticed Frida at the end of the boardwalk, sadly looking on as the Greek Captain sailed out.

That afternoon, Diocles arrived at the same dock. He showed up in a ratty boat filled with San Blas coconuts for the Santa Clara market. As soon as the boat touched the dock, he jumped out, seasick after a very rough trip. He was happy to be alive and with two feet on solid ground again.

As he recovered his balance, he walked to Ilona's restaurant, and on his way, he was teased about his dark tan, typical of summer tourists.

He was welcomed by Doña Cecy with a tea to ward off the motion sickness, which reminded him that he hadn't eaten anything but coconuts for the last few days. Ilona took him to the terrace, and Doña Cecy prepared a pulp risotto; his favorite.

Everyone had many questions to ask, but they waited until he ate. Bebéi and Irigandi arrived, and everybody wanted to know what Diocles had found out during his forced vacation. The smile on Diocles' face showed that news was good.

He started by saying that Irigandi's family had treated him very well, but he soon realized they also had secrets.

"Some of them speak Spanish, but there are things they don't like to talk about," and as he kindly touched Irigandi's face, he continued speaking. "The Kuna, regardless of where they live, don't like to talk about what their people do up in the jungles of Darien."

Diocles then paused for Irigandi to say something, but she kept quiet holding Zoubir's nose over her legs and petting his neck with her tiny fingers.

"Luckily," Diocles continued, "they also have Brethren, but not like ours who get drunk every day. Theirs only drink on special occasions when their women prepare a mix stronger than the hardest liquor and capable of making an entire island drunk."

Irigandi smiled.

"When the Kuna drink, they spill the beans and even talk about things they had long forgotten. One drunkard told me Mother Earth shared her secrets with their people, and only the spiritual guides like Irigandi's grandfather know about it."

Irigandi tried to stay still and distant as if what Diocles was saying had no relevance to her, but inside, her heart was bursting.

"Secrets, which, no matter how drunk they were, they didn't share with me. Something so important that they are ready to give their lives to protect."

Now, Diocles wasn't smiling anymore.

"They told me there are guardian families whose charge they pass down from father to son. And those are the ones who help Mother Earth protect these secrets." He then looked gravely at Ilona and Doña Cecy, trying to show how important what he was about to say was. "I found out that Irigandi's father came from one of those families."

Irigandi kept listening, still trying to mask her anxiety with a calm expression.

"I decided to visit the island where his family came from – a one-day journey from the island I was. And from what I could discern, many from that island had died protecting Mother Earth's secret."

Irigandi's stress was becoming evident.

"I also met a pleasant older woman, who liked to talk, like our Grená. This woman lived on this island, and told me that a little while back, a bald waga, who was ill, visited the island asking about an indigenous woman from Paya."

While Diocles kept talking, Irigandi left her chair and approached Ilona, sitting beside her.

"The man who was there," said Diocles "wanted to know more about that Kuna woman. She was a guardian who lived in Paya, guarding something that not even my friend, who rattled it all, could tell me. That made me think it must be something essential," Diocles joked and laughed. "Imagine something so secret that even Grená would keep quiet about it. My friend also said that the guardian woman from Paya had met a waga from whom she bore a son. And, as a big storyteller, she told me that the girl's family never forgave her for that – as a guardian, she should never have approached a waga. Anyway, she did it, and, sad and ill, the guardian woman had to return to the island to hand over the child to her family before dying. My friend told me that the guardian woman was her sister and that she had raised the son her sister left behind."

"What is her name," asked Irigandi abruptly. "Wagebingili," replied Diocles.

And as Irigandi heard the name, she stopped petting the dog to hold Ilona's hand tight.

"Wagebingili raised the boy," continued Diocles, "and sent him to the Kuna's school in San Blas. There he met a Kuna girl from another island, and while still in school and very young, they fell in love, and had a daughter."

Diocles kept on with the story, and all eyes looked to Irigandi, holding even tighter Ilona's hand.

"Since the boy came from a family of guardians, he wanted to become a guardian too, but his family didn't allow it since he had waga blood in his veins. However, the boy insisted – he wanted to honor his mother's tradition. Finally, the Kuna council allowed him to go, and his young wife went along with him. Their little daughter, however, was still a baby and could not go, so they left her with her mother's family."

Bebéi found it an opportune moment to interrupt Diocles' story and remind everyone present that his parents had also left him behind to confront the French in Algiers. Everyone nodded in solidarity with him.

"The young couple," continued Diocles, "died in the jungle. I never found out how, and nobody explained what they were defending, but my friend, who tells it all, confessed to me that they died defending Mother Earth's secret. When I asked if she knew where the girl was, Wagebingili said that the bald waga had asked the same question, and she told him that the little girl had gone to Santa Clara with her grandfather and that she was a blind Nele named Irigandi."

At this, Diocles grew silent, as did everyone around him. The only thing that moved on the terrace was Zoubir's wagging tail.

"So, what this means is that you, Irigandi, are Julio's granddaughter," said Ilona, breaking the silence.

Irigandi nodded assertively.

"I think so. I never met my parents, and people never talked with me about them, but Wagebingili is my aunt." That was all she could say.

Irigandi had trusted that Diocles would find out the truth, and he did it. She was happy. She had always felt a beating in her chest when Julio's name was mentioned. Still, she could have never imagined that the one who had died after the parade and caused Ilona so many problems was her grandfather.

Diocles didn't need to explain anything else. Everyone understood that Julio had returned to Santa Clara to find Irigandi. He knew that she was a blind Kuna girl who lived with her grandfather and to look for her, he had to expose himself, combing the streets of the old quarter with his dog. Too bad he never met her.

"And thinking more about it," Diocles added, "he could have never found her because before Irigandi had Bebéi and the dog, she rarely went out. And if it was not Julio, it was his dog that finally found her."

Zoubir wagged his tail as if understanding that everybody was looking at him.

Irigandi now felt at ease. A guardian could never fall in love with a waga, and that's why everyone always avoided talking about the waga blood running through her veins. She was proud of her native traditions but always felt she was unique. She was not pure as her ancestors, but she now could assert that the waga blood running through her veins was from Julio, who was Ilona's love, and instead of shame, she felt pride for being a native and, at the same time, Julio's granddaughter.

Ilona was surprised but happy. She understood that Julio had faked his death in the Dominican Republic to protect her. It would have been impossible to convince the narcs that he wanted to leave them, and perhaps he would have come back to be with her at some point, but cancer had overtaken him. And how ironic it was that Julio's granddaughter was the smiling girl who comforted and updated her with news from her friends for all those days while she was in hiding.

That same evening, Bebéi went to Irigandi's apartment to give her the urn with Julio's ashes, and later, while he walked with Zoubir, he felt deep satisfaction. He knew something that nobody knew.

Bebéi might be chubby and look like a goober with his short little tie and his habit of walking the dog through the streets. Still, he was the only waga to know what the guardians hid beneath the earth, underneath the Paya River at the foot of Takarkuna Hill. Something more precious than gold since it could reveal all of the ancestors' knowledge. Robespierre, the grand grandson of Le Breton, had told him in most secret confidence, and Irigandi's grandfather had confirmed it.

39

Peace is back in town. Finally, on a bright, sunny Sunday, Bebéi and Zoubir strolled the old neighborhood streets without a single concern on their mind. Life was back to normal. Grená was sharing the latest gossip under her umbrella while La Pajerita's son passed, peddling his ice cream cart, with a little monkey on his back dressed as Napoleon. At La Merced's steps, the Brethren members were asleep and drunk, except for Robespierre, who was speaking to a bunch of pigeons and ran, screaming his head off, when he saw the little monkey.

At the Cathedral Plaza, Diocles was feeding his cats watching Chombo Zen meditating, with his torso bare, seated in the lotus position. In front of the bookstore, Princess played chess with the priest.

Bebéi passed by and greeted them, ignoring that the previous day, Carmela had overheard the French Ambassador mentioning to his secretary that papers for Bebéi's transfer back to France were already on his desk.

"He has nothing left to do in Santa Clara," the French ambassador said. "Le Breton's papers are also going back to Paris."

Two days before, the Ambassador had informed his Ministry that he was resigning his post in Santa Clara to dedicate his energy to a mining concession he had gotten in the Darien. The papers he had bought from the Le Breton family helped him find where the gold was located, but now would be sent to the Ministry, where no one would look at them for the next several decades. And if the papers went, so would Bebéi, and he would stop raising questions about the hidden Darien treasure. The Ambassador was worried. At the party held by the Chinese, the Lady and her boss approached him to talk about the discovery Le Breton had made up in the Darien, and, of course, they had heard it from Bebéi. The questions seemed innocent, but the Ambassador knew that neither the Lady nor her boss would waste their time on idle questions.

Back to the street, the only thing on Bebéi's mind while walking Zoubir was the new gossip he heard at the Chinese store about Colonel Viera. It didn't look good. Rumor had it that his niece, the one with the big tits, was a hustler. She had told everyone she had studied in Miami, but Diana, who knew that city, discovered that the niece didn't even know where the university was.

When returning to Santa Clara, the niece had noticed that her uncle constantly gawked at her cleavage, and she had spread her legs a little to convince him she needed to pay off her debts and buy an apartment in Santa Clara. With his little Swiss hat and perky ass, the salsa-dancing expert Colonel fell for the story, and that meant big trouble.

The women in the neighborhood knew what was going on, but they didn't breathe a word to Otilia, the Colonel's wife. No one liked her. Otilia always acted as if she was better than the rest, and they were all waiting to have some fun the moment the Colonel found out the truth about his niece, and Otilia about his escapades. Everybody knew the old Colonel fell for her tits, but no one could have ever imagined that the Colonel was so enthused that he loaned her everything he had saved for retirement.

That Sunday, Bebéi also met Ilona, and she was emotional. Henry Moriarty had just given her the book Bebéi and Diana found at the hotel with the poems of Fernando Pessoa. Some verses were underlined by Julio himself, which seemed to describe the way he always wanted to live his life:

Rather a bird's flight, which passes by and leaves not a trace, than an animal track, imprinted forever on the soil.

The bird flies by and forgets and that's how it should be. Go by, bird, fly on, and teach me how to fly by!

Ilona was planning to spread Julio's ashes in the ocean with Irigandi. Just the two of them – his woman and his granddaughter. And the decision to do it in the ocean was Irigandi's idea.

"He lived so many lives and in so many places that it's best to let the ocean freely choose where to take his ashes," the girl said.

Doña Cecy was back cooking at the restaurant, and aside from feeding tourists, politicians, and residents, she now had to feed her ex-kidnappers and narc friends passing through Santa Clara. She was in great health, but her legs kept swelling up on her. Every night, when Diocles joined her to share the restaurant leftovers, and update her with news, she propped up her feet on the little bench. She enjoyed Diocles' company, and to her joy, everybody was saying that he had gotten chubbier.

At the La Merced steps, Null never explained why he had left his career, country, and family before showing up in Santa Clara to live on the streets. But there is nothing to worry about; we have already discovered so many secrets that, who knows, perhaps we'll find out why one day.

Robespierre kept running away from the monkeys, and La Pajerita kept walking in a hurry. Frida, after handling the restaurant, returned to La Merced's steps, showing her violent revolutionary soul after each emptied bottle.

The Lady at the American Embassy was even more powerful after her friend was promoted in Washington. Her only concern was Clara's intentions, which is why the Lady was interested in her whereabouts. Finding her was an easy task since all she had to do was to follow Pirilo, who, for entirely different reasons, couldn't take his eyes and hands away from Clara.

In the following weeks, Bebéi's problems at the French Embassy were resolved. Rumor had it that the Chinese Doll put pressure on the Ambassador. Still, according to Grená, who continued to hate the Chinese, it was thanks to Princess, and more specifically Lola Marlene, that the Monsieur l'Ambassadeur changed his mind. The gossip was that the French ambassador was in love with Lola Marlene, but no one was one-hundred-percent sure since the two kept meeting at the bookstore as two good friends. But Grená held on to the Gypsies' version. According to them, every Tuesday, the Ambassador would meet up with Lola Marlene in a hotel where Lola would show up in exuberant and exotic clothing. But until that version is proven, it will be added to Grená's pile of gossip, which we know is endless. Anyway, whatever the truth may be, we know that Bebéi stayed at the Embassy, and as he wasn't busy anymore, he began to help Diana and Micky in the backpacker hostel they opened.

Gigi went back to flying, but only for the narcs. No one else trusted her with her heroin rebounds, and as her passion was to fly, her only option was to work for them. The irony was that with each passing day and each crisis overcome, Gigi would come back even prettier, threatening all the austere men of Santa Clara. Luckily, the only one she often met up with for lunch and dinners at Ilona's restaurant was the priest, who, apparently, was serious about his priestly calling, at least that's what it seemed.

Grená was cheerful and exuberant again. All she wanted was peace to proudly enjoy her three sons: Lieutenant Pirilo, who to her surprise, wasn't that lazy after all; Silvino, who was now the secret lover of the Chinese ambassador's wife and could, eventually, became a respected international spy; and Rasta Bong, the eldest of her sons, who kept on with his successful businesses and had moved in with Ludmilla. Even though Ludmilla continued to make unexplained trips to Europe, Grená was at ease. After moving in with Rasta, Ludmilla never went back to pole dancing at *La Vie en Rose*.

"Better traveling around than naked in front of everyone," explained Grená at her shaved ice stand.

Hector was still depressed, trying to find a destiny that would suit him. According to Princess, he could only be happy in politics, and Hector was considering running against the Mayor in the coming elections.

Irigandi's grandfather was still sick and forced to go to the hospital every other day. Still, he was dedicating his free time to prescribing herbs and portions at Rasta's barbershop, and the lines at the door were longer every day.

Irigandi was happily splitting her time between Ilona, Bebéi, and Zoubir, and she was not worried about the French ambassador's mining concession in the Darien. As she explained to Bebéí, "The Ambassador and the Chinese are looking for gold and will find it, but much less than expected."

And when Bebéi asked if it wasn't risky that they could find Mother Earth's secret, she replied, "Don't worry. My people will continue to protect what is more precious than gold at the Takarkuna mountain, and my people will never let them get close to it."

That is all I have to tell you, and who knows, one day we could go back to Santa Clara by the Sea to find out what else they have been doing with their lives.

Printed in the USA
CPSIA information can be obtained
at www.ICGtesting.com
LVHW040243290224
772997LV00001B/1